Deadly Arrangements

The Flower Shop Mystery Series
Book Two

By
Annie Adams

Deadly Arrangements © 2014 Annie Adams
Book Two in The Flower Shop Mystery Series
All rights reserved

The book contained herein constitutes a copyrighted work and may not be reproduced, transmitted, down-loaded, or stored in or introduced into an information storage and retrieval system in any form or by any means, whether electronic or mechanical, now known or hereinafter invented, without the express written permission of the copyright owner, except in the case of brief quotation embodied in critical articles and reviews. Thank you for respecting the hard work of this author.

This book is a work of fiction. The names, characters, places, and incidents are products of the writer's imagination or have been used fictitiously and are not to be construed as real. Any resemblance to persons, living or dead, actual events, locales or organizations is entirely coincidental.

Published by Annie Adams

Cover Art © 2014 Kelli Ann Morgan
Inspire Creative Services

Interior book design by
Bob Houston eBook Formatting

ISBN-13: 978-1502340900
ISBN-10: 1502340909

ACKNOWLEDGEMENTS

I wish to express my most heartfelt gratitude to all of those who helped in the creation of this book. Thank you, Rich Hansen from the Utah Division of Wildlife Resources and the Farmington Bay Waterfowl Management Area. To Kandice and JD for doing the heavy lifting while I typed and then hit the delete key over and over again. To my family who put up with the "have to work on my book" excuse. To Lesli and Samwise who turned my wooden puppet into a "real book," to Lysa and Leslie for your keen eyes. To URWA chapter mates, who listened and chatted and hashed things out, who made suggestions, and spread the word.

To James who made all of this possible.

To Grandma Lola, who sat and read books with me only until I wanted to stop (which was never), even though she had so many other things to do.

CHAPTER ONE

"Quincy, you look…stunning," Allie said.

As corny as it was, I couldn't help feeling very much like Cinderella prepping for the ball as I stepped out of the dressing room of the Beautiful Bride Dress Shop. My mother and sister had waited patiently in the sitting room as I tried on dress after dress.

"If you ask me, this is awful soon for a wedding. Of course, no one ever asks me," Mom said. I glanced sideways at Allie who rolled her eyes just out of our mother's line of sight. I couldn't help but giggle.

"What's so funny?" Mom said.

"Oh, nothing," I said in a sing-song voice as I slipped back into the dressing room.

"Well, anyway, it's been what, two months since they met?" My mother made sure to use a loud enough voice so I could hear inside the dressing room and probably in Cleveland.

"I think it's incredibly romantic," Allie said.

"Oh, puh-lease," my mother said, the hardened edge to her voice as crusty as week-old bread. Her tone made my heart ache. She'd become a cynic about many topics, especially romantic love. Marriage and romance had become mutually exclusive in her oft-voiced opinion.

Of course, my mother will always nag about her younger daughters' marital status, whether any romance is involved or not. Once we're married, she'll move on to nagging about getting some grandchildren.

But, she had good reason to feel cynical about love and romance. My father had left my mother just after I got married—or should I say got married off? That's what it felt like, anyway. Nothing like a little societal pressure to make you feel like an old-maid in your early twenties. But, in Utah's religiously influenced culture, that's nothing new. At almost thirty, I felt like I was practically ready for the glue factory.

My ill-fated marriage had been the biggest mistake of my life. One abusive husband later, it may seem surprising I wasn't joining in the chorus with my well-intentioned mother.

I had escaped the marriage on my own. And I landed on my feet with the help of my Aunt Rosie, who decided to travel the world and turned her flower shop over to me. But the escape from the emotional cave I was living in had been much more difficult to accomplish.

I was out of the cave and seeing the daylight thanks to the beautiful hunk of a man that was now my…boyfriend?…Alex, with whom I had been spending as much time as our busy schedules would allow.

My dressing room attendant had disappeared, so I attempted to unfasten the gown myself as the marriage discussion continued.

"Like K.C. always says, there's no time like the present," I said. My delivery driver, Karma Clackerton, has a knack for handing out advice. She's one tough grandma who continuously amazes with wacky outfits and new additions to her weapons arsenal. "Besides, she's older than you, Mom. At least I think she is," I said, and then cringed at venturing into the touchy subject of my mother's age. "I think that's the reason she and Fred decided to get married so soon."

"You do have a point there, Quincy." Did my ears deceive me? Had my mother actually agreed with me? Would wonders would never cease?

"Neither of us is getting any younger. I suppose she should jump at the chance she's been given for happiness." I could hear the sadness in my mom's voice and I felt a tiny bit guilty for the gift of happiness I'd been given with Alex.

"Was that the last dress, Quincy?" Allie asked.

"Last one. But I might be in here for a while." The dress wouldn't be too hard to tackle, but then there were the undergarments I'd been instructed to wear by the attendant.

"You'll thank me later," she'd said. "Things will be firmed, lifted and separated in a way that your regular, *ahem, delicates* will never accomplish."

My regular delicates usually came with the words Fruit and Loom printed on them somewhere, so I was pretty sure things would feel different with this fancy underwear.

And actually, the attendant had been right. I felt incredibly sexy when I looked in the mirror. Almost every dress I tried on fit as if it were designed just for me, except for the length. No underwear would make a dress fit a 5'9" girl in the same way it fit a more vertically challenged one, but the curves worked in all the right places. It was going to be quite a feat removing the lace and mesh body sculpting device. Where was that attendant, anyway?

For her grand wedding extravaganza, with the help of Danny, my closest friend and fellow flower shop owner, K.C. had chosen an overall scheme of harvest colors, such as pumpkin spice, ochre, celadon, and aubergine, but she'd left the choice of bridesmaid dress style and color up to me. I was partial to a tea-length number in a burnt orange organza with a shoulder wrap, but I wanted to check another shop before making my decision.

"Speaking of romance, Quincy," Allie said, "how are things with Alex?" Her tone made me blush. I envisioned Alex the way he looked the last time I saw him. He was on his way to work in a navy fitted suit with a steel gray shirt, which perfectly accented his brown eyes and light golden brown hair.

"Things are—great. I mean, well yeah, they're great." Things were great when we were together, but he was currently on an undercover operation in the southern part of the state. That's all I knew. Alex worked in Internal Affairs for the Utah State Police, and much of the work he did was undercover. That's how we met—he was posing as a patrol officer while investigating the dirty detective who had framed me for the murder of a competitor.

I really liked Alex.

Okay—so maybe liked is an understatement. My knees turned to Jell-O at just the sound of his voice on the phone, not to mention all the things that happened to me when we were in the same room. But like was the only "L" word I could allow myself to use for a man, given my romantic relationship history.

I knew we had something together, although I couldn't quite pinpoint exactly what we had, because every time I thought I had "us" figured out, he would leave again. He also worked on a gang task force and traveled a lot for that job. Between dirty cops and gangsters, I was feeling part of a competition for his attention.

"Is he out of town for long?" Allie asked.

"I'm not sure," I called out, as I hung the dress on the satin hanger. *Now to remove the figure-enhancing Iron Maiden.*

"It must be hard not seeing him for that long," Allie said. "Heck, I miss seeing that fine man of yours."

"Allison!" Our mother had a lack of appreciation for the "color" of our conversation.

I caught myself smiling in the mirror. The fact hadn't escaped me that Alex was, shall we say, *appreciated* by fellow members of my gender.

Allie kept up the teasing with our mother. "Oh, Mom, admit it now. Alex is H-O-T, hot! It's okay to state the obvious. Quincy doesn't mind if you speak the truth. Do you, Quincy?"

"Of course not, Mother dear," I said.

"Well, he does have certain—physical—attributes." Mom cleared her throat, "Despite some differences I might have with him, he is quite easy to look at."

"Easy on the eyes? Is that what you're trying to say, Mom?" Allie said. "Quincy, our mother is blushing because she has the hots for your hot boyfriend."

Allie giggled again and my mother tsked. It was nice to have fun together again, even if it was at the expense of my—yes he was—my hot *boyfriend*.

I struggled with the hooks on the back of the bustier-entrapment device and realized I wasn't going to get it unfastened without tearing the delicate-yet iron-like support fabric. We had the dressing room and sitting area reserved for an hour, so no one else would be around to see me in my fancy skivvies, including the attendant, apparently. I unlatched the door and used my backside to push it open while my hands were occupied with the blasted hooks and eyes fasteners between my shoulder blades. "I'm going to need some help getting out of this thing."

I turned and looked in the direction of Allie and our mother, but my eyes landed behind them, directly into the dark brown eyes of a man grinning from ear to ear and casually leaning against the wall, ankles crossed, hand in the hip pocket of his jeans.

"I'd be happy to fulfill that request," he said.

"Ohmagosh!" I reflexively crossed my arms over my boosted breasts and then reached down in an attempt to cover the southern hemisphere with one of my arms in an awkward dance toward the dressing room.

"Who—wha—what?" I heard my mother exclaim.

"I'm so sorry," the familiar deep voice said without really sounding sorry at all. "The woman at the front counter told me I could find Quincy back here."

He was trying not to laugh—and failing.

"Alex?" Allie said in a high-pitched squeak, "We were just talking about you." I was sure her face was as scarlet as the face looking back at me in the dressing room mirror.

"I know," he said.

I threw my t-shirt and jeans on over the fancy underwear, which only added to the extreme discomfort of the situation. I admit it was thrilling to see Alex's face when he saw me in my sculpted and shaped glory. It was the closest to naked he'd ever seen me…on the other hand, my mother just had to be there for the big event. Ick. Blegh. Eew.

I escaped the dressing room as fast as I could to do some damage control.

My mother's face was not red as a poppy, as I had suspected it would be. It was, in fact, extremely pale.

"Alex," she said. "Hhh—how long have you been here?"

"Only a minute…or ten," he said, through perfect white teeth, which he was having an awfully hard time covering up because his smile was reaching epic proportions.

"We'll meet you up front, Quincy," Allie said. She and our mother slipped past Alex while twittering like a couple of thirteen-year-old girls who had just seen their latest movie star crush.

I bit my bottom lip when I finally approached Alex. He had an almost full beard of golden blond hair.

"What's this?" I asked as I reached up and stroked the furry side of his jaw.

"Ah, you like it? It's been part of my persona for the last little while." Truthfully, I hated it, but it didn't matter. He could have been wearing a dress and he still would have been the hottest cop on the planet.

He wrapped his strong arms around my waist and bent down to kiss me. I put my arms around his neck and held tight. His fingers wandered and fussed along my back where the tenacious hooks were still fastened under my t-shirt. He broke the kiss and leaned back just a centimeter. His warm breath passed across my lips, teasing.

"This little item is...inspiring."

He arched one eyebrow.

"Yeah, about that. How much did you actually see?"

What a dumb question. He wasn't blind.

"Just exactly enough, babe." The words slid out of his mouth in that deep voice, slow and deliberate. I swallowed and forced myself to start breathing again.

"Oh." A flutter started in my chest. I cleared my throat in anticipation of finding something to say. Things were getting warm in that little parlor. Actually, the warmth mostly seemed to be twirling around me. Why was my throat so dry?

"So, how much of our silly conversation did you hear?" I said, trying to appear nonchalant while my fingers toyed with the new curls at the back of his neck which had developed along with the beard during his absence.

"Um, probably just...all of it."

"Huh," is all that would come out, and that was followed by an excruciatingly long pause. I came up with a weak laugh, "Well, at least you know how everyone feels," I said and shrugged. He just stood there and grinned at me.

"What did I miss while I was gone?" he said, finally.

"Where to start?" I said. "I'll tell you what I missed..."

His eyes crinkled around the edges and he bent down and nuzzled my neck. "What's that?"

"Let me just show you." I kissed him, then he took over and kissed me back, long and slow. Electricity seemed to spark between our bodies.

He came up for breath. "Mmm, I like show better than tell. Seems like you've put some thought into what we talked about before I left."

Oh boy, had I ever. We had discussed the next step. *Theee* next step with a capital "T," if you know what I mean. Taking our physical relationship to the next level had been the topic after the hottest, handsiest, gropingest, make-out session two adults could have without moving on to more adult activities.

I had hesitated a nano-second when he asked about going further. I mean, who hasn't taken a pause before speaking once in a while? When someone asks you a question, isn't it polite to give a thoughtful response? So I hesitated. So what? Not that big a deal.

He took that hesitation to mean an absolute *no*. Despite my protests, he thought we should cool things down and wait until I was ready. I thought I was ready. My body was *certain* it was ready, and I was all set to prove it the next time we were together. But then he was called out of town for the job.

And now he was back from the job.

"Absolutely," I said. I looked into his brown eyes, "I'm ready."

"Are you sure?" He pulled away, which wasn't exactly the response I was hoping for. But then, we were in a public place.

"I'm sure." Wasn't I? Why wasn't he convinced? Was I sending out a vibe that I wasn't aware of? Like a dog whistle, the pitch only matching Alex's ears? "You just say the word—or make the move—or whatever else, and I am *there*."

He furrowed his brows and leaned back some more. Oh no. My inner dork had just taken over again.

I was ready. I had no reservations, no hesitations, no…no idea why I would have any reason to not feel ready.

"Quincy, hey, there's no pressure here. I understand." He completely let go of me. "Let's just keep things slow. I want you to feel comfortable with everything. You'll be ready when you're ready. And I'll be ready then too. Okay?" Then, horror of horrors, he chucked my chin like he was giving encouragement to a little leaguer. He might as well have called me "champ," and told me to get back in the game.

The temperature between us dropped as if we had just walked into my flower cooler. I rested the palm of my hand on his sculpted chest. "Thank you for being so thoughtful, but don't worry, I'm ready now. I mean, not now—now, like right here in the bridal shop, but now like from now on." I looked left, and then right. "I do still have about twenty minutes left on the room reservation, though. We could lock the door…"

He laughed and cradled my face with his hands. Much better than the chin-chuck for sure. "I've missed you, Q." He kissed my forehead then gave me a hug. "So, what are you doing later?"

I wanted to say, "Taking off your shirt," but I thought that might be pushing it. "Spending time with you, I hope."

"Let's go to dinner. No, better yet, let me make dinner for you at my place," he said.

This would be our chance. He was setting the stage.

"What day of the week is this?" he said.

"It's Saturday."

"My schedule is so off from the traveling, I can't keep track of the days."

"How did you know I would be here, anyway?" I said.

"I called K.C. when you and Allie didn't answer your phones. Great news for K.C. and Fred, huh?"

"Yeah, I guess you were gone when they made their big announcement. It's been a whirlwind ever since," I said.

"So, I'll go home and get cleaned up, and I'll lose this thing," he tugged at his beard. "I might not have time for a haircut, though. There's something I'm supposed to remember about Saturday, something I'm supposed to do. Oh well, I'll think of it. So, beautiful, do we have a date—tonight around six?"

"I can't wait. Hey, I kind of like those little curls, maybe you should hold off on that haircut."

"Whatever you say, babe. Your wish is my command."

CHAPTER TWO

I rushed back to the flower shop to help Daphne finish some of the closing duties. Saturdays were usually our slowest days at the shop, and I had considered putting the closed sign on the door early, but a slower day was perfect for our newest employee to go it alone for a while.

Rosie's Posies was still the name of the shop. After all, it was built on my great aunt Rosie's blood, sweat, and tears, not mine. Although, I'd shed my share of all three since I took over from her, especially in the last couple of months. In that short time, I'd been thrown in jail for assault with a deadly weapon, and K.C. had helped me rescue my sister from a psychotic, abusive boyfriend. Oh, and then there was the murder case. Two, actually.

All that action made quite a commotion in our little town. K.C. and I had become famous. Or is that infamous? Anyway, our new found notoriety seemed to have boosted the amount of customers we were seeing at the store. How being involved in a murder case increases a town's need for flowers, I'll never know, but I wasn't about to complain. I decided I needed to hire extra help. Daphne had appeared at just the right time, and with flower shop experience.

After going over the day's sales with Daphne, I told her I would finish up—but didn't tell her why I wanted to rush out of the shop! I buzzed back and forth, closing out the till and doing a quick sweep, but skipped mopping the floors. All the while, my mind hummed with the possibilities of what the evening might hold.

I couldn't help smiling when I thought about Alex. Not just for the obvious reasons—I did more than smile when I saw him—I practically drooled, although I tried not to in public. But I smiled thinking about *him* the person, not just *him* the body.

I hadn't exactly been trusting when we first met. He knew about my past with an abusive ex and the emotional baggage that came with it. And I admit, I really had hesitated at first. The leap from celibacy to intimacy seemed too difficult to fathom. I hadn't ever been physically intimate with anyone but the ex-husband.

So, even as wonderful as Alex was, I had been reluctant to trust him. It wasn't personal—I wasn't willing to trust anyone—or any man, that is. I was an equal opportunity distruster.

Deep inside, I knew he was worthy of my trust. It's just that I was emotionally gun shy, and still, even though I wanted to be with Alex in *that way*, there was a little voice in the back of my mind reminding me of the pain I had experienced before when I dropped my defenses and let a man get too close.

But tonight I would be on a mission to silence that nagging little voice in the back of my head. Alex was wonderful, handsome, and lovely in every way. I knew what happened after dinner would be something special. Whatever *it* turned out to be. I was hopeful for a certain *it*.

I placed the closed sign on the front door and retreated to the back to grab my things and shut out the lights. My fingers were poised above the light switch when I heard the front door chime. I looked around the corner hoping to see Daphne returning for a forgotten item. Instead, I saw a familiar face. All too familiar as of late.

I recognized the unforgettable scent of the favorite perfume of Jacqueline DeMechante. Jacqueline—not Jackie, not Jack-lean, but Jack-will-lean, unless you wanted trouble—was the mother of Jenny McQueen, a sweet bride for whom we were decorating a wedding. Jacqueline's daughter was getting married a mere two weeks after K.C. and Fred, and we were deep into the preparations for both weddings.

My nose twitched and the beginnings of an allergy induced headache crept into my forehead. If I hadn't been able to see Ms. DeMechante, I still would have recognized her. She was always preceded by a cloud of perfume which smelled of spice, musk, and exotic places. I might actually have enjoyed the fragrance if there wasn't so much of it. Hours after she'd left the shop we still smelled her. I'm pretty sure she bathed in that perfume.

"Jacqueline, what a pleasant surprise," I lied. Ms. DeMechante had made a habit of arriving at the most inopportune times to discuss wedding matters which had already been settled.

Now, as I was preparing to complete my mission with Alex, it was the *most* inopportune moment of *all* time.

"Ms. McKay, I realize it's closing time, but I was just driving by…and I've been considering our choices in the blue realm…and I'm just so concerned that you didn't quite get the essence of the tint that I want for Jenny's wedding."

Well since this is the fifteenth time you've brought the subject up, I don't see how it would be possible for me to have missed the ESSENCE of the tint.

I bit my lip and exercised some super-human restraint. "Well, Jacqueline, I do have the paint chips you brought in from the hardware store for color matching, and we picked the linens out of the catalog together, so I think I've got the idea. Would you like to take a look at the paint chips again?" What was I thinking? I was suggesting she prolong her visit?

"No," she said. She sighed while collapsing her shoulders, "I suppose I'll just have to trust you."

I fought back the eye roll.

"I feel confident that you've given me the most accurate color sample possible, Jacqueline."

"Oh, of course. Well, I suppose that's all for now." She placed one hand on her hip, her skinny elbow bending at a sharp angle. Her other arm hung in the air as if she held a long cigarette holder. The figure she cut reminiscent of an Erte silhouette. She swung toward the door with dramatic flair, disturbing the cloud of perfume, re-circulating it throughout the shop.

I immediately sneezed. And that sneeze was followed by another, and another, until I lost count. Through teary eyes, I saw Jacqueline pivot back toward me, which stirred up the atmosphere again.

"Is there something else...*sneeze*...Jacqueline?" I stumbled toward a box of tissues near the phone.

"Are you sick, Quincy?"

"No, no. It must be something in the air," I said, annoyed that she asked the same thing every time this happened.

"You should really find out what's causing your attacks," she said.

I blew my nose and grumbled to myself, "Oh, I have a pretty good idea."

"You know, Quincy, I just don't feel secure with the changes we've made."

What changes? My teeth clenched. If she only knew how long I had waited for this date with Alex. But if I tried to rush her out it would only make her want to stay longer.

"I really must speak with Jenny and then the two of us shall meet with you again. Perhaps we could bring her fiancé with us. I'm certain he'll want to be in on the plans too."

I was certain he wouldn't. He'd said as much at the last pointless meeting where we changed everything and then changed it all back to the original.

"I really don't think it's necessary to have a new meeting," I said, in the sweetest voice I could conjure. "If you're happy with the ribbons and sashes you've already chosen, we can just use those. All of them coordinate with the Nile blue sample you brought in."

"But it isn't Nile blue. As I've pointed out repeatedly, it's just Nile. And what about the Lapis? You didn't mention the Lapis. Is there a problem getting Lapis in? I was right. We must meet again." She turned toward the door. "We'll come in on Monday."

I took a deep breath and pasted a smile on my face. "Alright Jacqueline, we'll see you Monday."

I didn't bother asking her *when* on Monday, because she would, of course, come whenever she wanted to, which was *always* at the precise moment I was most busy.

I realized Jenny was Jacqueline's only daughter and that Jacqueline just wanted to provide the best wedding she could. Unfortunately, Jacqueline was an extreme micromanager with lots of time and money on her hands. I consoled myself with the thought that at least I had helped Jacqueline get out of the house, giving Jenny a momentary break.

Jacqueline formed her lips into a thin line, and then a kind of undulation, which was probably her closest imitation of a smile. The coral colored lipstick she wore smudged outside the boundaries of her lips and made her forced smile look all the more ridiculous. Her cobalt blue eye shadow, painted at sharp angles to the outer edges of her brow, deepened the shark-like quality of her gaze. She said nothing and elegantly strolled toward the exit.

Before she had a chance to turn back and start a new conversation, I sprinted to the switch on the wall, and as soon as her back foot broke the plane of the doorway, it was lights out. I had a long-awaited hot date to prepare for and no mom-zilla was going to stop me.

***

It was late when I pulled into my driveway in the zombie van. Zombie Sue had lived through a multitude of fender-benders, at least one hit and run that I knew of, and many dangerous delivery drivers. Not only was she my delivery van, but she was my sole source of transportation. Her odometer had broken long ago, so I had no idea how many miles she had on her. No matter, she was a zombie van. And unless someone cut off her head, she would last forever.

I'd purchased the Unique Support Item at the bridal shop after Alex left. I would need extra time to maneuver back into it after I showered, but now I had some experience with the mechanics of it all. So what if I missed a few hooks? I didn't think Alex would mind.

After undressing, I leaned over to turn on the water and shrieked at what I saw. My legs looked like something off of a rarely seen and never photographed urban legend from the woods. I hadn't shaved my legs since the last time Alex and I had gone out. Apparently he'd been gone a *long* time. I considered taking a picture of my leg and sending it to Allie to scare her, but I didn't have time to fool around now, or else I wouldn't have enough time to fool around later.

I propped my foot up on the old claw-foot tub so I could shave. The tub was quaint, its sides were deep, and the edge was slippery. My foot slipped off after the second pass with the blade, and I cut myself. As I searched through the linen cabinet for a new roll of toilet paper to dress the wound, I noticed the message light blinking on my cell phone.

Since I couldn't stop putting pressure on the bleeding, I hopped over to the vanity on one foot and played the message on speakerphone and then reached for my toothbrush.

"Hidey-ho there, Boss," came K.C.'s typically cheerful greeting. "I just wanted to see how the dress shopping went. I'm sorry I couldn't be there, but this wedding planning thing is hard work. I feel like a chicken out in the yard after it's head's been plucked. Listen, I know we had plans for the lecture tonight, but I heard your caliente cowboy is back in town, so don't pay me any mind. We'll make a rain check. Ciao!"

K.C. met her fiancé at a gala after we had installed all the floral decorations. A dead body had been shoved in Zombie Sue while we were there, but thankfully that hadn't had any effect on the start of their romance. She and Fred got engaged less than two months later and had decided to have a big outdoor wedding. They'd chosen a lovely spot at the visitor center at the Wetlands Conservatory, part of the marsh on the banks of the Great Salt Lake. Apparently, Fred was quite the birder and K.C. had taken up the addictive hobby.

I could've kicked myself for forgetting our plans. I guess my mind was on one track only and that track led to Alex's house and certain activities in his house. I would have to call her back after I brushed my teeth. The next message played.

"Hey Quince," my heart fluttered at the sound of Alex's voice—I also felt the instinct to cover up, since I was standing there naked.

Funny that. Given the things I had in mind for my mission with Alex and the preparations I was making, why did I feel the need put on a robe?

"You won't believe this," he continued, "but I remembered what it was that I was supposed to do on Saturday—I mean today."

I stopped brushing and scowled at the phone, willing it—or Alex—to stop talking about something that I just knew was going to end up ruining our plans.

"I got a call a few days ago from my old friend Sam who's in town for the weekend. We worked together back in California. Anyway, we were supposed to have dinner tonight and...well, just call me back when you get this message."

I nearly choked on my toothbrush. Mission failed. I considered calling him while still in the nude, but figured it would just add to my disappointment. I rinsed, spit, pulled on my robe, and made the call.

"It's okay. I understand," I said. "I forgot about the bird lecture with K.C. tonight. I guess we were both preoccupied."

"Why don't you come with us? I want you guys to meet each other." He sounded sincere, but I didn't want to play third wheel, especially not a sexually frustrated third wheel with something to prove.

"Well, I should probably keep my date with K.C. Fred's buddy is the lecturer and one of his groomsmen. K.C. wanted to check out a restaurant for her rehearsal dinner afterwards, too. Maybe I'll meet Sam some other time." I tried not to let the disappointment creep into my voice. I wasn't particularly thrilled about the prospect of hearing all about the Inland False Booby and its environs, but Fred was jazzed about it, and therefore, so was K.C.

"How about I cook for you tomorrow night? Sunday dinner. I feel really bad about this, babe. It's just that I haven't talked to Sam in like, three years."

"Go to dinner with your friend, have a good time. I'll come over tomorrow. It'll be better for everyone this way. Really, have a great night."

"Okay, you too. You're the best. Bye, Q."

It just wasn't in the cards for us to have our "big" night, and secretly—I felt relieved. Not that I wasn't ready! Okay, so maybe I wasn't so ready, but I was sure I could get over my hang-ups by morning. And heck, what would be so bad about waiting one more day? It wasn't like I hadn't been waiting for a long, long time already.

CHAPTER THREE

The crowd buzzed in the few minutes before the lecture was scheduled to start. I never would have thought this many people would be excited about a bird called the False Inland Booby. The lecture was supposed to have been held at the visitor center at the bird refuge, but the projected crowd was so large the organizers moved the event to Hillside High School, home of the Fighting Farmers.

"K.C., don't take this the wrong way, but why are there so many people here? I mean, I just expected a bunch of guys in plaid shirts and cargo pants, with maybe some fly-fishing vests sprinkled in, but the black-rectangle glasses crowd is here too. It feels like we're at an NPR lecture or something."

Fred leaned over K.C. "There are so many people here because this is a historical event. Jack Conway has discovered a bird that we thought was extinct!" His eyes glinted with excitement. "Jack is going to tell us all about how he sighted the bird and where he was. He was at our own bird refuge when he saw it, but I can't wait to hear the exact location. This is so huge. The international press is here and everything. Jack is world famous now, and just think, he is a member of our local bird society!"

An older couple came over and started a conversation with Fred. K.C. turned to me. "You know kiddo, birding is a high-stakes hobby."

"Really?" I said, waiting for the punch line.

"No, I'm serious. Take the Ivory Billed Woodpecker, for example. It was considered extinct, but then one day this guy says he saw one. No one in the bird world believed him. In fact, he had some people who went to the press and said they could prove him wrong." She paused to check on Fred's conversation, then sat there quietly, looking at the stage.

"So?" I said.

"Huh? Oh, sorry, Boss. Where was I?"

"They said they could prove him wrong..."

"Oh yes. Well, not soon after that, they found his main detractors dead. They'd been murdered. Come to find out, it was the man who says he saw the Ivory Billed Woodpecker. He was willing to kill to keep his reputation intact. Now that's hard core dedication."

I didn't know if I believed her or not, since she'd been known to spin a yarn or two, but the crowd began to stir as some movement was made in the curtain on the stage. A man in a suit and bow tie approached the lectern and gave an introduction for Jack Conway.

Jack entered the stage and the audience erupted in applause. He proceeded to tell the tale of the sighting of the False Inland Booby. A large screen rolled down from the ceiling on the stage and a painting of a white bird was projected on it while he spoke. Apparently Mr. Conway had only seen the bird once, and he had no photographic evidence, nor did he have any witnesses. The painting was from a bird book from the 1800's.

This lack of evidence seemed puzzling to me. Even in the most basic research papers in high school, we had to state our sources for the information. And I'm pretty sure none of my teachers would have accepted me writing "Because I saw it with my own eyes." But, as I looked from side to side at other audience members, none of them seemed to show any doubt in their expressions.

After the lecture the floor was opened for comments and questions. A microphone on a stand was positioned on the floor in front of the orchestra pit. A man approached the mic and introduced himself as Harold Busby. He trembled as he pulled his notes out of his pocket. He took a deep breath before he spoke. I noticed K.C. and Fred shifting in their seats. They looked at each other and K.C. rolled her eyes. Fred shook his head.

"Blowhard," K.C. muttered.

Mr. Busby's ruddy skin glistened with perspiration. "We all know that the False Inland Booby is extinct. The last known sighting of this bird was in 1947..."

"Now hold on, Harold," Mr. Conway interrupted from the podium. "You've known me for how many years? You know I'm not the type to make this stuff up."

Mr. Busby slapped his papers against the open palm of his other hand. "Jack, don't you interrupt me, it's my turn to talk. I know that you've made a pretty penny what with all these speaking engagements and touring all over the blasted world." Whispers spread throughout the crowd and people's heads turned toward the speaker. "You want all these people to believe that you didn't get any photographs, and that you were all alone when you sighted this bird?"

"Yes, I do. I tried to take a photo, but I went to point and click, the darned thing went dark. My battery was dead. Terrible timing, I know. But that's Murphy's Law, isn't it?" He attempted a weak laugh and held his hands out as if imploring the crowd, begging for sympathy, which garnered a few snickers.

A tall, slender man with a beak-like nose hurried up to the mic-stand and put his arm around Mr. Busby's shoulders. "Now, Harold..." Busby tried to shrug off the taller man's arm.

"You're not going to get away with this, Conway! You're practically a millionaire because of this lie, and I will go to my grave letting the world know that you are a charlatan—a snake-oil salesman." Busby's face had evolved to a frightening shade of fuchsia. The MC came to the podium and tried to change the subject by thanking Mr. Conway. While the crowd applauded half-heartedly, the tall man pulled Mr. Busby away from the microphone and led him toward the hallway exit.

"Well that was exciting, eh, Boss?" K.C. jabbed me in the ribs with a little too much force. "Nothing like a little showdown to give the lecture some juice. What did you think, Fred?"

"Old Busby's just sore. He's been in our bird club for years. His father was a founding member. I'm going to go see if Gordo needs help with Busby. In fact, I've got to talk to Gordon about that meeting we're going to have tomorrow morning. I'll catch a ride with him, sweetums. You girls go on and have dinner without me."

"But Fred," K.C. said, "we're going to your friend's restaurant so we can try it out for the rehearsal dinner."

"I know, my sweet, but I've already eaten there many times and can vouch for the place. I really have to talk to Gordon about this meeting. It's about," Fred glanced at me and smiled, then nodded his head toward K.C., "the thing I spoke about earlier, concerning Brock."

"Oh, yes, that. Well, Quincy I guess we ride stag tonight then. Alright with you?"

"Of course." I tried to ignore the cloak and dagger nature of Fred and K.C.'s conversation since it wasn't any of my business, but the mention of Brock's name was cause for some speculation. I just couldn't help it. Brock was Jenny McQueen's fiancé. I was curious as to why Fred would've mentioned him.

Brock and Jenny had met at the office, in a manner of speaking. Brock worked for the state Wildlife Management Bureau at the marsh, and Jenny was a marine biologist. They crossed paths in a salt water infused pond surrounded by brine flies and lake-stink. Such a recipe for romance! Despite the odd location of their first meeting, they were a truly sweet and loving couple. As were K.C. and Fred.

I decided I was almost glad Alex had come up with other plans for the night. K.C. and I could have a girls' night out where we could talk about all the fun parts of the wedding, and we wouldn't have to worry that we were boring poor Fred, who would never risk telling K.C. he didn't especially care about the wedding plans. He just wanted her to be happy, even if that meant sitting through hours of discussions about dresses, flowers and hairstyles.

But tonight, he wouldn't have to. I pushed thoughts of Alex out of mind as best I could and looked forward to a fun time with K.C.

***

We took K.C.'s little car to the restaurant in Salt Lake. "Hey, kiddo. Thanks so much for coming with me tonight. It was mighty nice of you to let Alex meet his buddy without making a fuss. You sure you're alright with me pinch-hitting?"

"I had plans to go with you to begin with. And I'm glad Alex gets to see his old friend," I said, hoping I sounded convincing.

"That's very sweet of you. I know I wouldn't be able to keep my hands off of Fred if he had been gone like that. Hell, he hasn't gone anywhere and we still light the house on fire most every night. It seemed like you two were getting pretty close by the time he had to leave. I don't want to pry, but I assumed you two might be doing the hokey-pokey by now."

"Wh…" Suddenly there was a blockage in my throat and I couldn't quit coughing. That song would never have the same meaning to me again. I tried to think of something—anything—that would keep me from imagining Fred and K.C. doing their version of that dance…ooh too late.

"There's nothing to be embarrassed about kiddo. It's a fact of life. It's just what nature intended for two consenting adults." She alternated her grip on the steering wheel as she talked with her hands, carrying on as if we were chatting about everyday things like the deliveries at work or how to make a rose arrangement.

"I really don't think we should be..."

"Shoot, I'm being insensitive to your predicament. You must have had an awful experience with that ex of yours. I wouldn't blame you for being a little gun shy, but you've got to get back up on that horse and ride 'im, if you know what I mean." Oh, I knew what she meant. How could anyone not know what she meant? "And you don't just have any old horse. You've got a fine stallion to mount..."

"Okay, K.C." I interrupted before I had to jump from the moving car to escape.

"I know—I know. I get carried away sometimes. But men aren't like you and me, Boss. They can't live without it. They *have* to have sex to survive, or at least to be tolerable. That's just the plain facts. I know you might be stuck in first gear because of the nasty ogre ex, but now you've got to move forward for both of your sake's. If you don't make your move, there's a lineup of cowgirls that snakes all the way around the block. They'll be knocking down his door for that bareback ride any chance they get."

Blegh.

When she actually used the word *sex*, it all just seemed so dirty. And then she threw cowgirls and snakes and bareback into the mental picture.

Double blegh.

But she was right about the competition. Anywhere I went with Alex, women stared at him, but I hadn't worried about it because he never returned their looks. He kept his attention on me.

"How did this restaurant make the list?" I asked, desperate for a subject change.

"Fred is a friend of one of the owners. They're supposed to be ultra-cheek…"

"Do you mean chic?" I said.

"That's what I said—you know, the place to be for anyone who's anyone. I'm sure their prices are sky-high too, but Fred said his friend wants to give us a deal for a wedding present."

"That's fantastic. Do you think we're dressed appropriately for such a nice place?" I wasn't wearing sweatpants, but I'd chosen a more casual top with khaki's and gathered my hair in a simple ponytail when I found out I wouldn't be needing to fix it up for Alex.

"You look cute as a kitten. What I wouldn't give to be as tall and slender as you. I rather like what I'm wearing. I think we look like two fashionable gals out on the town." K.C. sported a red floral print, ankle-length prairie skirt with a white knit top, a matching red scarf tied 1950's sock hop style, around her neck and her latest fashion statement, a hunter green Fedora she called her traveling cap, which she wore every time she drove her car or Zombie Sue.

We walked into the lobby and were instantly enveloped in a magical atmosphere. Rich tapestries and gauzy gold and purple sheer curtains flowed through the lobby and into the rest of the restaurant. Statues of camels and lions presided over every room. Furniture of dark, heavily carved wood and jewel-toned fabric dotted different spaces, while *world beat* music streamed throughout. Human electricity filled the air.

"This place is fantastic," I said after we'd been seated. "I hope the food is as great as the atmosphere."

The five-course *prix fix* menu offered numerous temptations for the palate. I didn't recognize the names of most of the things on the menu, but decided I could trust the restaurant, judging by the looks on the other diners' faces. Shortly after the first course of butternut cream soup was served, K.C. and I got down to business comparing notes about her wedding plans. I also told her about my surprise at the dress shop earlier that day. "I bet you had a grin on your face after that. How did he look after being gone that long? A sight for sore eyes, I'm sure."

A warm fluttering commenced in my chest as I thought about our embrace and his hair and the way his awful, scraggly beard tickled my cheek. "He looked…"

"Say no more, chickadee. I can tell what the answer is by the look on your face. That good, huh?"

I knew I was blushing and couldn't help but smile.

"He is quite a fella," she said. "And you're quite a gal. I see a rosy future for the two of you." K.C. scoured the room. "Gosh, there are so many interesting people here. I would love to be a fly on the wall to hear some of the conversations. Look over there to my left."

K.C. jerked her head in the direction she was talking about, probably thinking she was being subtle. In reality, she'd done a full body jerk, her blond bob flipped so sharply to the side it looked like she was in a shampoo commercial. She teetered on the edge of her chair after her weight shift and grabbed the table to avoid falling over.

Subtlety would rarely be a quality one would suggest when describing Karma Clackerton.

I waited until she righted herself and smoothed her hair. "What about them?"

"Phew. Who are we talking about?"

"The couple you just pointed out. On your left," I said.

"I bet he's in the mafia, and she's a femme-fah-tally," she whispered.

I didn't correct her mispronunciation of femme-fatale. "The Utah mafia, K.C.?" I rolled my eyes and we both had a laugh.

The entrées arrived and I tried to show some restraint instead of gulping down the delectable food. I'd chosen Provo River trout with crab and citrus couscous. K.C. had the Summit County filet of beef with garlic whipped potatoes.

"This beef just melts in your mouth," K.C. said. "I think I might have to come here for dinner every night."

All I could do was nod, as my mouth was never without a bite of my entrée.

Between mouthfuls of food and exclamations of appreciation for the meal, we compared notes about the wedding and coordinating plans with Danny, my good friend and fellow florist. Even though he was a competitor, we helped each other out and came to each other's rescue when needed. K.C.'s wedding would be large enough that I needed the extra help, and Danny was the event specialist. His help with the wedding would allow me to participate in the festivities. That wouldn't be possible if I was doing it all on my own.

K.C. had pretty much given me and Danny carte blanche on everything concerning the florals and décor. Previously, we'd all brainstormed ideas for incorporating symbols of both K.C.'s Dutch and Fred's Scottish heritage, and K.C. had injected some of her own unique but wonderful ideas that reflected her distinct personality.

The palate-cleansing cheese course was next, which almost could've have been served as dessert. Almost—but I'd rather miss my own wedding than miss dessert in this restaurant.

"Now there's a nice looking couple," K.C. said.

"Where?" I asked.

"Behind you, by the partition. Don't look! You can't see them from where you are. If you look it'll be obvious," said the queen of obvious.

"What's so nice about them?"

"It looks like he's a real gentleman. He pulled her chair out for her. And she looks at him like she really likes him. Actually, they remind me a lot of you and your beau."

"Oh, really?" I said.

"She looks like she could be your long lost twin—except for the breasts. Hers are much bigger than yours."

Of course they are.

"Oh, isn't that sweet," K.C. said as she looked over my shoulder. "You can tell she really likes him. And she's *good.*"

"What do you mean?"

"I mean she knows her way around a man. She reaches for something on the table just as he does so that their hands meet by *accident.* Wink, wink." She literally winked with her whole face as she said it. "She touches his forearm then laughs lightly as they talk. Oh my hell, I think she might have just grabbed his leg under the table. You should take some pointers from her. Learn how to really make your man growl."

"K.C.!"

"What?" She shrugged and continued eating.

I had no problem making Alex growl—or interested—or well, I mean happy in that way. Right? I recalled him suggesting we slow things down, not me. But maybe I *had* unintentionally been throwing off those silent delay signals. Apparently K.C. had picked up on them too.

I was deep into a dish of self-doubt by the time the dessert arrived. I'd been thinking how I wished I'd gone with Alex to meet his friend, no offense to my present company. We could have had dinner, said goodbye to his friend, gone to his place and…yikes. I was getting ideas.

"You okay, Boss?"

"Huh?"

"You're all flushed. Your cheeks look like my bare shoulders after ten minutes in the sun."

I shoved a bite of warm *Tarte Tatin* in my mouth, "Mmm, I'm fine. It's just this *dessert*." It really was that good, but not the cause of my elevated heartbeat and sudden sweat. The homemade vanilla bean ice cream helped to cool things down.

K.C. spotted Fred's friend at the maître d's station and went to express her delight with the restaurant and confirm her desire to book the rehearsal dinner there. I followed just behind her. As she spoke with the man, I surveyed the other guests in the room and my eyes stopped, along with my heart, on one couple in particular.

K.C. was right. They were a lovely couple. And half of that *lovely* couple was a still-bearded, suit-clad man with a death-wish named Alex Cooper. The other half was a woman who looked very much like me. Obviously tall, even though seated, her long, platinum blond hair fell over her shoulder as she leaned toward Alex to talk. Her sapphire blue wrap-around dress clung to *all* the right places and plunged so far down in the front, I could see her navel lint from across the room.

I tugged at K.C.'s arm before she got away from me. "I think I'm going to be sick."

"What's the matter, kid? Is it the food?" she whispered. "Please don't tell me it's the food. I love this place."

"No," I whispered back. "That couple you thought was so cute, that looked like Alex and me, *is* Alex and sluttier me."

The corners of K.C.'s mouth turned down and she squinted. "Well I'll be snookered. I thought you said he was with an old work pal."

"That's what he said."

"There's only one way to find out what's going on. Come with me." She grabbed my wrist and yanked me in the direction of their table. I couldn't protest in the restaurant without making a scene.

"K.C.!" Alex exclaimed. "What a surprise. What are you doing here?" He stood in the presence of the lady. *What a gentleman.* "Congratulations on the engagement." He encircled her for a hug and his eyes grew huge as he saw me standing behind her.

"Quincy?"

"Alex." I looked at him coolly then turned my gaze toward the woman at the table.

"What—are you two doing *here*?" he asked.

"I was just wondering the exact same thing," I said. K.C. still had a grasp on my wrist and she squeezed hard enough to give me carpal tunnel syndrome.

"Easy cowgirl," she whispered over her shoulder.

I stepped up to the table, slapped a barely passable smile on my face, and extended my hand to the other woman. "Hi, I'm Quincy McKay."

"Samantha Ross," she said as she shook my hand. Ah, the old friend from California, "Sam." Silly me to have assumed Alex's old cop buddy was a man. But he certainly hadn't gone out of his way to make a clear distinction about "Sam's" gender.

"Sam, this is Quincy and K.C." Alex motioned for us to sit down at their four-top table. "Quincy owns a flower shop and K.C. is her driver. I just found out today that K.C. is getting married."

I owned a flower shop? Is that all I was to him? A flower shop owner?

"Oh congratulations," Sam said sweetly. She exuded confidence. And sex appeal. *A lot* of sex appeal. "So, Quincy—is it?" I nodded and smiled ever so sweetly back at her. "How do you two know each other?"

Everyone looked at Alex, who despite having his mouth open, said nothing. Obviously he hadn't told her about us. I mean, why should he? Having dinner with a woman like that didn't lead to a man talking about his girl—friend, or female friend, or whatever kind of friend I was.

I was the kind of friend he was ready to sleep with, just not the kind he could remember to mention to an old "friend from work."

"We, um—well we..." he stammered.

My jaw dropped open. What was his hold up?

"I've ridden in his police car a time or two," I said in the most provocative voice I could manage. Unfortunately, the only model for inspiration that came to mind was Ginger from Gilligan's Island. "Oh, and I stayed in his jail once."

She looked me up and down then laughed dismissively. Apparently I didn't come across as a street walker or stranded Hollywood actress. I returned her fake laugh and smiled. Everyone was laughing and smiling...smiling and laughing...the muscles in my face ached from smiling so much. Then I looked at Alex and dropped the smile.

"You know, Alex," K.C. said in an obvious attempt to cut the tension, "Fred asked me if I thought you would be interested in being a member of the wedding party. And I thought that was a swell idea. He's really developed quite the man crush for you after everything you've done for all of us."

"Wow, that's flattering, K.C. I would be honored."

"Fred will give you a call now that you're back in town."

After that, the uncomfortable silence settled down into the spaces between us.

"So what brings you to town, Samantha—was it?" I said, and then looked over at Alex again.

"Please, call me Sam. I'm in town for a law enforcement symposium. I knew Alex had moved out here to a quaint little city, so I sent him an email a while ago asking if we could meet up and talk about old times. We've had plenty to catch up on, haven't we, Alex?"

He didn't respond. He seemed distracted by the effects of a certain blue dress. Or was it the places on her where the dress didn't cover?

"Did he have that sexy goatee when you knew him?" K.C. asked and then winked at Alex.

Samantha reached across the table and put her hand on Alex's forearm as she spoke. "No, he didn't, but I think it's a great addition to perfection. You had much shorter hair then too. I think I like it shorter."

I thought I might puke. Alex made a show of waving away her compliments, yet I noticed he didn't move his arm too quickly until he glanced over at me.

"Oh, Quincy, before I forget, your mom called me looking for you," Alex said. "I told her I would pass the message along." Cue the record-scratching sound. As if this restaurant situation wasn't humiliating enough, my mother had ensured that I could now die from embarrassment.

"That's so sweet," Samantha said as she placed a hand over one of her ample bosoms—making sure to keep Alex's attention and his eyes on the merchandise. "A mother that checks up on her daughter like that. I can't imagine my own mother ever calling my guy friend to get a hold of me."

Guy friend?

"I guess I left my phone on my kitchen counter. I'm sure there must be some emergency, she wouldn't call for no reason." Anyone who knew my mother would know I was lying. "She probably just assumed since Alex just got back into town, and came looking for me at the dress shop earlier today, that he would be *spending the evening with me.*"

Point for Quincy.

K.C. put her hand in the middle of the table. "Uh—how long will you be visiting, Sam?" K.C.'s attempts to steer the mood or the conversation were futile.

"A few days. The conference only goes through tomorrow afternoon, but I think I'll stick around and see the sights." She looked at Alex and winked.

"Oww," K.C. said. I hadn't realized the vice-like grip I'd had on her forearm.

"This has been so great," I lied, "but I'm feeling kind of ill. It was a pleasure meeting you, Sam. Goodbye, Alex." And I meant goodbye.

"Quincy…" Alex said.

"No, no, don't get up. We've got to get out of here—to plan a wedding—right K.C.?"

My eyes were welling up and I knew I wouldn't be able to stop the flow of tears once they started, and I couldn't let the she-wolf have the satisfaction of seeing them. I calmly walked to the lobby. Once out of Samantha's sight, I rushed outside as fast as I could, hoping K.C. would come along too.

The ride home was long and quiet. K.C. had none of the usual words of wisdom to impart.

"Well, didn't you say he invited you to go with them for dinner?" she finally said.

"Yes, but people never mean it when they make those kinds of invitations. He was just being polite. I mean, did you *see* the way she was dressed? Tell me she was dressed for just meeting with an old work buddy. *Please.* Makes me wonder what kind of *work* they were doing."

"Are you absolutely sure he didn't mention she was a female co-worker?"

"He told me his old friend Sam was in town and that they had worked together in California."

"So, in actuality, he never told you his co-worker was a man. You jumped to that conclusion."

"Well yes, but obviously it was more than a co-worker type of relationship. You saw the way she pawed at him…and the way that he…*let her.*" My throat seemed to be closing off. It physically hurt to swallow and my chest ached.

"Now hold on just a minute. Alex seemed pretty shell-shocked at that table. Maybe he was just frozen like a poor little rabbit cornered by a bobcat. Maybe he just didn't think. They don't think about things. Men, that is. Well, at least they don't think with their noggins most of the time. They think with their little…"

"*So* not helping, K.C."

"Right. You can't let this eat you up inside. You've got to talk to Alex and get his side of the story. It's only fair."

K.C. dropped me off at home and I got ready for bed. I found my cell phone where I had left it. The light blinked indicating I had voicemail.

He better have left me a message. But I was so mad at him, I didn't know if I wanted to listen right away. I scrolled through and saw that my mother had called several times. I thought I should listen to at least one of her messages now that she'd made me look like a junior high girl at the high school senior's party, whose mommy shows up with her forgotten retainer.

"Quincy, please call me. It's an emergency." Oh no. Even with all the guilt-laying and exaggerating tactics my mother used in her usual messages, this sounded like a real emergency. My heart raced and I couldn't get the messages to play fast enough. Another message said, "Quincy, I wish you would answer your phone. It's an emergency. It's your father." Oh no, oh no. Once again, tears welled up in the corners of my eyes. "He..." she sighed and paused for a painfully long time. "He called me, Quincy. *He says he wants to come home.*"

Oh boy.

CHAPTER FOUR

My father had gone on tour with his bluegrass band, "The Salt Flat Lickers," at the same time I had moved away from home. Either the tour never ended or my father just never came back from the last gig. I didn't have a lot of contact with my family then because of the serious issues I had with my wife-beating husband.

After I returned to Hillside, I only brought up the subject of my father once. My mom refused to talk about it, so I never brought it up again. I realized I had been awfully self-centered since I had come back, worrying about the flower shop and my lack of a personal life. Given my mother's tendencies to—what would one call it, annoy?—it had been easy to avoid trying to talk about my dad and how hurt my mother must have been.

And how about my father? I had lost contact with him completely. My marriage had been only one of the many subjects he and my mother had disagreed upon. And after learning the hard way, I understood why my father had been completely against my marriage.

Even though it was late, I called my mom. After several rings her message picked up. Maybe there wasn't such an emergency after all. Maybe she'd gone to bed, although knowing what a worrier she was, I didn't think she would be getting much sleep.

***

I awoke to the sound of the phone ringing and contemplated not answering. Angry thoughts of Alex and Samantha and the awful scene at the restaurant had kept me up most of the night. But I answered in case it was my mother.

"Hello," my voice creaked out.

"Good morning, beautiful."

"Alex?"

"Should I know about any other guys who call you that?"

"I don't know. Are there any other previous *co-workers* I should know about?"

"My, my, my, are you jealous, Ms. McKay?"

"Who, me? What would I have to be jealous about?"

"How about I come in and talk to you about it?"

"Where are you?"

"I'm in your driveway. I have breakfast."

Bribery, I thought. But it was food bribery. At least I could let him in for that. I ran into the bathroom and looked in the mirror. "Oh!" My hair was sticking out at odd angles, and a pimple had appeared next to my nose. No time to fix it now. Nor the makeup smeared around my eyes. I pulled up my striped tube socks and made sure my Star Wars t-shirt wasn't tucked into the back of my cutoff sweatpants.

Alex looked his usual sexy self in worn-out jeans and a t-shirt that fit just right over lots of hard-earned muscles.

He still had the goatee and it looked fantastic. And really, what wouldn't look great on him? But Samantha had overtly talked about how much she loved it the night before. So it had to go.

"Are you feeling any better this morning?" he asked.

"What do you mean?"

"You left because you weren't feeling well, remember?"

"Oh. That's right. I was feeling pretty sickened last night."

He pulled a frilly pink calico apron out of the drawer next to the sink and put it on, then placed a pan on the stove. He came over and wrapped his arms around me, pulling me into him. "Don't be mad at me, Q. What exactly did I do wrong, anyway?"

"Well, first, I feel like I'm supposed to be turned on by my Aunt Rosie right now, since you are wearing her apron. Which is *so* wrong. And second, I will be mad at you as long as you have that incredibly hot-looking thing on your face."

"C'mon, if it's so hot, why should I get rid of it?"

"Because your *old* girlfriend thinks it's a 'Great addition to perfection,'" I made air quotes and spoke in a mockery of Samantha's voice.

"She's not my girlfriend, Quincy."

"No. She's not. And apparently no one else is either. *Sam* had never heard of me before I got to the table."

"Yes she had. She was just kidding around—I had been talking about you all night."

Yeah, she's a real jokester, that one.

"I told you, we used to be co-workers. She's in town for a conference. That's all." He kissed my forehead then went back to the stove to start some bacon. I supposed he was right. If she was just a co-worker, why would he have any reason to tell me her gender? We were both adults. Maybe it was a coincidence she looked like me?

And probably she dressed like a slut all of the time.

"Okay, so she's just a former co-worker, but she sure is a hands-on kind of gal."

"Who could keep their hands off of this?" he asked as he fluffed the shoulder ruffles on the apron.

"I could, unless that apron didn't have a t-shirt under it." Did I say that out loud? I was still supposed to be mad at him, wasn't I?

He put a pitcher of juice on the table and pulled me into him again. "As long as you're wearing those socks at the same time." His hand slid slowly, all the way down from my waist to the back of my knee, then he bent my leg and pulled it up to rest on his hip.

This was not how I pictured our first—encounter. Me with raccoon eyes and him wearing my aunt's apron. I couldn't do it. Not like this. I at least needed to comb my hair, and maybe change out of my cut-off sweatpants.

"The bacon!" I shouted. Smoke was pouring off the pan. Alex jumped over to deal with it. Ahh, sweet bacon to the rescue—both tasty and heroic at the same time. "I'll be right back."

This was my chance to run to the bathroom and tidy up. The phone rang just as I passed it in the kitchen. The caller ID said it was my sister, Allie, and I thought she might have news about our mother.

"Have you heard from Mom yet this morning?" she said.

"Um, no I meant to call her but I…" but I was prepping to get it on with my boyfriend and hadn't had time to call her yet.

"I talked to her on the phone yesterday, but I haven't heard back from her today, which is weird. So, I don't know if I should be worried or not. This is my weekend to stay over with Mimi, so I haven't been home." Mimi was an elderly neighbor who needed someone to stay with her at nights. Allie and my mother rotated weekends staying at Mimi's house. "Anyway, I'm substitute teaching in Sunday school today and I've got to run, so I wondered if you could call and check up on her."

This was unusual behavior for our everything-just-so mother. "Okay, I'll call her right now." Best to get the call out of the way so I wouldn't be interrupted by Allie, my mom, or guilt for letting down all of the above, later on.

I looked down at my outfit and back at Alex. If I didn't change out of my sweatshorts, I could still brush my hair and wipe the makeup from under my eyes while I talked to my mom on the phone. I would just have to cut the conversation short.

"Is everything okay?" Alex asked.

"Oh, it's great, I—just need to make a quick call to my mom. Allie and I are kind of worried about her. I'll just be a second."

"I'll be right here," he said.

I dialed the phone and ran to the bathroom. I grabbed a bottle of Visine and dabbed some on my zit. I'd heard somewhere that it shrinks them down. After several phone rings I assumed mom just wasn't picking up. I would leave a message telling her I'd come and see her later.

"Hello." A sleepy male voiced answered.

"*Dad?*"

"Quincy girl, is that you*?*"

"Yeah, what are you—you're back."

"Got in late last night. Oh boy, I can't wait to see you and your sisters.*"*

"Where's Mom?"

"She's sleeping in. We were up pretty late. She's still got it, your mother."

"Dad! Are you—did you two—blegh, never mind. I don't want to hear." An involuntary shudder passed through my body. Apparently I was right about my mom not getting any sleep the night before, but not for the reason I thought.

"What's the matter?"

"You've been gone all this time and now it's back to 'nothing wrong, business as usual?'"

"Listen, honey, your mom and I have had our differences, but deep down we still love each other. We've been talking on the phone for a couple of months now and we missed each other—a lot." Oh, geez, did he mean....?

A mental picture popped into my brain and it was not good. Thinking of your parents having sex is like imagining yourself wading in a swimming pool full of squid parts. It's like when you keep your eyes open in the gory scenes of a horror movie. No amount of mental scrubbing will remove those disturbing pictures from your mind.

"Dad, I've got to go. Tell Mom I'll call her later."

"Bye, favorite girl." He called each of us that when the others weren't listening.

I hung up the phone and shivered with the willies. I went back to the kitchen without washing my face or brushing my hair. I looked up to see Alex, sitting at the table, grinning and wearing Aunt Rosie's apron...and nothing else.

***

My teeth found my bottom lip while I beheld the sight in front of me. I took a step toward him. My pulse pounded throughout my body and I had to remind myself to breathe.

Bam! Bam, bam, bam, bam, sounded on the back kitchen door. I tasted blood from where my teeth had pierced my bottom lip.

"Boss! Are you there?" K.C. bellowed from the back stairwell.

I heard a groan of frustration coming from the direction of the pink apron.

I held up my hands in defeat. "What should I do?" I whispered.

"Ignore it. She'll come back later," he whispered back.

"Boss, it's an emergency. I can't find Fred anywhere."

Anyone in the world would have understood Alex's sigh about our unfulfilled moment without need of translation. "Give me a second to get dressed." He picked up his bundle of previously discarded clothes and carried them in front of his...midsection. I caught a peek of gorgeous gluteals adorned only with ribbon tails that dangled oh so tantalizingly betwixt tight mounds of perfection as they left the room.

I staggered at the sight and leaned on the doorknob for a moment to regain my bearings.

Bam, bam, bam, awoke me from my daydream.

"Just a second K.C.," I called through the door. "I was just getting dressed."

I paused a beat longer and then opened the door.

"*This* is what took you so long?"

I glanced down at Han Solo and sighed. "You said there was an emergency?"

K.C. pushed past me and walked into the kitchen. "I haven't heard from Fred since we left him last night."

Alex finished pulling his t-shirt down over his bare chest as he entered the room.

"Oh, Alex! I noticed your truck outside but I—were you two...?" She tugged at her own shirt tails, subconsciously mirroring Alex. She turned to look at me and grimaced. "Was I interrupting—something?"

"No!" We both said in unison, with far too much volume.

"You weren't interrupting *anything*." The frustration practically oozed out of his pores. "What's wrong K.C.?" His tone had softened.

"I can't get a hold of Fred. The last time we talked was yesterday after the Booby lecture."

Alex's eyebrow shot up and his mouth curled into a smirk. I could see the wheels in his mind turning. "I'm sorry the...did you say...what kind of lecture did you two go to?"

"It's a bird," I said.

He tried to look at me through glazed-over eyes.

"The Booby—it's a bird."

"Oh." His face relaxed. Given our recent interruption, I was sorry to ruin his fun. I could only imagine what images were conjured when he thought it was a booby lecture of another kind.

"Sorry, K.C., we interrupted you."

"Oh, yes...well, before Quincy and I left for Salt Lake, I told him I would call when I got home. Of course I did just that, but he never answered. I tried all night and figured he must have zonked out or something. We were supposed to meet for our regular breakfast and bed, but he never came over and he's still not answering his phone."

Alex looked at me with a puzzled expression. "I'm confused. You were supposed to meet Fred at a bed and breakfast?"

I mouthed the word "no" and waived at Alex out of K.C.'s line of vision. But I was too late. I braced myself for the forthcoming explanation and *all* the unsolicited details. I wondered with a great deal of sympathy, which of those details she would share with Alex.

"No, we spend Sunday mornings together; just like you two lovebirds were, until I barged in. Sorry about that." The embarrassment made it difficult to meet Alex's gaze, but once I did he winked at me and I noticed the crinkles around his eyes had returned. "But Fred is missing and we need to find him. Can you two help me?"

"Are you sure he isn't just sleeping in?" Alex asked.

"I'm sure. He would never miss our Sunday School sessions."

Alex's face reddened. "I'm sure you're right about that." A vicious frog seemed to have taken residence in his throat. "Ahem, mhh—have you been to his house?"

She had been to his house and his car wasn't there. It was too early to get the police involved yet, as Fred hadn't been missing long. It just didn't seem quite right for Fred to disappear without word. He and K.C. had spent every possible moment together since the night of the gala when they met.

"Didn't Fred say yesterday that he was going to meet someone about—Brock—wasn't it?"

"Yes, he was going to meet Gordon Hawkes early this morning at the bird refuge to talk about an issue with an employee."

"Who is Gordon Hawkes?" Alex asked.

"He's the area manager at the wetlands. Fred is on the board of directors for the refuge and they know each other very well through the bird watchers group."

"It seems kind of an odd time for a work meeting—early Sunday morning," Alex said.

"That's what I thought, but he told me it was the only time old what's his name—Brett, Bart, Bobby, could get away from his fiancé."

"You mean Brock," I said.

"Yeah, that little cutie patootie who works with Gordon. Besides, they could do some primetime bird watching while they talked."

"I'd schedule my appointments so that Brock Jensen could show up too," I said, waggling my eyebrows in an attempt to lighten the mood.

"Who is Brock Jensen?" Alex said.

"He's the assistant manager to Gordon Hawkes," K.C. said. "I don't know why, but Fred said they needed him to be there too. Something about a personnel issue is all he would tell me.

"Anyway, while we're doing all this yapping we're not finding Fred. What am I going to do?" Her voice caught. I knew there was probably a perfectly normal reason K.C. couldn't locate Fred, but seeing her rattled left me frightened along with her.

Alex put his arm around K.C.'s shoulders in a sideways hug. "I'm sure there's a logical explanation for him being gone. Don't worry, we'll find him."

"Thank you, sweetie. You're a real gentleman, you know that?" Alex's face reddened just enough to be utterly charming.

"K.C., why don't you try calling him one more time on all of his phone numbers, even his office. Then, drive over to his house and check again, just in case. Quincy and I will head down to the bird refuge and see if we can talk to anyone down there. Maybe some of his bird watching friends will still be there. He's probably looking through his binoculars, not realizing the time...searching for Boobies."

I gave him an exaggerated "Ha-ha," and made a face.

"Oh, thank you, Alex," K.C. said. "If anyone finds him, we'll call each other so we can cancel the search party."

I changed into some real clothes and quickly tended to my appearance while K.C. called all of Fred's numbers with no luck.

CHAPTER FIVE

"So who is this *Brock* guy you two were going on about?" Alex asked as we drove to the bird refuge.

"My, my, my, Mr. Cooper. I do believe it sounds as if someone is jealous."

He grinned. "Merely collecting facts to help K.C., that's all."

"Brock Jensen is a very handsome and charming young man who is engaged to one of my brides. They met working at the bird refuge, which is kind of cute. He works for the wetlands and she's a biologist."

"That *is* very cute," Alex said in an exaggerated tone.

I stuck my tongue out at him. "Anyway, the two of them came in for a wedding consultation with her mother, and let me tell you…I don't think there's any love lost between Brock and his future mother-in-law."

"Is he as handsome and charming as say—your boyfriend?"

"Which one?"

"Hilarious," he deadpanned. He reached over and rested his hand on my knee. "I am sorry, you know."

"About?"

"About Sam—and last night. I should have told you about her before we went to dinner. I didn't sleep much if that helps."

"What, did you two stay up reminiscing?"

"Very funny. As a matter of fact, I told her I had to beg off after dinner. I felt bad at the way you left and I thought I should go home."

"How did she take the news?"

"She was disappointed."

Poor girl.

He didn't have anything more to add to the conversation and I didn't want to talk about her anymore, so I turned on the radio. His preset landed on a "new country" station. A strong female voice with a fake, overemphasized twang belted out a song about revenge on the woman who stole her man. Talk about art imitating life—or was it the other way around? In either case, it was a nasty reminder of what I was trying to forget.

Alex bobbed his head to the rock beat that didn't belong in the country song. I don't know what annoyed me more—the obnoxious singer or the way Alex was oblivious to the lyrics. I snapped.

"I give up," I said.

"What do you mean?" Alex roused out of deep thought. Reminiscing about the night before, perhaps?

"Did you sleep with her?"

"Who?"

"Oh come on!"

"I told you, I went home after dinner."

"I'm not talking about last night. I'm talking about ever."

"We worked together. We were partners, for crying out loud."

"You guys were too familiar with each other last night. That wasn't coworker physicality."

"What the…you just made that up. That's not a thing, *coworker physicality.*"

"So you never ever exceeded the boundaries of a work relationship?"

"No! Quincy, I told you—oh…"

"Oh?"

"I forgot this one time…"

"You did." *He'd lied to me.*

"I—we did." His voice was laced with what I thought sounded like regret. But I wasn't sure exactly where the regret came from, whether it was that he remembered or that he had forgotten.

"Oops, you forgot? As much as I'd like to be snarky here about how forgettable she must have been, I can't. I don't know what to say."

"We were drunk. Sloppy, stupid, drunk—at least I was. We were at some convention at a hotel and I had just gone through a bad break up."

My face was hot and my throat constricted so that I couldn't swallow. *You are not going to cry!* "Wasn't she your partner?"

"No! I mean she was at one time, but by then she had long since moved to a different job, in a different city. It was a mistake. It was convenient—and stupid. Thoughtless."

"So you were at a convention like the one she's at now. Tell me, did she ask you to go back to the party with her last night?"

"What does it matter? I didn't."

"So, she asked you."

"I guess she did, but I said I was heading home and that was that. Listen, Quincy, I'm sorry. I'd pushed it out of my mind. It was a mistake to sleep with her. I knew her too well to even…think about it. I guess I didn't. Think, that is."

"You shouldn't be apologizing for sleeping with someone before you met me."

"Then what are you so upset about?"

I actually felt my nostrils flare as my teeth ground together.

"Well, let's see. Am I more angry that your *not*-ex-girlfriend was putting on the full court press when I saw the two of you last night and you acted like you barely knew me," my hands moved around as I spoke, and became more frenzied the more worked up I got. I crossed my arms in front of me to contain them. "Or, am I mad that you went out last night with your *not*-ex-girlfriend and coworker who you have slept with in the past, but then lied to me about it?"

"I think you mean whom," he said.

"What?"

"I didn't lie to you about anything. And I'm just trying to lighten things up. It's not as bad as you're making it out to be."

"This is a joke to you?"

"No, babe, it isn't. But we didn't do anything wrong, so I still don't see what you're so upset about."

"You didn't tell me your old friend was a woman, for starters. Or that she's a certain... *kind* of woman."

"I didn't tell you about her because I knew you would get like this. For no reason. And besides, I invited you to come with us, and you said no."

"If I'd known who she was, I might have come. I could've slapped her paws away the first time she tried to put them on you."

"I would have loved to see that," he said, the corner of his mouth curling up into an obnoxiously handsome grin.

Ungh. Unbelievable.

We arrived at the bird refuge then and no more words were exchanged. Fred's car sat perfectly parked near the front entrance of the visitor center next to another car. Fred wasn't inside.

Neither of us spoke as Alex rolled the vehicle to a stop and we exited. The stillness of the refuge hung heavy in the air as soon as I stepped out of the Scout. I closed the door carefully, fearful of breaking the reverent silence. Alex seemed to feel the same stillness and quietly closed his door. He didn't look at me before taking long strides to Fred's car. He looked inside the windows, tried the handles, which were locked, and placed his hand on the hood. "Cold," he said.

Both of us walked toward the boardwalk that encircled a large portion of the marsh, but we didn't walk in tandem. I found myself a half-stride behind him. It wasn't intentional, but it felt more comfortable there.

A wooden tower loomed in the distance. The three-story structure formed a look-out for viewers, much like the night watchman towers in prison movies, but it was open at all levels and a winding spiral walkway wrapped all the way around. Waist high panels prevented children or less than cautious adults from falling in to the reed-filled waters. The space above the panels was completely open allowing for bird spotting and breezes crossing the marsh to pass through. The top of the tower provided a completely unobscured view of the Great Salt Lake and its islands to the west, or the Wasatch Mountains to the east.

After taking only a few steps on to the boardwalk, we emerged into a mythic new world. A world much like in fairy tales, where you felt as much a sense of fear as you did wonder and excitement.

Either side of the walkway was flanked by reed grass topped with silken pompoms, cattails, thistle, and prehistoric equisetum. A small shred of fabric provided a small reminder of our modern world as it played on the breeze, anchored at one end to the barbs of a thistle.

The grasses and reeds towered over the two of us, even over Alex at six foot four. The wooden slats we walked on looked to be less than a foot above the water in most places. I wondered how deep the water was, then tried to push away the thoughts of drowning.

Even though neither of us spoke, we both walked toward the tower. It just seemed the logical thing to do. It also seemed quite logical that Fred probably just got distracted by observing the birds he so loved, and had lost track of time.

The sun glimmered through Alex's golden hair and intensified the bronze in his skin. I so wanted to stop him and talk through everything that had just happened. We would work through this tough spot, he would have good reasons for deceiving me—which he would share—and we would move forward. I didn't look forward to the difficulty of all of it, but to the outcome—the feeling of balance restored.

I looked at him without really looking at him during all of this introspection and as if he had read my thoughts, he stopped walking and turned toward me. Just like that, he'd flipped a switch. The "get the job done" cop exterior vanished and his features softened.

"Quincy," he whispered and took my hands in his. "I hate feeling this way. I am truly sorry. Let's hurry up and find Fred so we can talk about this. Okay?"

I nodded, then made the mistake of looking into his eyes. I had to let go of one of his hands to wipe the tears that came without warning. He gently moved my hand away then used his thumbs to clear the rest of the tears. He wrapped his arms around me and rested his chin on top of my head. I felt like I could melt into him if only I pressed hard enough. The tears flowed for a few seconds more, but they were tears of relief. I buried them in the fabric of his shirt.

We continued on to the tower and climbed the stairs encircling the outside of the structure until we reached the first viewing level. No Fred, just the remnants of a few owl pellets on the overhang of the ledge of the first safety fence. I looked up to see where the owls might have perched before leaving their leftovers and spotted something fluttering on the second level ceiling. I looked again. It was only a reflection of the sun, yet something would have to have been on the floor to cast a reflection on the ceiling.

I nudged Alex to get his attention then pointed at the reflection. He watched it for only a moment then took off at a run up the stairs. I followed and noticed a rust colored smear next to a droplet of the same color on the landing.

When we got to the next level, we found two men crumpled on the floor, one with blood drying on his head. Alex kneeled over him while I hurried over to the other man. A sick feeling rose to my throat, as I recognized the form on the tower floor. It was Fred. He lay on his side, groaning. His hands were tied behind his back and his ankles were bound with cloth.

"Fred, are you alright?" *What a stupid thing to ask.* "Are you hurt?"

He groaned then said in a hoarse whisper, "K.C."

He must have had a head injury, he wasn't making sense.

"Fred, I'm Quincy. K.C. isn't here. Are you hurt?"

"No, K.C....please call her. She's hopping mad by now."

He was making perfect sense. Now that Fred was alive, K.C. was going to kill him for not calling her.

"Let me untie you," I said. "Are you hurt anywhere?"

"They hit me hard enough to knock me out, but Gordon needs help."

I could hear that Alex had already called for medical help. He relayed Fred's condition after he told them about Gordon. I reached over Fred to untie his hands. He held a pair of glasses in his rusty-colored fingers.

"Fred, are your hands cut?"

"No, it's Gordon's blood. I got it on me when I rolled over and took his glasses off."

We kept Fred and Gordon warm as best we could. I took Fred's key fob and ran to retrieve blankets out of his trunk, being careful not to touch anything but the blankets. When I returned I could see Alex had covered the wound on Gordon's head with the fabric that had bound his wrists.

I retreated to the corner when the medical personnel arrived. I heard some of the conversation Fred had with the police before he was taken in the ambulance as a precaution. He told them that he and Gordon had met early that morning at the parking lot of the refuge.

He said they had arranged to meet Brock Jensen at the tower to discuss some official business for the marsh. A few minutes after they arrived at the tower, Harold Busby showed up and he seemed really upset about something regarding the marsh and the board of directors. Gordon told him he would arrange to meet with him in a few days to talk about whatever it was he was so upset about and then Harold left.

They had thought Brock wasn't going to show, but he arrived about twenty minutes late. The men were all on the upper level, leaning on the railing and looking out over the marsh, when someone behind them told them not to move. Fred said he heard a click that sounded like it could have come from a gun. Suddenly, Brock, who was standing between Fred and Gordon, jerked backward, and Fred heard a man tell someone else to tie him and Gordon up. That's the last thing Fred remembered.

The walk back to the car along the planked boardwalk was eerie enough after finding Fred and Gordon, but a dense fog rolled in causing mental shivers as well as the real goose bumps on my skin.

"What happened to Brock?" I asked.

"We don't know," Alex said. "Fred doesn't remember anything after he heard the one male voice telling someone to tie them up. It could have been Brock he was talking to, or another person."

"Oh, we have to call K.C.! I'm sure she's worried sick."

I spoke with K.C. on the phone while Alex drove me home. I told her not to come in to work the next day, but she told me I was "speaking nonsense," and now that she knew Fred was okay, she was okay.

Once we arrived at my house, Alex walked me to the back door and we agreed to talk later about our other issues that just didn't seem so pressing any longer. It was a good time for us to take a break anyway—just for the day, of course.

CHAPTER SIX

The crisp coolness of late September mornings hadn't begun in full force yet, but the swift breezes and occasional flyovers by honking geese promised a change in the weather was just around the corner. I grabbed a jacket before I left for work Monday morning.

After the trauma of finding Fred, I said a silent prayer of gratitude for my full and happy life. I reflected back to a mere few weeks before, when I could think of nothing but how I was going to keep the doors of my flower shop open. I wouldn't be rich anytime soon, but I could meet payroll, pay for supplies, and keep the lights on. For now.

"K.C., I'm always happy to see you, but what in the heck are you doing here?" I said as she came through the front door of the shop.

"Now that I know where Fred is, and that he's okay, I'm glad to be here. It's a return to normal. And it helps keep my mind off of thinking about how bad it could have been. Besides, I think Fred's getting sick of me doting over him. His daughter is visiting with him now, so he'll be just fine."

"How is Gordon doing?"

"He's alright. He's a tough old buzzard. He's still at the hospital though."

"Do you think we'll need to make some changes to your wedding plan so that Gordon can attend? It's only a couple of weeks away."

"No way, no how. We won't need to change a thing. Gordo will pull through and be right there standing up for Fred at the altar. I'm not going to let some dirt-bag, piece of trash disrupt my wedding plans or get away with hurting my future husband or his best man. Things will go just as planned and that's all there is to it."

She put her cap and purse away in the back room. "What have we got on the docket for today, Boss?"

"I was supposed to have another wedding appointment with Jenny McQueen and her mother and fiancé. But her fiancé went missing Sunday morning, so now I have no idea how to proceed. They can't very well have the wedding without the groom. Have you heard anything more about Brock?"

"Not a thing. I was hoping you might have the low-down from Alex."

"I haven't talked to him since he dropped me home after we found Fred."

"Oh no! I knew I had interrupted something yesterday morning. I had hoped you two would get back to it once you got home."

Ergh. "Um—thanks for that, but some things actually came up on the drive to the refuge…but, it's fine. We're fine. We're going out tonight and I'll talk to him then."

K.C. looked up at the ceiling, "If you say so."

"What?"

"You sound like you're trying to convince someone of something, kiddo. I don't need convincing that you two are hunky-dory. So, who were you *really* trying to convince just now?" She looked over the top of her red, cat-eye glasses at me.

I shook my head. "You've got it all wrong. We're...we've got a lot of work to get to today. We should get started."

"Uh-huh."

Thankfully the phone interrupted.

K.C. gathered order slips for the day's deliveries while I took a new order over the phone.

"Sally VanBuren wants a fall arrangement like the one on the cover of *Best Homes Magazine*." I looked up the cover on the computer and found a picture of an arrangement composed of cattails and various natural grasses and reeds.

"You know where we could find a lot of those grasses?" K.C. said.

"Don't say it."

"Why not?"

"Why would you want to go down to the place where Fred and the others were attacked? And besides, it's still a crime scene."

"We don't have to go onto the tower. I just want to go down there and see what it was like for poor Fred. And I can check in at the visitor center and make sure they've got everything ready to go for the ceremony while you take some cuttings."

"I don't know, K.C. Can't we get in trouble for cutting plants out of a preserve? Isn't it protected land or something?"

"We'll just get them from the ditch banks on Clint Wheeler's property, right next to the refuge."

"Won't we get in trouble for cutting things from his property?"

"I'm sure we won't, but if you want to be Miss Goody Two Shoes, you can go knock on the barn door and ask his permission. He won't care."

"I'll think about it. The arrangement is going in a terra cotta planter on her porch, so it'll be big. We'll need lots of different kinds of stuff to fill it. I guess we could plan to go take some cuttings sometime soon."

I prepared arrangements for delivery while K.C. began cleaning out the walk-in cooler. She wore a bright yellow apron with a black smiley face logo on the front, and she whistled as she brought all the buckets out of the cooler. When I finished with the arrangements, I helped her with the cooler job, which required cleaning from ceiling to floor and in every nook and cranny with a mixture of bleach and water.

K.C. left me to finish the ceiling, since I could reach it more easily, and she went into the back room to tackle the tower of dirty buckets. The bleach fumes were almost overwhelming, so I had to leave the door hanging wide open for enough air circulation. As K.C. passed, she bumped the door enough to latch it.

There's no way she would have known about my little phobia about being trapped inside the cooler. I tried to remain calm. I knew full-well that the release latch was put inside the door for a reason. This is knowledge I didn't have when my cousin Tyson locked me inside of the same cooler when we were six years old.

I didn't want to look like a wimp by busting out of the cooler like a caged beast breaking free from captivity, so I calmly walked over to the door and gently pushed the plunger.

And nothing happened.

I pushed again, more forcefully, and nothing gave. I pounded on the door and K.C. opened it right away.

"We have to get that fixed. Now."

"Are you okay, Boss? You look a little pale."

"I have a thing about getting stuck in the cooler. Until we get it fixed, we can't close the door while someone is in there. Ever."

"Okey-dokey. Would you like me to take over for you? You seem pretty spooked."

"No, I'm fine. Sorry to get all dramatic. I'll finish up in here if you'll finish the buckets, and then we need to put together the roses for Kyle Mangum's wife."

We continued with our respective jobs, and I made sure to keep the cooler door wide open.

Hands above my head, I wiped the ceiling with a rag drenched in bleach water, dodging the droplets that flicked off with every swipe. I worked my way backwards so I could finish at the doorway. A big droplet splashed on my cheek and into my eye and stung like crazy. The bleach smell was smeared all over my face and I started to gag. I headed toward the door, using memory and groping to find my way toward the restroom. As I stepped out, I smelled something new and familiar. I forced my eyes open. "*Geez!*"

My nose rested about three inches away from the heavily penciled arch of Jacqueline DeMechante's right eyebrow.

"Jacqueline, you startled me. I'm sorry, I didn't realize you were here." Just how long had she been standing in the doorway staring at me with those freakish shark eyes?

"Apology accepted," she said. "I'm here for my appointment and since no one greeted me at the counter, I thought I would just come and find you."

"Everything all right in here?" K.C. called out before she came in from the back room.

"We're just fine. I must not have heard the doorbell," I said, more for Jacqueline's benefit than K.C.'s. "Jacqueline, this is K.C., our delivery driver." I turned to K.C. "We're doing the wedding flowers for Jacqueline's daughter, Jenny, and her fiancé, Brock."

"Oh, yes…about Brock, he and Jenny won't be able to join us for today's appointment." She closed her heavily shaded eyelids. "They're otherwise engaged."

I looked at K.C. whose mouth hung open, mirroring my stunned expression.

"Have they found—Brock, then?" K.C. asked.

"No, he hasn't returned yet. He's a very…unreliable young man. I suppose he'll turn up soon. But that isn't my concern. I need to nail down these wedding plans."

"Excuse me, Jacqueline, if I'm not understanding correctly, but wasn't Brock kidnapped? We can reschedule the flowers for whenever the wedding happens. Whenever he's safely home," I said.

"My daughter's wedding will happen in twenty six days, and that's what I'm here about today. Shall we get started?" She turned and walked toward the consultation table at the front of the room.

K.C. swirled her index finger next to her temple and mouthed the word "cuckoo," then returned to the back work room.

Jacqueline and I went over the wedding contract one more time, and just as we had on her three previous visits, we ended up visiting the ribbon racks in the middle of the shop. The racks were similar to bookshelves filling one wall, except instead of flat wooden shelves, there were quarter inch dowels holding up rows and rows of colorful ribbon. The ribbon bolts ranged in size from fifteen to a hundred yards and the styles varied from sheer to double faced satin to lace and picot trimmed from the eighties when Aunt Rosie ran the shop. There were rolls of jute twine, grosgrain, and even two inch wide ric-rac.

K.C. rejoined us as we perused the blue-green family of ribbon. Jacqueline reached to unravel yet another roll, of which she had no intention of using in the wedding, and her large gold bracelet snagged on one of the strands she had left unfurled.

"That's quite a piece of hardware you've got there," K.C. said. "What is that on your bracelet—a beetle?"

Jacqueline's eyes closed and she straightened her shoulders, seemingly gathering herself against the indignation she suffered as a result of K.C.'s remark.

She turned, slowly, toward K.C., eyes still dramatically closed. "This—" she placed the bracelet on her heart, her arms crossed in an "X" on her chest like a mummy, and flashed her eyes open, "is a gold enshrined scarab. Earthly representation of Khepri, The Morning Sun."

"Oh, and here I thought it was just a beetle on a bangle," K.C. said, ironing her lips into a tight line.

"Um…did you get that beautiful bracelet in your travels to Egypt?" I asked. No need to start a fight over a beetle bracelet.

"Yes," Jacqueline said, then closed her eyes again while a smile spread across her face. "I only wish I could return." The smile disappeared. "But, there's a wedding to get out of the way before that will happen."

I turned to K.C. "Ms. DeMechante is an Egypt enthusiast. Isn't that right, Jacqueline?"

She sighed heavily. "Yes, speaking of which, I've got work to do. I'll take the dark Lapis and the Nile, Quincy. That is all."

"Those are beautiful choices, Jacqueline. You'll let us know if there are any changes in the plan…I'm sure."

"Hmm? Oh, back to work, yes—Lapis and Nile, those are my color choices."

I looked sideways at K.C. and shrugged. "O—kay, we'll talk to you soon then, Jacqueline."

"Mmm-hmm. Adieu, ladies."

K.C. and I exchanged confused glances as Jacqueline left the store. "What in *thee* hell is wrong with that woman?" K.C. said.

"I don't know. She must be in shock. She's been stressed out with the wedding and Brock's kidnapping has probably pushed her over the edge. I'll call my wholesalers today and tell them what's happened. I think there's just enough time that we can cancel the flower order. Surely a kidnapping will be enough to sway them my way, even though I'm officially past the cancellation deadline."

She wrinkled up her nose and waived her hand in front of her face. "Phew. I hope so. That would be a big bag to be left holding. Sheesh, she left the gift in our air that won't quit giving. That perfume is awful." We both worked on re-rolling the chaos of all the ribbons Jacqueline had left in her wake. "So what's with the colors she's talking about? It seems I've heard them mentioned a thousand times already. Did she change them?"

"Oh no, it's been dark Lapis and Nile from the start. And she has made it clear I am not to confuse those colors with teal of any kind."

"So what color is dark Lapis?"

"Teal."

"How about Nile?"

I looked at her pointedly.

"Don't tell me," she said.

I raised my eyebrows.

"Teal?"

I touched my index finger to my nose.

K.C. shook her head and chuckled. "That woman is one piece of work. She wears a dead dung beetle on her wrist, for crying out loud."

"So that's what a scarab is? How did you know that?"

"I've studied a few things in my day. I may not be an Egyptologist, but I know a thing or two about a ball of dung being pushed around by a bug. I've studied lots of bugs, actually. I just don't dip them in gold and wear them as jewelry."

"You're fascinating, K.C. You know that?"

She pushed at her page-boy blond haircut. "I do try."

We finished cleaning and K.C. carried the dozen yellow rose arrangement to the delivery staging area near the back door.

"So what's the deal with this delivery for the Mangums?" K.C. said.

"I did the wedding flowers for Kyle and his wife. He came in later and ordered a monthly delivery of a dozen yellow roses on the date of their anniversary," I said.

"Oh, so you've seen the wife then?"

I paused to think. "You know—that's interesting. I haven't ever seen her."

"But you said you did their wedding flowers."

"I did, but Kyle came in one day and said it was a second wedding for both of them, so they were just having a small ceremony. She couldn't come to the shop for some reason, so he just ordered a bouquet of yellow roses for her and a boutonnière for himself. He said those were her favorite."

"Huh," she said.

"Why do you ask?"

"I'm just being nosy, I guess. I've only delivered there twice, but I've never really seen her."

"Do you just leave the flowers on the door step?"

K.C. picked up the delivery slips and the van keys. "No, she comes to the door…let me hold that thought, I left the delivery log in the van." She went out the back door and then returned a few moments later. "Boy, it's still so hot out there. I'd better get the AC running before I take these flowers outside."

"So you were telling me about Mrs. Mangum…" I said.

"Oh, yes. Both times I've delivered to her, she barely opens the door just wide enough to fit the arrangement through." She held up one of the delivery bouquets in front of her face and peeked around the side of it. "Like this. And then, I don't know what kind of work she does, but both times, she was wearing latex gloves and goggles and a bandana over her hair. I couldn't get a good look at her."

The phone rang and interrupted our conversation.

"Rosie's Posies, how can I help you?" I answered.

"Where is our blushing bride?" said a familiar voice.

"Danny, how are you?"

"The question *is* how are you? And how is our officer of the law?"

"Oh, he's fine."

"Well, I know how he looks, sweetie. I'm just wondering how y'all are doing?"

"Ha ha, let me get K.C. for you."

I overheard K.C. going over Fred's story with Danny and her protestations about postponing the wedding.

After she returned from the delivery, I convinced K.C. to leave early and go visit Fred. When she finally admitted how anxious she was to see him, it reminded me about my plans with Alex for that evening. The last time we spoke, he was dropping me home after the awful experience at the bird refuge. Before that, we were on our way to—well who knows?

Something fluttered up in my stomach, but it became more of a banging around that came up into my chest. I wouldn't describe it as butterflies—it was more like wacked out birds. The Inland False Booby, perhaps?

Instead of figuring out what was bothering me, I opted for distraction. I fired up the Internet and looked at ribbon catalogs until it was time to leave.

***

Alex was supposed to pick me up and we were going to go for a hike. The leaves on the trees were just hinting at changing colors in the foothills of the mountains. It would become chilly as soon as the sun went down, which would cause the need for cuddling—something I *wouldn't* be hesitant to do.

Since I'd had advanced notice of his arrival this time, I made preparations for his visit, including getting my mind right and deciding what I was going to tell him when we had our talk.

When I heard the knock on the back door, the nervous stomach was back, but there was some excitement mixed in there too.

Alex stood on the back steps, his smile gleaming as the lines around his eyes gathered in their charming way. He held a gift bag up as he came in.

"What's this?"

"A peace offering."

"Why would you need one of those?" I asked.

"I was thinking about how hard I've made it for you to trust me—"

"No. It's me that has the problem. I don't trust people in general. But, I can't make excuses based on the past any more. The past is gone. You're here now and I should trust you. I do—trust you."

"No. You shouldn't."

A feeling of panic rushed to my stomach. "Why?"

"No—I mean, you should, but—okay, I've made it hard lately. I didn't tell you about Sam. I've thought about what you said, and you were right. I should have told you about our—well, that time." He ran his hand through his hair.

I gently tugged on his arm and motioned to the kitchen chair.

"The truth is, I hadn't totally forgotten about it, but I wished that I could. It was a mistake for both of us. She was involved with someone at the time and I had absolutely no interest in her."

I sat, assuming he would too, but he stayed standing. "I've given you all kinds of reasons not to trust me. And you still do. That's why I l…" He reached into his pocket and pulled out his phone. "Sorry, I'm not supposed to be on call, but—hang on just a sec." While he checked his texts, I ran all kinds of scenarios through my mind.

He'd started to say an "L" word. And what if it was THE "L" word I was worried about? It was way too soon in our relationship to be saying those kinds of words, especially *that* particular word. All this business with Samantha had thrown him off. He wasn't thinking straight. And now, here he was, standing in my kitchen, not wanting to sit down, probably with a rehearsed speech about "L" words like love and life that were way too serious for either of us to deal with right now.

Yeah, that Samantha had really screwed things up.

The possibility of our future might have crossed my mind a time or two, but only for a moment until I pushed the thought out as fast as it came in. I couldn't even commit to getting bangs cut in my hair. How could I commit to marriage and kids and a mini-van? And what would I do with Zombie Sue? She didn't have enough seats for kids, and I couldn't just get another van. I couldn't betray her that way. Suddenly it was a hundred degrees in my kitchen. I took off my jacket and fanned my face with a folded up placemat.

"Quincy?"

"I can't."

"Can't what?"

I got up to get a glass of water. "I can't get a new van." I chugged down the water like it was a beer at a frat party.

"O—kay. Is something wrong with your van?"

I sucked in a breath. "Did I say that out loud?"

He gave a short laugh. "Yeah, is everything all right?"

"I—never mind." I shook my head. "What were you going to say—before your phone…?"

"Sorry about the interruption. It turned out to be nothing. So, where was I?"

"You were saying you l…" Excruciating.

"Oh yeah," his cheeks reddened and he cleared his throat, "I know it's hard for you to trust people, and I didn't realize how the whole thing with Sam would make you feel until after it was too late. So I'm sorry for that. I—like um—being with you, Quincy."

Relief. We were in just the right place in the relationship.

"Anyway, I saw this at that new mall in Salt Lake and thought you might like it." He held up the gift bag.

"Yay, presents! Thank you."

I reached inside and pulled out a black t-shirt. Interesting choice, I thought to myself, until I unfolded something glorious. A character from the original best TV show in the world appeared before me. The sparkling eyes and gleaming white teeth of Dirk Benedict—Starbuck—twinkled back at me.

"Where did you get this? How did you know?" I threw my arms around Alex, the t-shirt clutched in one hand and the gift bag in the other.

"Wow, if I knew this is all it took, I would have brought it much sooner." He wrapped his arms around me and drew me in close. He smiled as he leaned down and kissed me. Just as I'd imagined DB Starbuck would've back in the day. Watching old sci fi reruns with our dad was something me and Allie had looked forward to every week as kids.

Alex put his cheek next to mine and whispered, "Notice anything different?" He nuzzled my ear with his smooth, whisker-free chin.

"I'm not sure, I think you need to kiss me again," I whispered back.

"I think you're right."

He tilted his head down and stopped, his lips resting a breath's width away from mine. I realized my lips were puckered up like a cartoon character.

"What's wrong?" I said, with a little too much desperation. I may have felt nervous before this date, but now that Alex was here, the engine was running and ready to roll.

"I just...are we good? I mean, you feel okay with everything?"

I felt myself smiling. I searched my thoughts and realized I had no hang-ups, no niggling little thoughts, and no hesitations. I had overcome whatever it was in me that made me stall before. And now that the time seemed right, it was full steam ahead.

I planted a kiss on Alex he would never forget. Then I dropped the gift bag and moved my now free hand onto his perfect posterior.

I watched his eyebrows shoot up. "Whoa, so all it took was a t-shirt…"

"Not just any t-shirt. It's…a *DB Starbuck* t-shirt."

"Should I be feeling jealous right now?"

"Oh no, I'm just appreciative of the gift," I said as I squeezed the non-t-shirt-holding hand.

"Quincy!" he said, half gasping, half laughing, "What's gotten into you? Not that I mind…"

"I've just—done some thinking, that's all. And now the thinking is done and it's time for other stuff."

"Other—stuff?" His face lit up like he'd just won the lottery. He reached back and coaxed the t-shirt from my hand. "You mean—after we get back from our hike?"

I slowly shook my head.

He draped the t-shirt over his shoulder, slid his fingers down my arm, and took my unoccupied hand and placed it behind him, next to my other hand. "Do you mean—now?"

I bit my lip and nodded slowly.

He wrapped one arm around my waist and pushed my hair behind my ear. His fingers trailed slowly down my neck, past my collar bone.

My breath caught up in my throat and my hands did some caressing of their own.

His fingers stopped just shy of the swell of my breast and he bent down and brushed his lips under my earlobe in that magical spot, then he whispered, "What kind of other stuff?"

I could feel his lips curling into a smile on my neck as I tipped my head back to release the agonizingly delightful tension.

He moved his kisses down my neck and his hands worked at my waist, moving under my shirt. He stopped abruptly.

All my nerve endings protested at once.

"I think you should try this on." He held the t-shirt up in front of me and his eyes sparkled.

"Okay. I think it's kind of long, probably don't need any pants with it."

He shook his head, his face grave with mock seriousness. "Probably not."

I grabbed the t-shirt and headed for the living room, toward my bedroom. Alex kept hold of one end of the shirt and followed me in. He tugged at the shirt and I turned into him.

"You're sure?" he said.

"Absolutely." I stood on my tiptoes and leaned into him for a passionate kiss, then said, "I'll be right back." I turned and flung the shirt over my shoulder, then looked back at him and smiled.

I went into my room for two reasons. One was to change into my gift, but more importantly, I needed to do one last visual check for any stuffed animals. This was not the time to look up from our anticipated activities and see Mr.Snuffles watching our adult—um—relations. Mr. Snuffles or his companions just wouldn't understand.

I re-entered the living room wearing the t-shirt, which was just long enough for some lace to peek out from underneath. I think someone might have planned it to fit this way.

I did a sharp inhale when I saw Alex wearing only his faded jeans with the top button undone.

I slowly walked toward him until I was close enough he could just reach me with his outstretched arms. He groaned, then said, "Don't stop there." He pulled me into him and slid his hand down, over my hip and then the back of my thigh, lifting my knee up to the side of his hip. He slid his hand down my calf to my ankle.

"No socks this time." He grinned.

"No socks."

My hands rested on his bare chest and I traced circles with my fingers. "No shirt," I said.

He placed both hands around my waist and then slid them down over my bottom, toying with the edge of the shirt. "No shirt?" He looked down at me with a devilish grin.

"No shirt," I said confidently.

He kissed me while his hands worked under my shirt and down my leg. One hand traveled up my side, his thumb brushing the side of my breast.

"Babe," he whispered, "do you want to go to the bedroom?"

"Mmhmm, in a minute." I didn't want to stop long enough to walk the five steps to the bedroom. I grabbed the front waistband of his jeans and pulled him toward me as I stepped backward. We both fell onto the couch, him on top of me.

"Ouch," he pulled his hand out from under me and shook it, as if trying to shake loose the pain I had just inflicted.

"Sorry," I said.

"It's fine. You okay?"

"Oh, I am *so* okay."

"Good." He sat up and straddled my hips with his bent knees. "Quincy," he said, his voice raspy and breathless and oh, so sexy.

"Uh-huh," I said, mindless as to what my hands or any other part of me was doing to him.

"Take off your shirt, I can't look at that guy anymore."

"Mmhmm."

I reached down and grabbed the edges of the shirt, tugging it out from under Alex's knees. He held my bare waist as I lifted the bottom edge, the skin of my belly extra sensitive to the exposure.

The real exposure was next. The point of no return. The path that can never be uncrossed, the bell that can never be un-rung. I had one last fleeting thought of whether I was going for it or not. I ignored that thought.

Bam! Bam! Bam! sounded on the front door.

"For the *love* of ..." Alex said through his teeth. "I swear, you live in freaking Grand Central Station."

I lowered my shirt.

"Nooo, no, no," Alex protested, "just wait. We'll be quiet and they'll leave."

The knocking on the door continued.

"Quincy-girl, are you home?" a voice said, from outside the front door.

Before I could say anything Alex gave a weighty sigh, and climbed off of me then stomped toward the door.

"Who in the hell..." Alex said.

"Alex, that's my..." before I finished the sentence he yanked the door open and suddenly I was lying on my back in lace panties and a t-shirt, just around the corner from where my father stood. I bolted up, ran to my bedroom, and jumped into my pants. I hurried into the living room to find shirtless Alex staring at my father.

"Dad," I stepped in front of Alex, breathing heavy from my sprint, "what a—surprise." I conjured a weak laugh. The heavy breathing probably didn't help with the picture that had already been painted for my father, who stared past me with furrowed brows at Alex's bare upper body.

My father filled the doorframe, his red-streaked-with-gray mane putting a cap on the intensity of his presence. He had let his hair grow out when he started with his bluegrass band, and now he wore it loose, cascading down just past his shoulders. His thick eyebrows matched his hair. If his physical stature wasn't enough to scare people off, his deep base voice usually did the trick. On the outside he was a fierce lion, but on the inside, he was a tame little kitty-cat.

"Dad—this is Alex." I stepped aside then looked from one man to the other.

What happened next was something you might see on the Nature channel. It was just like watching two dogs sizing each other up. First there's the sniffing, then the grunting and pawing, and then the looking each other up and down, making appraisals.

"Angus McKay," my father said, then stepped inside, "but everyone just calls me Mac." He extended his hand to

Alex, which I took to mean he had accepted him to his pack, or pod, or whatever a group of men is called.

"Good to meet you, Mr. McKay—Mac," Alex said, then nodded in male non-verbal code. He placed his hands on hips—subconsciously bracing himself for a father's wrath?

Apparently my father had accepted Alex's nod, because he clapped him on the shoulder and returned his own nod.

"Annette has told me all about you, Alex. Good to finally meet you."

I looked at Alex wide-eyed and he returned the same look to me. I thought after hearing all about him from my mother—in her unique style of describing someone who doesn't meet her standards—my dad would have punched him in the face upon meeting him. I think Alex had felt the same way, given how relieved he looked after my dad only smacked him on the upper arm.

"Quincy-girl. What a sight for sore eyes." He kissed the top of my head like he always did when I was little. "I hope I'm not interrupting anything." He raised an eyebrow and glanced over at Alex then back at me.

"No," Alex said before I had a chance to chime in. "I was just…fixing…Quincy's…"

My dad looked at me and I could see his eyes twinkle over his wry grin. "No need to explain. I came over unannounced. I just wanted a chance to see my middle girl again."

"Dad, I'm glad you're home. Let's go sit in the kitchen."

Alex took advantage of the moment to put his shirt on then joined us at the kitchen table.

After about fifteen minutes of polite conversation between the three of us, my father broached the subject of his recent, extended absence from our family's lives.

"You know," Alex said as he stood, "I've been putting off some stuff at home and I've got to get up early, so I'm going to leave you two to visit."

Oh no. He had "stuff" to do? He had to get up early? I had just been served a cliché sandwich by the man I had very nearly—missed it by that much—slept with only minutes before. I knew Alex was frustrated, but how about me? What was I supposed to have done when my long-lost father showed up on my doorstep? It wasn't my fault he appeared at precisely the wrong moment.

Fate obviously didn't want me and Alex to come together, if you know what I mean.

I walked with Alex to the front porch. He turned to face me and put his arms on my shoulders. Not an embrace, but not a cold handshake either. Just kind of in-between. Stuck. Stuck between passionate and cordial. He leaned down and kissed me quickly, like it was a required formality before he could leave. I found myself longing for a chin chuck.

"Alex…"

"I'm sorry, Quince."

"I realize this isn't what we had planned, but I had no idea he was coming over. I'm just as frustrated as you are…"

"I don't know if that's possible," he said with a sad laugh.

"Hey!"

"Don't worry, I just—felt awkward sitting in on your family's private business."

"I appreciate that, but now you don't even want to kiss me. Did I do something wrong? It seemed like you liked me a lot when we were on the couch."

"Quincy, your *dad* is in the kitchen."

"So what? We're out on the porch."

"It's Mantown Rules. You don't kiss your girlfriend in front of her dad, unless it's on your wedding day. Even then I would be extra careful to keep it clean. Have you actually seen your father, by the way? I would not want to be on shift if he was the bad guy. He actually saw me with his daughter, in the house he grew up in, with my *shirt off* and my *pants* unbuttoned!"

"So it was awkward." I shrugged. "Very, very, excruciatingly awkward," I muttered. The thought of the look on my father's face when he stood at the front door made me shudder. "But we're still—you know…?"

A smile returned to his face. The cute, crinkly lines around his eyes came back. "We're still *you know*. But not within a five mile radius of your dad. No matter what you say, he told me with his eyes that if he ever sees me even touch you, he'll rip my still-beating heart out of my chest and squeeze it front of my almost-dead eyes."

I rolled my own eyes.

He kissed me on the cheek, then whispered in my ear, "Goodnight, Beautiful." He stepped back, "I'll call you tomorrow."

I sighed for lack of a better response. "I'm keeping the t-shirt." He smiled at me as he backed down the steps. "I'll be sleeping with Starbuck tonight."

"Ouch." He blew me a kiss and left.

CHAPTER SEVEN

There's nothing like a fresh start and a new day. New day at work—a chance to do more business and make a living. New day in a relationship—a chance to heal wounds and become closer. I'd had a good talk with my father the night before and we'd come to an understanding. Things weren't going to continue on as if nothing had happened, because that would be impossible. You can't undo the past, you can only move on in a different direction. So that's what we agreed to do. Dad asked me about Alex, who he really seemed to like despite finding him "half-nekked" in my house.

With Alex—there wasn't so much of an understanding. But frustration—there was plenty of that to go around.

The trouble with getting closer to Alex was that for him, it meant getting closer to my family. A little too close, as was proven the night before. I wanted to find a balance between good relationships with my family and with Alex, and I wanted to succeed in my business too. I just wanted it all. Is that too much to ask?

I drove Zombie Sue to work and parked in the back lot. Cool morning air filled my lungs as I stepped out of the van.

Hillside Creek, which curled behind the back parking lot, bubbled and sang loud enough to hear over the morning traffic. Birds chirped and twittered and their light chatter traveled through the clean, delicious air in melodious, twinkling notes.

I walked around to the front entrance so I could pick up the mail and the newspaper from the community mail bank in the middle of the building.

Two customer checks had found their way to our box, along with some bills and catalogs. It's always a great start to the day when you get paid before you walk in to work.

The newspaper was there too. Lately we'd had a thief. I'd never called to complain, because I thought maybe the person stealing the paper needed to look through the classifieds for a job. Maybe they'd found their job. New beginnings for everyone today.

Allie and Daphne walked in to the shop together. I'd found out about Daphne through Allie, who had decided to take classes at Weber State University in the fall semester. She met Daphne in a night class and found out she had moved here from Florida, where she'd worked at a busy flower shop.

We split all the opening duties and began the preparations for our regular orders. Allie fielded phone calls while Daphne and I chose the containers to use and gathered greenery and flowers.

"We'll need to get new roses today from Keith to make the Mangum order," I said.

"I can take the deliveries when they're ready," Allie said.

"No need for that, dear. Your delivery gal is here." K.C. stood in the doorway to the back room in a Superwoman pose. "How is everyone this morning?"

She wasn't wearing her traveling cap. Today she'd opted for a white scarf, which covered her hair and ended in a knot tied at the chin. She removed her electric blue-framed cat-eye sunglasses and hung them on the front collar of her shirt.

"I thought you weren't coming in today. You have the day off," I said.

"I would go stir-crazy if I stayed at home. And Fred says he's fine on his own. Besides, *I've got something to show you ladies*," she sung, a la Ethel Merman.

She led us outside to the back parking lot.

"Mama's got a new baby."

Her outstretched arms directed us to a classic car painted white and the same bright blue as her sunglasses. Sunlight sparkled off of chrome bumpers, wheels, and trim as if there was a giant disco ball in our back parking lot.

"Wow, K.C., it has fins!" Daphne said.

"And it's a convertible," Allie said.

"It's a '58 Dodge with the La Femme color package. That means it was made just for the ladies. There's a matching umbrella, purse, and lipstick cover. Ain't she a beaut?" K.C. beamed.

"When did you get this?"

"Yesterday, after work. A woman in my apartment complex had advertised in our newsletter that she was selling her late husband's classic car collection. I didn't think anything about it until I saw a picture of this one. I just had to have her. It's a wedding present to myself."

"Oh, K.C., it's beautiful," Daphne said.

We took turns sitting in the passenger seat to get a closer look inside. "Hey, K.C.," Allie said as she emerged from her turn in the seat, "what's this thing with the buttons and the cord?"

"C'mon kid, you're just teasing, right? You don't know what that is?"

Allie shook her head.

"That's a CB radio with an 8-track."

"A what?" Daphne said.

"Quincy, tell them what it is," K.C. said.

"I don't know." I shrugged. "I think Grandpa had one in his farm truck."

"Gads," K.C. shook her scarf covered head, then reached in and pulled out a couple of her 8-tracks. "An 8-track is like those whatchamacallits—cassettes. They play music."

"Those are massive," I said.

K.C. paused for a beat, glanced at the boxes in her hands, then frowned at me before she continued. "The CB is for talking to other cars who have CBs. It's like calling someone on the phone."

"Why don't you just call on your phone?" Allie said.

Allie received a frown too. K.C. planted her hands on her hips and sighed. "The previous owner must have installed it. He left his 8-tracks too. I've got George Jones, Waylon Jennings, Loretta Lynn…"

Blank stares abounded.

"Oh well." She clasped her hands together. "Who wants to go for a spin?"

After everyone had a turn riding in the new car, K.C. took the deliveries in my van and stopped at our hospital gift shop cooler to check on things. It was lunchtime when she returned.

"Mrs. Mangum handed me a check when I delivered the monthly order. Was I *supposed* to pick up a check?"

"No," I said. "I usually send Kyle a bill and he mails a payment."

She handed over the check. "I'm telling you, something is up with this customer. If it were just this check today, it wouldn't be odd, but—I can't put my finger on it—she just seemed so strange when she came to the door."

I studied the check. "Kyle usually writes the payment out of his account, but the name on this check is Lori Hoffman. It's the same address as the one you deliver to, though. Maybe he ran out of checks. I bet this is her maiden name. It's signed Lori Hoffman. That's probably what's happened—he ran out of checks, so he had her write it out for us."

The corner of K.C.'s mouth hitched and her eyes shifted. "Not very romantic to sign the check for your own flowers." She shook her head slowly. "Mark my words, something weird—weirder, I mean—is going to come of this order. My creepy-crawly senses are tingling."

"You mean spider?" Allie said.

"No, I mean creepy-crawly. It's all encompassing. I don't discriminate based on number of legs, antennae, or the lack thereof. Somebody or *some thing* is behaving like a creepy-crawly and I can sense it."

"Oh." Allie glanced over at Daphne and they exchanged smirks.

The front doorbell chimed and I looked up and froze in place. Allie was nearest the customer counter, so she greeted the guest.

"What is *she* doing here?" K.C. whispered.

"I have no idea." I could feel the skin on my cheeks growing hotter with each passing second.

"Let's go find out," K.C. said.

Samantha wore another cleavage-popper with a black leather jacket gathered at the waist. She was painted into a pair of artificially faded, designer-looking jeans tucked into knee-high black patent leather boots with three-inch heels. A sparkly, crystal teardrop pendant came up for air from between her breasts.

"Quincy and Kayleen, it's good to see you again."

"It's K…" I began.

"Don't waste your breath," K.C. said through her teeth, "she doesn't care." She smiled and tilted her head to the side.

I plastered on a smile of my own. "What brings you here—to my store? Samantha—was it?" K.C. and I stood behind the customer counter, while Allie retreated to the back with Daphne.

"Oh, call me Sam. Alex mentioned you had a little hobby, I thought I'd come check it out. I bet it's so fun getting to play with flowers all day."

I heard a faint, "Uh-oh," come from the designer's table. Allie knew that if there was one pet-peeve I had in this world, it was people talking about my business as if it were some flight of fancy-decide to be in business after a day of strolling through a flower garden-so easy and fun any idiot could do it-hobby.

I held back the verbal tirade that foamed and swelled within, and kept on smiling. "Thanks so much for stopping. I didn't know you were still in town, or I would have suggested the three of us get together." I felt a shooting pain, and realized my fists were balled up so tight in my pockets that my fingernails had cut into the skin of my palms.

"Oh, these necklaces are divine! I must have one."

K.C. leaned over and spoke out of the side of her mouth, "There's plenty a' room to fit another necklace in that canyon."

Samantha plunked her giant purse down on the counter while she looked through the jewelry display near the cash register.

"I'll go ahead and ring you through," K.C. said. She was obviously trying to diffuse the tension and I didn't mind. "That'll be sixty-two fifty-nine."

"Now, if I can find my credit card in here..." She opened an expandable wallet with several credit card slots and flippable photo holders.

"What have we here?" K.C. pointed to the top photo. "Who is this adorable little one?"

"That's my son," Samantha said. She smiled, her face beaming with pride. "He's three years old. I miss him like crazy."

"Look at this photo, Boss. Handsome little tyke." The little boy in the picture had a beautiful smile, blonde hair, and the most distinct chocolate brown eyes. I had only seen eyes like that on one other face before.

"He's adorable," I said. My legs felt like spaghetti and something similar to K.C.'s creepy-crawly senses were tingling in my stomach. Lucky I hadn't had lunch yet.

"I just need your John Hancock here and you'll be good to go," K.C. said.

"Will you be here long, Sam?" I had to know what her up-to-no-good plans were, even though it didn't matter, because I trusted my boyfriend to tell me if any of them involved him.

"You are so sweet to ask, Quincy, but I'm afraid our schedules won't sync. Alex has some meeting tonight, so dinner is out. I'm leaving tomorrow afternoon...maybe we could all have breakfast together. I know Alex has to go to Salt Lake tomorrow for work, so maybe we could meet there somewhere. I'll be sure to give you a call after I talk to him." She smiled at me with her hot pink glossed lips and winked.

K.C. grasped my wrist with her left hand and shoved the bag at Samantha with her right. "Here ya go, drive safe now, bye-bye."

"Ta-ta," Samantha said, then wiggled her way out of my store.

"You can let go. As much as I wanted to, I wasn't going to hit her," I said.

"I wasn't worried about you. I needed something to occupy both hands so I couldn't punch her in the kisser. Where's my taser? If she comes back in here, I'm gonna light 'er up like the Fourth of July. How dare she come in here and tell you what your man's schedule is?" She took a few deep breaths and blew them out hard. "Ya know, she was probably just making it all up to get your goat, Boss. I bet that's all."

I walked to the back design room and pulled the top cardboard box from a stack of empty ones to the floor. I repeated the mantra "*I trust my boyfriend*" over and over while I stomped down the entire stack of boxes. "There. Ready for recycling," I said, and looked up to see K.C., Allie and Daphne crowded together in the doorway, watching me. "What?" I shrugged.

"Are you okay?" Allie said.

"I'm totally fine. I'm sure she tricked Alex into telling her everything about himself, including his schedule, and his entire *life*," I stomped the boxes again for good measure, "during dinner while she had him hypnotized with her— necklace."

K.C. nodded to Allie and Daphne while cupping her hands out in front of her chest.

"Who's hungry?" I said. "I'm headed over to Skinny's." Nothing like a noggin-sized scone slathered with honey butter to soften the sting of a she-wolf invading your territory.

***

K.C. insisted I was too upset to drive and offered to take me to lunch in her new car. I needed to stop at the bank across the street to make a deposit and put an arrangement on the counter. After only eight different warnings during the two minute drive about spilling the water from the arrangement on her upholstery, we made it to the bank. Next stop, Skinny's.

"Now listen, sis, just because the little boy in that picture had beautiful brown eyes and blond hair, doesn't mean he has anything to do with Alex."

"Oh," my shoulders slumped and I buried my face in my hands, "I forgot all about that when she started blathering on about Alex. I remember now though."

"Sorry."

"No, no, I don't mean it that way. It's just...ooh I can't stand that woman. She's already caused so much trouble between Alex and me, and now this."

"Well I don't mean to pry, kiddo, but do you think there's any way Alex could be—you know—*related* to the little cherub?"

I rolled down the window to let in some air since it felt like there wasn't much available inside the car.

"Boss, are you all right?"

"I'll be okay, we're almost there. I just need some water, and a scone, and a vat of honey butter."

K.C. turned the car into the parking lot of Skinny's.

"They have a history," I said. "I don't know how much I should tell, I..."

"Stop. Go no further." She shut off the car and turned to look at me. "Do you trust him?"

I paused a moment and looked her in the eye. The answer struck me as clear as an autumn morning. "Yes." I trusted him.

"Good. Then nothing else matters. You'll work it out. He may not even know the boy exists. And they might just look incredibly similar. It might just be a one in a million coincidence that they look exactly alike, but hey, there's always that chance, right?"

I felt a smile tugging at the corner of my mouth.

"Right." She was right. I trusted Alex no matter what. Maybe for some people that feeling was a given, just as ordinary as waking up in the morning and brushing your teeth. But for me, the realization that I trusted a man—this man—without any more hesitation, felt amazingly, and for the first time, monumentally *normal*. My insides swelled with happiness—or maybe it was just hunger.

I unbuckled the seatbelt and reached for the door latch.

K.C. touched my shoulder. "Now, just because you trust Alex doesn't mean you can trust her. And it sure doesn't mean we can't mess with her." She nodded toward the entrance of the café. Samantha stood just outside the door talking on her cell phone.

"What's she doing *here*?" I said. "We can't go in there now."

"Why not?"

"Because she'll think we're following her. I don't want to give her the satisfaction of thinking she got to me."

"Hey, chickadee, all we're doing is going out to lunch. She just happens to be going to the same place." K.C. tapped her fingernails on the steering wheel. "It's odd though…"

"What is?"

"Skinny's is a local canteen. I mean, not that other people can't come here, it's just that they don't that often. So, I'm wondering how Miss Thing knows about the place. Someone she knows must have told her." She slammed her lips shut as if she'd tried to keep the last few words from escaping. She'd been too late.

"I suppose it's possible Alex told her about this place. So what? She's good at snaking information out of people."

"Ooh, I know. Maybe she's been stalking him and happened to see Skinny's when she drove by. A stalker's gotta eat too."

I couldn't help but laugh. "I guess I'm just a little jealous. But it's not like they're having lunch together. He would have told me." I basked in the glow of my newfound confidence in our bond of trust.

"You really do trust him then?"

"One hundred percent." I glanced around the car and found the 8-tracks behind the seats. I raised my right hand and placed my left on a Willie Nelson. "In fact, I, Quincy McKay, announce that I will no longer subject myself or others to the misery of living a life filled with suspicion or distrust of my boyfriend. I do solemnly swear on this holy record of the Red-Headed Stranger."

"You swear huh?"

I made an "x" across my chest with my pointer finger. "Cross my heart and hope to die, stick a needle in…"

"Boss…"

"…my eye."

"Oh boy." K.C. leaned forward and reached toward the windshield with both hands. Her blond bob fell forward, covering her face.

"What are you doing?"

"Who, me?" She patted down the dashboard and then leaned to her right, invading my personal space to an uncomfortable level. "I'm just looking for um—my tire gauge, because I—want to—gauge a, the amount of air, in the, a—whatchamacallit…"

"The tires?" I leaned back, against the door to get out of her way. "K.C.! You're squishing me! What's going on?" Backed against the car door, I leaned to my left to avoid breathing in some platinum blond hair. "Hey, is that..."

"No!" K.C. threw herself back into her own seat. I strained to get a better view out the windshield. "No, no, no, that is not who you think it is." K.C. thrust herself up and over the steering wheel like a porpoise propelling out of the water.

"That's him, isn't it?" I leaned forward to the windshield so I could see around K.C. until my nose bumped the glass.

"No, Quincy..." K.C.'s bosom smashed into the horn on the steering wheel and the sound echoed off the building with such force and volume the bison on Antelope Island probably covered their ears.

I didn't notice whether Samantha got a good look at my pig nose or K.C.'s blond hair stuffed up against the windshield because I ducked as far under the dashboard as a tall girl could get as soon as the horn honked.

I hadn't spied on a boy since when I first got my driver's license and offered to run errands for my parents just so I could borrow the car and drive past Scotty Bennett's house every night for a month. But it looked like that was exactly what I was doing, except this wasn't Scotty and this wasn't just a school-girl crush.

Now it appeared I was childish and crazy and that I didn't trust my boyfriend, which wasn't the case at all. I thought about texting Alex, but that would just add to the crazy Quincy show. He already had incentive enough with my family interruptions and my general weirdness to run away as fast as he possibly could. Texting would just encourage him to run faster.

"So," K.C. sat back and smoothed her hair, "Bulgy Burger drive-through, then?"

I nodded from my crouched position on the floor.

A tapping sound came from the driver's window.

"Jumping Josephine!" K.C. said, startled.

I looked up and saw a man tapping on the window. It was the man who had lectured about the Booby bird. K.C. rolled down the window. I unfolded myself from the floor.

"Jack, good to see you," K.C. said.

"I'm sorry if I startled you," Jack said as he eyed the interior. "Wow, what a swell car. Hey, I heard about Fred and Gordon. How are they?"

K.C. gave him the rundown of everyone's condition and the story of the assault and probable kidnapping of Brock.

"Let me know if there's anything I can do," Jack said before leaving.

"It was real nice of him to stop," K.C. said as she rolled up her window.

"It sure was, but now that he's gone, can we go?"

"Yeah, let's blow this Popsicle stand. Uh-oh."

I followed K.C.'s gaze and saw Elma, the grumpy, and only, waitress at Skinny's walking toward the car. Just the person I did not need to see. She carried two foam drinking cups. "Oh, what does she want?" K.C. said.

Elma tapped the driver's side window with a poison-green fake fingernail. She chomped on her gum hard enough to make her rouged jowls jiggle and shake.

K.C. rolled down the window and Elma leaned in, her stiff beehive hair impeding her full progress into the car. Elma shoved the cups under K.C.'s nose.

"Sweetcheeks told me to bring these out here to you two." Elma grinned and chomped on her gum.

"Do you mean Alex?" K.C. said.

"If that's the cop with the nice butt who hangs out with Quincy...then no."

"Who, then?" I asked, my eyes scrunching down to slits. I knew full well who'd sent them.

"Sweetcheeks is the girl he's with. Now if I'd said Sweetass," she winked, "you'd know I was talking about *him*." She licked her lips and I held back a gag.

I reached across K.C. and took the containers from Elma's green-clawed hands. "Does Alex know she did this?"

Elma shrugged. "Beats me." Her face filled the window as she looked me up and down then slowly shook her head. "Tsk, tsk, tsk. Sure is a shame, Quincy." The glitter on her false eyelashes caught some sun and the flash blinded me.

I sighed. "*What* is a shame, Elma?"

"Wasting your chance with a man like that. Looks like he's moving on to a new model."

"Oh, what do you know?" K.C. said. She started to roll up the window.

"I know you're about to be banned," Elma said. She pulled a digital camera out of her apron pocket.

"K.C.!" I whispered frantically, through unmoving lips. "Think of the scones! Roll it down! I can't lose my scones." Banishment from scones would push me over the edge. Life without Skinny's scones was unfathomable.

"Oh, all right," she muttered and rolled down the window.

"We're sorry, Elma," I said.

"Hmmph." Elma pursed her lips and glared at K.C. "Fine. I'll give you another chance." She pointed a pudgy index finger at K.C. "But watch it. You're this close to having your face plastered on the wall."

The wall of shame was a new feature at Skinny's. If Elma or Skinny got fed up with someone, the camera would come out and the victim would find their mug shot pinned to the wall behind the cash register. I don't think Skinny was actually responsible for any of the photos populating the wall.

"Stick a sock in it sister," K.C. said as she backed the car. Hopefully it wasn't loud enough for Elma to have heard.

After finishing our Biggy Bulgy Burgers with bacon and tater tots with fry sauce, we drove out west. We'd decided to take a trip to the marsh to check out the availability of greenery we needed to cut for the big grassy arrangement that had been ordered.

K.C. and I drove to Clint Wheeler's dairy farm just outside the road leading to the bird refuge.

Neither of us were dressed for mucking along ditch banks, but that didn't stop us from going. We pulled up to a cinderblock and metal building which looked to be the milking barn. A beautiful Victorian house with a wraparound porch loomed in the background. Gingerbread woodwork decorated doorways, window frames, the roofline and any available corner. Someday, my little house would be restored to look like this one.

A large garage made of metal siding stood across the way from the milk barn. I grew uneasy and shivered at the memory of a similar building in which I was almost killed a couple months before. We got out of the car and went to the front door of the milk barn. K.C. knocked then pulled on the handle.

"It's locked," she said. "C'mon."

I followed her to the garage building and found myself slowing down and falling further behind K.C. the closer we got to the entrance.

K.C. knocked and opened the door. A gruff voice called out "yeah," after she had already walked in. Inside, a sixtyish year old man stood at a workbench. He wore tan work gloves and gripped a pair of pliers in one hand and some kind of mechanical part in the other.

"Hello, Clint," K.C. said.

He looked up at K.C. then me and paused for a long moment. "Oh, Karma Gale is that you?"

"Yes, but it's Clackerton, remember?"

"Right, right, right. How is the old boy?"

"I'm afraid he's moved on to greener pastures. It's been a few years, now."

Mr. Wheeler winced. "I guess I did know about that, now that I think about it. Sorry."

"Not to worry. Actually, I'm getting remarried soon to a great guy. Fred Carr." The farmer's black, bushy eyebrows perked up and promptly knitted into a scowl. K.C. didn't seem to notice.

"Did you say Fred Carr?" he asked.

"Yes, do you know him?" K.C. said.

"I...well no. I was thinking of someone else, I guess. So what brings you here?"

"This is my friend and my boss, Quincy McKay. She owns the flower store in town and she wants to ask you something."

"Hi, yes, I need to cut some long grasses and cattails for a floral arrangement, and I noticed you have some on your property. I just wanted to ask your permission to cut some down."

"You mean ditch weeds?"

"Yes, that's pretty much what we need."

"Hell, you don't need my permission—pardon my French. Cut down as many as you want. I don't care."

"Thank you, Mr. Wheeler."

"Oh, it's Clint," he said.

"We better skedaddle, Clint," K.C. said. "Thanks a million."

"Say," he held up a gloved hand, "you said you have a flower shop?"

"Yes, it's called Rosie's Posies," I said.

"Well..." His ruddy cheeks developed a new shine. "I have this uh—lady friend and she's coming down to visit from Evanston..."

"I would love to trade some flowers for the grasses." I had to put him out of his misery, talking about flowers and romance.

"No trade, those grasses are weeds, I'll pay you."

"We can work that out later. When would you like them?"

He led us through a side door in the barn, which opened to an office. He used his arm as a plough to push a pile of magazines off of a giant desk calendar. He confirmed the correct date and I agreed to deliver a bouquet on that day.

"I told you we didn't need permission," K.C. said as we drove away from the farm. "Clint and I go way back. We went to high school together. I haven't seen him in years, but he knew my husband too. He probably came to the funeral, but I guess it's an easy mistake to make. Once you get old like me, you can assume anyone your age might have died already."

"I think he might know Fred," I said.

"Don't you remember? He said he didn't know who he was."

"That's what he said, but that's not what his face said. His face said that he knows Fred and that it might not be too friendly a relationship."

"Really? Well who wouldn't like Fred? Maybe his face is just stuck that way. He's always been kind of grouchy at first, until he warms up to you. Ah, here we are. Would you look at those."

We pulled over to the side of the narrow road and got out of the car. Beautiful brown cattails pierced the sky, like spires on a castle, on the opposite side of the ditch. I took a careful step toward the bank and my weight shifted in the mud. I felt the slightest pang of discomfort in my big toe, which had been broken when I was trapped in a barn similar to the one we had just left. I changed my footing and slid in the soft ground again.

"K.C., it's pretty muddy out here and I'm not going to be able to jump across the ditch with my toe the way it is. I can't get my footing. Maybe we could come back later with better shoes on."

"Agreed. Just look at this." K.C.'s foot had sunk about two inches into the ground. We cleaned the mud off as well as we could, threw our shoes into a plastic storage bin in the trunk at K.C.'s insistence, and went back to the shop.

"Why don't you take the rest of the day off?" I said. "If we get any more delivery orders I can take them. Allie and Daphne can watch the shop until closing time."

"I thought those gals were staying so you could leave early and get ready for the big date with your beau tonight."

"Oh, after our show today, I don't think Alex will ever want to be seen in public with me again."

"Don't be silly—he's used to you."

"What does that mean?"

She pursed her lips and glanced sideways, as if searching for an excuse, "It means he likes you, that's all. You two are just fine. Anyway, since you're offering, I think I will go see my sweet-ums. But don't you work late. Go spend time with Alex."

***

I sat down at the desk in my office once inside the store. Allie and Daphne were cleaning the melted wax out of over two hundred glass votive candleholders we had used to decorate a recent wedding reception. We'd hung them all over the church gymnasium to create more wedding ambiance and less sweaty basketball playing ambiance. Combined with the other décor, they had been stunning, but now they were stubbornly holding on to all of that melted and hardened wax. I had supply catalogs to go through and orders for glassware to place with vendors and preparation plans to get to before the local high school's homecoming dance, which would be the week after K.C.'s wedding.

Yep, there were plenty of reasons I wouldn't be able to see Alex after work. So what if one of those reasons was me making a fool out of myself in front of him and the beautiful woman who was trying to win him over—despite K.C.'s contrary version of what had happened. I did smile at the fact Samantha's recitation of Alex's schedule included a meeting later that night. It was our date. At least he'd kept that tidbit from her. Unless he was having second thoughts about our date. Maybe "a meeting" was code for something he would try to get out of.

As frustrated as he must have been, maybe the prospect of an evening with crazy, hesitant Quincy was more than he could stand. And maybe the thought of spending it with Samantha was more appealing. She wouldn't hesitate about doing *anything*, I was sure.

I buried my head under my arms on the desk.

I really did need to get the grasses and cattails cut and ready for the large autumn arrangement in a couple of days. I would need time to harvest the greenery, of course, but also to clean and de-bug the stems. I sat up in the chair and pondered my schedule. The more I pondered, the more wide open it looked, since my current boyfriend would be my ex-boyfriend soon—right after he started dating Samantha.

And what about her son? Alex was an honorable man. I couldn't imagine him ignoring the fact that he had a child in California who was without a father. He would probably want to move to California as soon as he found out about the little boy.

I looked up at the computer screen and noticed the pointer circling around and around. I had been tracing circles over and over again with the mouse. I needed something else to focus on.

"Quincy. Yoo-hoo, hello in there."

I looked up at Allie, who clutched a phone to her chest.

"Are you okay?" she said.

"Oh, yeah. Sorry, I was just thinking about something."

"It looks like it." She smiled. "Here's something else to think about. Mom wants to talk to you." Before I could respond, she handed the phone over.

"Hi, Mom. So...what's new with you?"

"Very funny, my dear. Your father told me he came by to visit. He sounds pretty impressed with Alex."

"That's great." Alex claimed he liked my father too. He just didn't dare look at me when in the same room as my dad.

"Listen, I know it's late notice, but we want to invite you two to dinner tonight."

Dinner. With my parents. And Alex. Not great timing at all. I didn't want to explain why Alex might not be attending.

"By you two, you mean me and Allie, right?"

"No, of course not. Allie is already coming."

"Oh, you mean, K.C.? To talk about wedding plans?"

My mother's forced sigh came through the phone so loud I think I might have felt her breath hitting my face through the receiver. "I mean Alex, of course. Ah, wait a minute, you're teasing me, aren't you? I'm afraid I don't have time for jokes, honey. I've got to get everything ready."

"I don't know if he'll be able to make it...short notice and all..."

"I know it's not much time, but we really want him to come to dinner, and I've already cleaned the house and made all the preparations. There's something we want to discuss with the two of you."

There it was. It took her some time to come around to it, but the ulterior motive had just presented itself. She wanted to lecture us about church, or maybe the neighbors had been tattling on me for who knows what.

My mother's secret army—or not so secret depending how you looked at it—of friends, neighbors, and church ladies was always up for a good sharing session of the intel they had gathered while out and about town. The secret society gals had hit pay-dirt with the events occurring in my life as of late. One of them had probably seen Alex with Samantha this afternoon and couldn't wait to phone up my mother and share the good stuff.

"Mom, I'm sorry you've gone to all the trouble, but..."

"No buts. We're leaving the house at seven."

"I thought you cleaned the house up for dinner."

"I did. What if someone needs to use the restroom?"

I'd forgotten that any sign of a visitor to the house warranted a top to bottom, thorough scrubbing and scouring. Just on the off-chance someone might ask to use the powder room before leaving to their destination.

"Oh, and one more thing," Mom said. "Quinella, please dress up a little bit. No t-shirts."

Well now I *really* wanted to go.

I gave a weak maybe to my mom and got off the phone.

"What's with this dinner thing?" I asked Allie.

She shrugged. "I don't know. I meant to tell you about it earlier, but I got distracted and then, well you know, I kind of forgot."

"What's mom got up her sleeve? Why the sudden desire to have a big family dinner?"

"I don't know. I've been so busy with school lately, I haven't been home much. And to tell you the truth, I've kind of avoided the situation there. Not that anything's wrong—it's just very different with dad there again. I kind of don't know where I fit in, really."

Though I didn't live at my parent's house, I sympathized with my sister. We didn't have much time to talk about our current domestic and family issues though, because Jacqueline DeMechant walked in the front door accompanied by a man I'd never seen before.

I approached the front counter and before I could greet anyone, Jacqueline spoke up.

"Quincy. I have some news."

My stomach dropped. She was going to tell me something bad had happened to Brock.

"Jenny's wedding is off."

I waited for her to say why, to talk about her daughter's feelings, about her daughter's missing fiancé—something. But nothing came, except the peculiar giddiness she exuded.

"Oh dear. Is it Brock?"

"Well of course it's Brock. He's disappeared. We can't very well have a wedding without the groom."

"You mean there's no news about him?"

"No, and I don't have time to wait around any longer. All isn't lost though. Quincy, this is my fiancé, Bruce Tanner."

"Hi there." The man nodded at me quickly. It wasn't unfriendly, but it wasn't an overly warm gesture either.

"Bruce and I have a proposal for you. We've spent all this money on wedding flowers and we don't want it to go to waste."

"This is an extreme case, Jacqueline. We can issue a credit to be used when they find Brock and the wedding is rescheduled."

"Brock isn't coming back," she said.

I stopped short and a cold shiver ran down my spine.

I paused. "I see." I didn't see, but I played along. "You were talking about a proposal?"

"Yes," Bruce said. "I live in a plain old bachelor pad. Jackie…er…Jacqueline has a much better eye for decorating than I ever will. You go on and tell her." He looked at Jacqueline with a trained-dog expression.

"We purchased so many permanent botanicals to decorate with and now they're just sitting, gathering dust. I'd like you to make some centerpieces and accent pieces with them to use at Bruce's condominium."

"What the heck are permanent…what did you call them?" Bruce said.

"Botanicals. Their more common name is silk or artificial flowers," Jacqueline said.

"Oh, par*dun*-a-moi," Bruce said, then chuckled at his own joke.

Jacqueline slowly glanced sideways at him, then closed her eyelids as if seeking relief from the tedium of Bruce.

"We could definitely do that, if you're sure, Jacqueline."

"I am sure. Also, I would like you to go through the condominium and look through the space. We will need some non-floral accent pieces such as paintings and statuary. I've added a few pieces of my own, but I'm getting ready for a trip and just won't have time to do the running around."

That's what she had me for.

"I must tell you, Jacqueline, I'm not an interior designer."

"I have every confidence in your abilities, Quincy."

A vote of confidence from a customer, even a condescending and sometimes difficult customer like Jacqueline, was a great ego booster, especially on a day when there wasn't much besides ego blasters going on for me.

We scheduled time for a visit to Bruce Tanner's condo to do a first walk-through and take measurements. I worried that I shouldn't have agreed to continue working for Jacqueline, because of the whole situation with the groom and the kidnapping. But I reasoned that the police were doing everything they could to find Brock. Jacqueline was acting strange about the whole thing, but I reminded myself that she acted strange all the time.

The couple left behind a pungent remembrance. Her perfume and his cologne combined into a nostril-insulting stew that remained in the store as a dense fog.

"Wow, I'm feeling dizzy from that smell," Daphne said from the back workroom. "What is it?"

"It's just Jacqueline's calling card. I wouldn't be surprised if one day, she and Bruce left their car closed up on a hot day and it spontaneously combusted from the fumes left inside. How do they not smell each other?" I said.

"Maybe they're both hard of smelling," Allie said. "Each one is over-compensating for their own lack of smell."

"You're probably right. By the way, did you hear us talking about an interior design job?" I said.

"I heard bits and pieces. Isn't it strange they don't seem to care that Brock is missing? She made it sound like he got cold feet. He didn't just leave, did he?" Allie said.

"I don't know. Brock was with Fred that morning and while Fred's back was turned, Brock disappeared. At least, that's what Fred said. I don't know what to think. I'm sure Jacqueline has more information than we do because of her daughter being Brock's fiancée, but you would think we would have heard by now if he really just left. It doesn't all make sense to me, but I'm just the florist."

"Oh sure, just the florist," Daphne said. "I heard about you solving a murder case."

"That was just a case of dumb luck, or *un*-luck, really. As odd as Jacqueline might be, she is our customer and she's put her trust in us to do the job that she's paying us to do. And that means flowers—and maybe some decorating, but it doesn't include investigating."

"I guess the boss has spoken," Allie said.

I looked at Daphne. Her eyes were wide open and unblinking.

"Don't worry, Daphne." I smiled. "Allie's just teasing. And sometimes I do get too bossy, but in this case it's not just that I'm concerned with serving our customer. From experience, I know I don't want to be involved with any more crime fighting. I got a concussion, a black eye, and a broken big toe, not to mention fearing for my life a few times." I sighed for dramatic effect. "Detective work is just not all it's cracked up to be." I winked at Daphne then turned and stuck my tongue out at Allie.

The phone interrupted our conversation. I answered, "Rosie's Posies, how may I help you?"

"That's a loaded question, Sweet-pea." My stomach did flip-flops at the sound of Alex's voice.

"Hi." I wasn't sure how to reply. Had he seen me in Skinny's parking lot with K.C.? And what was he doing having lunch with *her*? And why was I worried? I trusted him…didn't I?

"Are you there?" he said.

"I'm here. I—sorry, I…"

"Um—we missed you at lunch today."

"We who? You knew I was there?"

There was a pause. "Quincy, are you okay?"

"Yeah, why?"

"You told Samantha you wanted to meet for lunch, but then you told her you couldn't come at the last minute. Ring any bells?"

Anger flashed through my mind. "I told her what? She told you I said that?"

"Yeah, she told me you hadn't had a chance to meet with her and that you asked her to come and meet us for lunch before she went home."

"That lying, sneaky, little—ooh I just want to strangle her with that stupid pendant she wears in her boobs." I felt like I could breathe fire.

"Whoa, slow down. What are you talking about?"

"You know, the necklace that squishes between her..."

"No, I didn't mean that. It's not that attractive anyway—I mean, I hardly noticed—why are you calling her names?"

"I went with K.C. to Skinny's today so we could grab lunch and talk about the awful visitor we'd just had at the store."

"Who?"

I did a head slap. "Sam! She didn't say anything about lunch, or you. She said enough to piss me off and then left. I thought it meant at least she'd be out of my life for the next five minutes. Guess I was wrong."

"But she told me you said you couldn't come."

"Well, news flash, she lied."

"Hey!"

"I'm sorry. I didn't mean to sound so—mean. I'm just tired of her interrupting our lives."

"Sorry, Q." He sounded empathetic.

"No, it's me. I'm the one acting like a jealous girlfriend."

"When you say it that way, it's kind of a turn on—women fighting over me."

"Stop waggling your eyebrows—I can tell you are through the phone. There's no fighting here. I don't understand why guys get such a thrill over that, by the way." The change in conversation was enough to relieve the tension. "I was going to call you about something. I got so worked up about her, I can't remember what it was about."

"I called for something too..."

"Oh, I know, I was going to ask you—and you could totally say no and I wouldn't mind one bit. My mom called to see if we—me and you I mean—want to go to dinner with my parents and Allie tonight."

"Dinner with your family?"

"Yeah, I know it sounds like a million laughs..."

"I'd love to go." He sounded downright perky.

"You would?"

"Yeah. Your father can see us together with all of our clothes on. It'll be great."

Great was not the first thing that came to my mind when thinking about this dinner plan. "Huh. That was not the response I expected. What did you call about, by the way?"

"I was reminded of something at lunch today and I need to talk to you about it, but it can wait."

"What is it?"

"I'd rather talk in person."

"Oh. We don't have to go with my family tonight. We can just meet after work. I wouldn't mind missing the family outing." I wouldn't mind spending some time with Alex all to myself, either.

"It's okay. I'm looking forward to going with your family tonight. I'm sure we'll get a chance to talk."

Don't bet on it. We were going out with my mother after all.

CHAPTER EIGHT

Searching through my closet felt like an expedition through the wilds of an unexplored jungle. Half of the things didn't fit, but I was too sentimental to throw them away. I wanted new clothes, but lacked the funds for any major overhaul, and I was most comfortable in the same five shirts and two pairs of pants that I always fell back on anyway.

My mother had said no t-shirts tonight. I considered wearing one just to make a point. I didn't know which point exactly, but there had to be some good reason to defy her orders. I picked up Alex's gift and caught myself smiling at the memory of the first time I tried it on. My insides warmed when I replayed the scene and recalled the feeling of Alex's hands caressing, and well, other things.

That is...until my recollections reached the point where my dad entered the scene, unintentionally—Dad alleges—providing an emotional cold shower for us. So much for that trip down memory lane.

I decided to keep the t-shirt at home, where I could slip into it and think about Alex after we'd spent the evening together. As for the outfit, I found a retro floral print skirt and a coral colored shirt with a fabric ruffle-rose. It wasn't show stopping, but it was a cute ensemble that I finished off with a slipper-style flat. I didn't own any heels because of my height, but I could wear a one-inch lift and still be shorter than Alex.

I drove to his place since he'd had to work late and was short on time. He lived in a little white cottage that stood behind another house. The cottage had been the house of Alex's landlady until she and her late husband built the newer home in front of it. Mrs. Bernhisel liked renting the smaller house to a policeman because she felt safer living alone in her big house. I think she liked having someone to dote over as well. Alex regularly found full dinners and baked goods on his doorstep when he would come home from working in Salt Lake.

I walked through the screened-in porch and knocked on the front door. I heard a loud, "Come in, Quincy." I walked in and felt the humidity from a shower throughout the air, which held the delicious scent of Alex's aftershave.

"Where are you?" I called out from his living room, taking in the scarcity of any objects in the room that weren't dedicated to daily practical use. There was dark leather sofa, a recliner, and a black metal coffee table with a tray holding a remote control. A large TV sat on the fireplace mantel.

The freshly shaved fragrance grew in intensity behind me. "I'm right here." His arms reached around me and I felt the dampness left on his bare chest as it soaked into the back of my shirt. He kissed my cheek just in front of my left ear. The sweet spot. Actually, at that moment, any spot would have been the sweet spot.

I turned in his arms to look at him.

"Oh my gosh."

"What?" he asked through a grin.

"I can't see you like this, in just a towel. I might have certain thoughts."

His grin widened and his eyes sparkled. "What thoughts?"

"Thoughts that don't involve a towel being anywhere near you." I slid my hands up and placed them on his chest.

He groaned softly then slid his hands down my arms and grasped my hands. He leaned away. "Sorry, I shouldn't have started things up like that."

"Why not?" I protested.

"We don't have a lot of time."

"We could not go," I said with entirely too much enthusiasm.

"Mmm, Miss McKay, you're trying to seduce me." He kissed my forehead. "And I love it. But, it won't work—this time."

A small wave of insecurity flashed in my mind, or was it guilt? *I shouldn't be pursuing sex like this.* It went against everything I'd ever been taught. But many things had changed in my life since childhood, and life experience had moved the line between right and wrong and good and bad. The line that had been drawn for me was becoming rather fuzzy and didn't really seem to fit into my vantage point anymore. I had to draw my own line. Having the picture painted for me had been easier in many ways, but it wasn't necessarily better. And I didn't feel like living in someone else's picture anymore. I had to create my own landscape.

"You're sure?" I asked.

"Yes," he said, but he shook his head at the same time. He leaned down and touched his forehead to mine. "I—I…"

Again with the "L" word? Now?

"…look," he said, "we can't have a quickie for our first time. And even if we had plenty of time, there's no way in hell we could go have dinner with your family afterwards."

I laughed. "Why couldn't we?"

"Your father would know."

"Oh, c'mon! He wouldn't know. How would he know?" I put my hands on my hips.

"He just would." He turned toward the hallway entrance, then looked back. "It wouldn't matter if it were hours later." He disappeared into the hall and then peeked around the doorframe. "He would know." He left again and I started toward the hallway myself. His head came around the corner. "And I like you, and I would like for your father to like me too." His head disappeared and his towel came at me through the air.

I walked toward his bedroom, stopped halfway, and leaned back against the wall. "What about the rest of my family?"

I could hear the sound of hangers screeching across the closet rod as he moved things from side to side. "What about them?" he said. "You mean would they know too?"

Blech, I shuddered at the thought. "No. I mean, do you care if they like you?"

"Sure I do," he called from his room, "but I'm not too worried. I think your sisters like me."

A drawer opened and closed. Socks, I thought. "What about my mother?"

There was a long pause and then Alex appeared in the doorway. The ends of his tie hung loose down his chest on either side of his unbuttoned shirt and he held polished loafers in one hand. "Oh there's no worry about your mother. She *loooves* me. I heard what she said at the dress shop." He waggled his eyebrows and I lobbed his towel at him.

***

We met everyone at the restaurant, using *lack of time* as an excuse for not going to the house first. My parents had chosen Tony's Italian restaurant, a family friendly place with large tables to seat many, or intimate booths for couples. Red checked table cloths and lit chimney lights for heating handmade pizza adorned every table.

We followed the hostess in a single file line to the back seating room of the restaurant. Everyone looked at each other awkwardly, not knowing where to sit. My brother in law, Rick— always the leader—sat first. Alex held the chair for me while my father helped my mother take off her jacket. Rick looked up at us and leaned over and whispered something to Sandy, who then stood up and took over helping with Mom's jacket. Dad looked at Rick, paused, looked behind me, then rushed over to the chair next to me and held it out for Allie.

"Oh—um thanks, Dad," Allie said with a funny look on her face.

Rick stood up and helped Sandy with her chair as she returned to her spot.

Allie nudged my arm. "What in the heck was all that about?"

I shrugged. "I guess chivalry isn't dead?" My family didn't really *do* things like pulling chairs out for people. We had foregone those types of formalities many moons before.

"Something's up. I mean, Rick and Dad both *pulling out chairs* for people?" Allie said and then reached for one of the two water carafes on the table.

"Allow me," Alex said. He reached across me to pour Allie's glass. "Q, how about you?"

A loud "ahem" sounded across the table from Alex, where my mother sat.

Alex spilled some water next to my glass. "I mean—Quincy."

"Oh, Annette. Quinella's an ugly name," Dad said.

"Angus! That was my grandmother's name. It's a lovely name. Isn't it, honey?" She looked at me with imploring eyes.

"Your grandmother went by her middle name, Pearl. She didn't like her first name either," Dad said.

"Oh, I suppose you're right. I'm sorry, Alex."

Allie, Sandy, and I traded glances with saucer-sized eyeballs. Our mother had just admitted fault *and* apologized to my boyfriend.

"I think we should put a thermometer to the ground," I mumbled.

"What do you mean?" Alex said.

Allie giggled. "We think Hell has frozen over."

"Hey, did you see old Harold Busbeak at the bar?" Dad said.

"Angus!" Mom's mouth pursed in disapproval.

Dad shrugged. "What?"

"The poor man is under enough duress, he doesn't need to be called names and he probably doesn't want the whole town to know he was sitting in a bar."

I choked on my water. The commander in chief of the neighborhood spy network was worried about a person's feelings about privacy?

The server came to take our drink orders and I watched the apprehension in my mother's eyes along with disappointment in Sandy and Rick's when Alex stuck with water. Sandy and Rick don't get out much; they were probably hoping to see Mom throw a fit when Alex chose a more adult beverage.

"So who is Harold Busbeak?" Sandy asked.

"It's Busby," Mom said. "He's been talking to the papers about Jack Conway's bird discovery."

"The Inland False Booby," Dad pronounced in a regal tone.

Sandy smirked. "*What* in the heck is that?"

"It's a bird," Alex said. "Only a bird." He looked at me and made a face.

"Jack Conway sighted a bird that they thought was extinct," I said. "It's a big deal. All over the national news. Harold Busby is calling Jack a liar, and says he'll prove him wrong."

"Doesn't K.C.'s fiancé have something to do with the whole thing?" Allie asked.

"Well, they're all in the same bird watching club based at the marsh," I replied.

"Do you think it all has something to do with what happened to Fred?" Mom said.

I shrugged. "I don't know, but it seems kind of suspicious that Harold showed up at the scene and left just before the attack. I should go ask him if he saw anything weird before he left."

Alex put his arm around the back of my chair, leaned down and whispered, "It's none of our business, Q. Leave the poor man alone and *stay* out of it," he said with syrupy sweetness.

I frowned at him and he smiled and winked. Hard to stay mad at that face.

"What are you two love birds whispering about over there?" Mom said.

I felt my cheeks heat up. "Oh, nothing," I said. Alex grinned even more.

"Now, Annette. Leave them alone. They were just whispering sweet nothings to each other. Isn't that right, Quincy?" Dad wrapped his arm around Mom's shoulders and grinned at her.

"We...were just...talking about...nothing. No sweet nothings," I said.

As the meal progressed, I noticed Rick awkwardly draping his arm across Sandy's shoulders and her shrugging it off in order to be able to eat. I nudged Allie to get her attention and nodded toward the unusual display.

"Something's definitely going on," Allie whispered.

We ate our dinner without incident until my mother cleared her throat loud enough for the entire restaurant to hear. Apparently she had something important to tell us.

"Your father—uh—Angus and I have invited all of you out tonight to talk about something very important. With all the wedding planning that's been going on around our family, especially with you, Quincy, we've been reminded of how important and sacred the bond of marriage is for a couple." My mother trained her eyes at me as she spoke.

The waiter came to the table with the dessert menu, providing a welcomed interruption.

"Allie, what is our mother up to?" I whispered.

"I don't know. It's been like this since dad came back. I have no idea what she's going to come up with next."

"Did Dad say anything about me and Alex the other night?"

"I don't know. Like what?"

"Nothing, never mind."

"Quincy, your father came to visit you the other night," Mom said.

Here we go.

"And we were reminded how there's been so much change for everyone lately, and we thought this would be a good time to talk about marriage." She clasped her hands in front of her.

I reached for Alex's hand under the table and squeezed harder as my mother's speech became more difficult to bear, like when I squeeze the arms of the chair at the dentist.

"Married relationships are difficult, but when two people decide to commit to each other," she nodded toward Sandy, "like your sister and Rick have—"

"Ow," Alex whispered.

"Sorry," I said. I squeezed pretty hard with that last bit.

"We just think a couple should take a long hard look at what they want before they make decisions that could affect the rest of their lives," Mom said.

While my mother spoke, my father pushed back his chair, and fumbled with his pockets. He stood and walked around the back of Mom's chair and stood on her other side.

"Annette," Dad began, "after I visited with Quincy and Alex the other night, I knew I had made the right decision. You see, I've spoken with all three of our girls and talked about the time I was gone and why—"

"Angus," Mom said with the aside voice she reserved for our father when he said something she deemed inappropriate in front of us kids. "I thought you wanted to have a talk about marriage."

"Oh, I do that." He awkwardly knelt to one knee.

"Angus, what on earth are you doing?" Mom's face was scarlet. She glanced frantically from side to side. My father was committing the number one sin in public; he was making a scene.

"Annette, I've had plenty of time to think about our relationship, and we've talked things through. I've decided I need to make an honest woman out of you, and a decent man out of myself."

"But you said…"

"I said I wanted to get everyone together and talk about marriage. And that's what I'm doing now. Annette, will you marry me?" Dad pulled out a little green box.

"Angus McKay—I—you said you would never tell," Mom said.

"Annette! If I don't stand up soon, I'll be permanently frozen in this position. This is a killer for my bursitis. Will you or won't you?"

"Oh, Angus." Mom placed a hand on either side of Dad's face. "Yes, of course I will." She leaned down and kissed him.

The people sitting at the other tables nearby clapped and cheered. Everyone at our table exchanged stunned glances with each other. Our chins would all be bruised from hitting the table, except for Alex, who clapped along with the rest of the restaurant patrons.

Dad made an attempt to stand up and Rick got up to help him, which Dad promptly eschewed. He finally stood and ambled back to his chair. "These old bones are getting creaky," he said. "I need to exercise more."

"Um—Dad," Allie said, "what exactly did you mean just then?"

"I was thinking about taking up boxing again. There's a class for old men like me at that gym downtown."

"No. What did you mean about...making an honest woman out of Mom? You just want to renew your vows, right?"

Dad looked at Mom, who sighed while her shoulders drooped in resignation. "I guess we have to tell them now, don't we, dear?" she said.

"Cat's out of the bag, Annette. Sorry to surprise you this way."

"What are you two talking about?" Sandy asked.

"Your mother and I were never legally married," Dad said with complete nonchalance.

"What?" Sandy cried out, in a rare display of any emotion other than calm.

My father told us a story that twisted everything I thought I knew about my parents upside down and sideways like a corkscrew roller coaster. The after effects were just as unsettling.

My dad joined the Air Force after high school, just after he and my mother started dating. This much I already knew. What I didn't know is that the quickie wedding they did before he went to basic training wasn't the wedding we all thought we knew about. It wasn't even a legal wedding. My father's parents were Scottish immigrants who worked a farm. I found out that my parents did a Scottish hand-fasting ceremony in my grandparents' back yard. When I was a kid I'd asked my mom why there were no photos of her wedding. She'd told me they couldn't afford a photographer. Sounded reasonable. I didn't think to ask whether or not any of their friends took pictures. Hey, I was a kid. What did I know?

Everything I knew about my parents had been called into question. But I wasn't the one I was worried about. My poor religious sisters. How would they handle the knowledge that my parents hadn't really been married for our entire lives?

Alex gave my father hearty congratulations, and then we made our escape. I would have to process everything later.

It still seemed like I had just woken from a dream when we pulled into Alex's driveway. I'd done some calculations in my head as we drove. I was no math wiz, but I was pretty sure my parents' "wedding" had occurred after my sister Sandy was conceived. *My mother,* of all people, had been lying to us our whole lives. Not that it mattered when and how and who came first. But the last person who would ever be suspected of having a secret pregnancy was my mother! The same woman who had tried to lecture her daughters—actually one daughter in particular—only an hour before about avoiding the very thing she had done herself.

Alex turned off the car. "Tonight was certainly…"

"Entertaining?" I offered.

"I was going to say *interesting*."

"Leave it to my family. Hey, we never got to talk about your thing."

"What thing?"

"You know, whatever it was you wanted to talk about when you called today and I interrupted you."

"Oh…that," he said quietly. The mood in the car chilled like the early evening air outside.

He got out and came around to open my door. "Mrs. Bernhisel has been watching us through her kitchen window. I'm afraid she's going to break her hip. Let's go inside."

I looked at him, confused.

"She asked me to come look at her kitchen faucet once. While I was there, someone pulled into the driveway. She climbed on top of a box of laundry detergent so she could peek over the curtains instead of moving them aside to look out the window. She thinks no one notices she's watching when she does that."

We sat on the bench swing on Alex's back porch, despite the cool air, wanting to witness the last pink streaks in the western sky. I snuggled into him for warmth and he held me in his arms.

"So, what did you want to talk to me about?" I asked.

"It can wait. Tonight was eventful enough for you, with your family, I think."

"About my family. Don't internalize the crazy too much. It always seems worse than it really is."

"Don't worry about me. I like your family. I think they like me. What about you? Pretty intense with your parents, huh?"

"I'm not sure what I think about all that. I had a good talk with my dad that night he came over."

"Did he tell you then about living in sin with your mom?"

"Hey! They're not living in sin," I punched him lightly on the shoulder.

He leaned away from me and laughed. "It's your mom's term, not mine. When you were checking out of the hospital after I found you..." My body did an involuntary cringe at the memory of when he found me, injured, in a barn in the middle of nowhere. He pulled me closer. "I told her I was worried and wanted to stay with you at your house, since you wouldn't stay with anyone else. She told me it would be over her dead body she would allow her daughter to live in sin with some police imposter."

"She said that?"

"Yeah, no big deal. She was just doing her job as a mom. I think she's been trying to be both parents to you guys for a while."

"I guess so. When Dad and I talked after you left that night, he didn't say anything about their wedding or asking my mom to renew vows. He just talked about how he felt about her, how he'd felt since he left, and how he wanted to give it another try." I began to shiver, relenting to the chilly night. "I better get going," I said.

"Yeah, I've got to get up early tomorrow."

"How come?"

"Early meeting. I think I'm getting another out of town assignment."

Heavy sigh from me. "All of your assignments are out of town, aren't they? I mean, since you don't really work for Hillside P.D., Mr. Imposter."

"Yeah, well this imposter caught the bad guy didn't he?"

"Yep, and I'm really glad he did. Prison wouldn't have been very fun. Where will you be going?" I silently pleaded for it to be somewhere within the state and not for longer than a few days.

"I'm not sure yet. Just got word today."

"Is that what you wanted to talk about?"

"Kind of. There's more. How about we talk about it tomorrow? I'll come get you after work."

We walked together to my van. "I have to go to the bird refuge while it's light tomorrow," I said.

"Why? You're not snooping around a crime scene with K.C., are you?"

"Of course not. My crime solving days are over. I'm actually getting some grasses and cattails for a really large arrangement, and Danny needs me to get some measurements of the front of the visitor center so he can plan the decorations for outside the building."

"Outside the building too?"

"Oh, you have no idea. This is going to be an event unlike any other ever seen in these parts."

"With Danny and K.C. involved, I have no doubt about that." He held my hands and clasped them to his chest. "Your hands are freezing. You need to get inside. How about we go to the refuge to talk tomorrow?"

"Okay." I paused, thinking he would kiss me goodnight, but nothing happened, so I climbed into the van. Maybe he was just cold—from the temperature, of course—so he just skipped the long embrace. Yeah, sure.

"Quince?"

"Yeah?"

"I..." He leaned into the car and kissed me. Our lips must have been blue, because it felt like two trout had bumped into each other, rather than two passionate sets of lips. "I'll see you tomorrow."

The light from my headlights glinted off Mrs. Bernhisel's giant glasses as I passed her window.

"Sorry to disappoint, Mrs. Bernhisel," I said as I drove away.

CHAPTER NINE

It was almost a relief Allie wasn't working the next day. The big wedding bomb our dad had dropped had been shocking to everyone, but it was probably more so to her. I was the black sheep, Sandy was married and living in her own home, but Allie was still living at home with our mother. She had been the closest to mom and her religious household. Being the black sheep, I didn't feel like I was the first person she would feel the most comfortable confiding in at the moment. I would call her later, after I figured out how to talk to her.

Once Daphne arrived, I went with K.C. to deliver lunch to Fred. His apartment was actually a nice condo on the east end of Hillside. After enduring a five minute eternity of exchanges of "snookums," and "chi-chis," and all other manner of made up terms of endearment between the two love-birds, we all sat down to eat and visit.

"Any word on the investigation, Fred?" I said.

"None. I hear that Gordon is improving, though. Apparently it was real touch-and-go there for him the first day. He's still at the hospital, but his wife thinks he'll be home soon."

"Quincy is supposed to do the wedding flowers for that boy that went missing," K.C. said. "Hard to have a wedding if the groom isn't there. It seems as if the mother of the bride doesn't really care if he's there or not."

"Oh," I said, "I forgot to tell you, she finally conceded that they wouldn't be able to hold the wedding without the groom. We're going to decorate Jacqueline's boyfriend's place with the wedding money. It's all such a weird set of circumstances, and no one seems to care that Brock is missing. What possible reason would anyone have had for attacking you guys?"

"Yeah," K.C. said, "just what were you boys discussing that it was so important for you to be there?"

Fred exhaled slowly and shrugged. "I guess I can tell you two about it. I've already told the police what I know. I was trying to be discreet, so...you can't discuss this with anyone else while the police are investigating."

K.C. crossed her heart and made the zipper motion across her lips. She nodded toward me and I did the same.

Fred looked at both of us, then looked from side to side, as if someone might be hiding in the condo, listening in. Apparently satisfied we were alone, he began his story. "A little bird had told me—"

"Hah, good one, honey. A bird told him," K.C. said.

"Oh, yes, a bird. How interesting. I didn't mean to make a pun," Fred said.

Were these two made for each other or what?

"Anyway," Fred continued, "someone in the Friends of Feathered Friends group mentioned to me they had seen someone dumping their waste water into the marsh, along with some other toxic stuff—"

"You mean Harold..." K.C. said.

"Now, cuddlekins, I didn't mention any names."

"We all know if there's any tattlin' you can bet Harold is the one a rattlin'," K.C. said.

"Be that as it may, my dear, I had to report it to Gordon in case it was true. I told Gordon everything the informant told me," Fred glanced pointedly at K.C., who rolled her eyes. "Gordon said we should meet to talk to Brock about it."

"What does Brock have to do with this?" I asked.

"Brock supposedly witnessed the polluting, or had knowledge of it," Fred said.

"Who was the supposed polluter?" K.C. asked.

"I'd rather not say until we find out if it's true. We never got to talk to Brock about that. He'd just arrived when it all happened."

"So, this informant," I glanced at Fred, who grinned pleasantly at my choice of words, "how does he know that this dumping happened and that Brock knows about it?"

"That man has eyes on the back of his head and everywhere else, I tell you," Fred said. "He runs around those marshes with binoculars and top of the line recording and photography equipment. As unpleasant as he is, he is a valuable asset to FOFF. He's a human encyclopedia when it comes to any bird species, and he knows that land better than any of us. He has no life other than the marsh and the bird refuge."

"And neither you nor Gordon remember anything about the people who attacked you?" I said.

"No. Gordon doesn't even remember walking up to the tower. He has a terrible head injury. I just hope he can fully recover. I remember all three of us leaning on the railing, and then hearing someone telling us not to move. Wait..." Fred held up a finger. "Harold showed up before Brock. I don't know how he knew we were there, or when he got there. He came stomping up the stairs and he was going on about Jack Conway being a liar about the Booby sighting."

I stifled a giggle about a booby sighting and thought of Alex and his response to the Booby lecture. I loved the goofy look on his face.

"You said Harold stomped up the stairs. You could hear him coming. Do you remember if you heard the bad guys coming?"

"That's what's so strange. I didn't hear anything. There was absolutely no warning. We were talking, though. Brock was actually pretty animated as soon as he approached and was talking loudly. Gordon asked him how he was doing, and he started in about his mother-in-law and the wedding and the pressure. Poor kid. There were a lot of financial expectations coming from his fiancée, according to Gordon. Gordon said he felt sorry for the kid because as his boss, he knows how much the kid earns."

"So there was some extra financial pressure on Brock," K.C. said. "Maybe someone was paying him to look the other way when he saw someone polluting the marsh?"

"That could be tempting. Pleasing Jacqueline isn't an easy job," I said, knowing first hand.

"Do you think it could have been Harold that grabbed Brock?" K.C. said.

"No, not old Busby. He came by the hospital to see how I was doing the same day that I got there."

"That sounds suspicious to me," K.C. said. "He knew you were in the hospital because he put you there."

"Harold couldn't have done it. I've known him forever, and besides, how would he have been able to knock out the two of us and whatever else happened to Brock? No, it wasn't him. And what would be his motivation for taking Brock? Harold's a tattletale. I can see him coming to see if he got Brock into trouble, but that would be his reward, not hurting Brock."

"Harold does seem to love the marsh," I added. "Maybe his anger over the polluting and Brock—a person who is employed to protect the marsh—turning a blind eye to the polluting pushed Harold too far. He lost it."

"I see where you're coming from, Quincy, but it's just not the Harold I know," Fred said.

K.C. bolted up, hands raised. "I've got it. It's the polluter. He or she had motivation to stop Brock from talking." K.C. paced back and forth in front of the coffee table. "He wouldn't know how much Brock had shared with you, so he conked you both over the head, not caring what happened to you—the bloody bastard!"

"Karma, dear! You're so upset—calm yourself. We don't want your blood pressure to get too high."

"You're right, sweetums, but I've got to know who that dirty polluter is. C'mon Freddie, please tell me who it is." She sat down next to Fred and cuddled up, then batted her eyelids.

"I can't tell you, honeybun. I don't know that I have all of the facts. Until they find Brock and we get to talk to him in person, I won't substantiate what's only gossip at this point."

"Well darn your integrity right now—no offense. When I get my hands on the guys that did this to you..." K.C. said, her hands wringing the imaginary neck in front of her.

"Thank you, sweetcake. I don't even know if there was one guy or a gang of them. I think I heard someone telling another one to tie us up. But now, I'm not even sure about that. I know I didn't hear them coming, that's for sure. Anyway, it's all in the hands of the police now." Fred clapped his hands together. "So, let's talk about something new. We've got a wedding coming up soon, haven't we girls? What still needs to be done about that?"

***

Despite just having had lunch, K.C. thought dessert at Bulgy Burger would be just the thing, and I agreed. Scones at Skinny's wouldn't be on the menu for a while, at least until Elma cooled off. She wouldn't ever forget, but maybe the banishment threat would lessen in intensity over time.

"We'd like..." I started to say at the drive-through speaker.

"You just want the regular?" the voice from the speaker box said.

"How can you be so sure you know who this is?" I said.

"Please. It's two o'clock and you're in a white Astro van. You want bacon on your Bulgy Burger this time?"

How depressing was this? "No, actually, we want dessert this time." *So there.*

"A large Iceberg with chocolate chip ice cream and hot fudge—hold the cherry, and a peanut butter Avalanche with almonds instead of peanuts, then?" Though his voice was tinny because of the speaker, I understood what he said.

I blew out a sigh. "Yep that'll be it." I turned to K.C. "We're pathetic."

"So we're predictable when it comes to our junk food, so what? That Iceberg's still gonna taste like good sin," she said.

"I got some bad news in the mail today," I said.

"Oh no. It's not the paternity test, is it? Alex *is* the father. I knew it. I'd hoped against it, but it was too obvious, wasn't it? Well, at least you're not on one of those TV shows where they announce the results over the air to the whole world and someone does the happy dance all over the stage. Oh, kiddo, I'm so sorry. What did Alex say?"

"No!" I almost shouted. "The check you got from Lori Mangum the other day bounced. I tried to call Kyle but he didn't answer. I thought maybe I'd just stop by the house and return it. We can work out some kind of repayment later on. That's all. I just hate having to tell people their check bounced."

"Oh. That's a shame. Well, I never really suspected Alex was the father anyway," K.C. said. "Have you talked to him about…you know?"

"Not yet. He had something important to talk about yesterday, but my parents provided a big enough distraction. He thinks he'll have to go out of town again. He finds out at work today."

"Oh no! How long will he be gone? He won't miss the wedding, will he?"

"I don't know. We're meeting tonight. I imagine he'll have more to tell me then. We're going to the bird refuge so

I can cut some grasses and take final measurements for Danny. I'll keep you posted."

"Say, since you're going to the marsh, you could look around for clues at the tower."

"First of all, I'll be with Alex who has already warned me against snooping around. *Not* that I was going to anyway. That's probably why he volunteered to go there with me. But secondly, the police have already been there. Alex was there when we found Fred and Gordon and I'm sure he wouldn't have let the sheriff miss anything. Our snooping isn't going to help."

"You're probably right. I just wish I could hurry up the investigation and find the punks who did this to Fred and Gordon and Brock, and bring them to justice."

"I'm afraid your brand of justice might exceed the limits of the law just a teensy bit," I said.

"You might be right about that too."

***

"You sure it's okay to cut this stuff down?" Alex said.

"Yeah, K.C. knows the property owner and we got his permission. He acted like we were silly to ask. I guess it's all just weeds to him."

Alex steered the Scout around the numerous holes in the hard packed dirt road. Every time we hit a larger bump, a groaning noise emanated from the bottom of the truck and Alex beamed with joy. Now, I do appreciate the satisfaction one feels when they drive a reliable car—Zombie Sue, for instance. She just drives and drives and never asks for more than a little gas and oil once in a while and just a little love. Clearly, I have strong feelings for Zombie Sue. 'Strong feelings' doesn't even begin to scratch the surface when describing Alex's car crush for his Scout.

As we bumped and bounced along, a tire landed in one particularly large rut and a giant wheat colored bird flew straight up out of the ditch, only three feet from the car.

"Whoa, what was that?" Alex said.

"That's a Sandhill Crane."

"How do you know?" he asked.

"My Dad used to bring me and my sisters out here when we were little. A Sandhill flew right out in front of us once, and Sandy started screaming and wanted to run away. Dad taught us all about them so we wouldn't be scared anymore." I looked out the side window and another stretch of long silence took hold.

"They mate for life, you know."

"Really?" he said. "How do they know they've found *the one*? They all look the same, don't they?"

"They dance in the spring to attract a mate. It's avian romance," I said.

"I guess humans do our own kind of dance too, don't we?"

I thought of my parents. "Yeah, you could put it that way."

We stopped just before the gate to the refuge, where Clint Wheeler's property extended to the border. I'd brought clippers and heavy scissors and a bucket with clean water for the grasses I planned to cut, but a lot of the water had splashed out during the bumpy ride. Alex opened the tailgate and the spilled water dripped onto the ground. Transporting things in water is often a challenge. No matter how well you think you've secured your arrangements, every once in a while, you open your car door to a flood.

I shook the water off my gloves and tool pouch. "Why would somebody dump their waste water in the marsh?"

"What are you talking about?"

"I was talking to Fred and K.C. today about someone polluting the marsh. I just wonder why anyone would drive all the way out here, down that bumpy road. I imagine it would be a large quantity of water, so it would be obvious you were carrying it. Someone would have to see the vehicle you used to drive it. Doesn't make sense."

"It seems more likely it's someone next to the marsh. It's probably convenient for them to dump it. If it's toxic stuff, they have to pay to get rid of it legally, so they take the cheaper shortcut. It's big time fines if you get caught dumping on protected land, though. Probably prison time."

Alex jumped over the ditch, then pulled on my outstretched hand as I made the jump. We found some beautiful cattails and grasses with stripes and tufts of brown silk on their ends.

"Oh look at this gorgeous equisetum!"

"Gesundheit," he said.

"Very funny. Isn't it pretty?"

"I've never thought of it as pretty. I always saw it as a weed. But if you say it's pretty, then it's pretty. You're the expert. Beauty is in the eye of the beholder, isn't that what they say?"

After gathering armfuls, we figured out how to transport everything back across the ditch without landing in the water and put our small harvest in the back of the Scout.

Although we didn't get wet, our shoes did get muddy. Every time I landed after jumping across the ditch, my feet sunk in to the squishy ground about two inches deep.

"I can't get in like this," I said as I stood at the open car door.

"Why? What's wrong?"

"Look at this mud. I don't want to get it all over your car."

Alex looked at me and laughed for what I considered way too long.

"This baby was made for mud. Hop in—no wait. You've got something on your cheek, hold still." He swiped his fingers across the side of my face. It felt cold and wet where his fingers had traced. I reached up and found mud on my fingertips.

"You..."

"What?" He laughed and ran to the other side of the car and got in.

I got in on my side and stomped my muddy feet all over the floor while flashing a mischievous smile.

"Is this pretty?" I pointed to the floor.

"Gorgeous!"

"Beauty's in the eye of the beholder, that's for sure."

He looked at me for a long few seconds. "Come here."

"Oh no, I'm not falling for that again."

He held his palms up so I could see. "Look no mud."

I leaned toward him and he met me halfway. He kissed me and just as I leaned in for more, he pulled back. It could've been a coincidence. It wasn't an abrupt retreat, but noticeable nonetheless.

"You've got something on your face," he said and started the Scout. A smile curled into his profile. In the time we'd been together, I'd learned how much he loved to tease. "We should get going. It'll be dark sooner than we think."

I wanted to protest and stay right where we were, doing right what we had just been doing, but time was ticking.

"So why is it that you're the florist, and K.C. works for you, but Danny is in charge of the flowers for her wedding?"

"Hmm," I had to think of the best way to frame my response. "Danny is just Danny. Besides, he's kind of the creative consultant, if you will. He's the wedding planner, who also happens to be a florist, so he has his vision of the overall wedding and I'm providing the flower portion of the wedding. It's really a help to me. Even though I'm working, I'll also be able to enjoy the event too because of his staff pitching in. There's no way I would be able to be a bridesmaid and do all of the usual wedding day floral duties. I look at it as a team effort."

"I see," he said.

We pulled into the visitor center parking lot at the marsh and I commandeered the rearview mirror to look at my face when he turned off the car.

"Let's go get the measurements you need first, then walk around the boardwalk," he said.

"We can talk then," I said.

He nodded and smiled, but the smile was short lived, turning into something more like a reluctant grimace.

I took as many measurements of the exterior as I could think of, knowing Danny would want me to be thorough.

Alex was a great help, but my frequent reminders to bring him out of his thoughts and back to planet earth made it obvious something else occupied his mind.

We held hands as we walked slowly around the boardwalk, but it felt more like I was carrying his hand with me, like a five pound dumbbell, rather than sharing in an affectionate act.

"So, what is it you're avoiding telling me?" I said.

"Who me? I'm not avoiding anything." He put his arm around my shoulder and pulled me close to him. "I just wasn't sure how I should tell you that...I...have to leave town again." He winced and leaned away from me as if he expected me to throw a punch.

"What's the big deal? You already told me you were going to talk about that at work today."

"Yeah, that...I am going to Boise for a job, and it starts just as I'm finishing in California."

He stopped walking where the boardwalk came to a "V" and split into two paths. He turned to face me, holding both of my hands in his.

I narrowed my eyes. "You don't work that far away—do you?"

"No. Well, Boise, yes. But California...no. That's why I haven't been able to...I don't know how much I can tell you. It's some family business that I just found out about, and I need to go to California to straighten it out."

"Family business. In California." My hands had found their way to my hips without my noticing until just then. I left them there. "This wouldn't have been brought to your attention by an old *work buddy*, would it?"

"That's the part I'm not sure how much I can tell you about," he said.

"What kind of family business would *Samantha* be telling you about?"

Now, because I had vowed my trust in Alex on the holy 8-track of Willie Nelson, I reminded myself to calm down and let Alex explain.

"It's a relative of mine who is close to Sam, and she's worried about him. She told me in confidence."

"A relative? That's what you're calling him? A *relative*." I stomped my foot, and instantly regretted it. My healing big toe throbbed with pain. My teeth were clenched and my mouth was drawn so tight it hurt. "Willie Nelson or not, there's no way you can expect me to trust a thing that you're saying. I can't believe you would call him a relative, like he's some distant cousin or something. Unbelievable!"

"Quincy, what in the hell are you talking about?"

"Unbelievable!" I took the boardwalk path to the left and kept walking. "I can't talk to you...I've got to walk."

Alex called after me, "You're not making any sense. And what does Willie Nelson's cousin have to do with anything?"

What kind of person calls his own son *a relative*? And besides that, what kind of boyfriend would make up some story after finding out this kind of news instead of just telling his girlfriend—his *trusting* girlfriend—that he had fathered a child? How could someone who seemed so normal, in fact wonderful, turn out to be so—un-normal—when it came to relationships?

My brain buzzed into numbness, and all I could do was walk along that boardwalk. The breeze started up stronger and made the grasses overhead rattle. After a while, I slowed down, thinking I heard voices.

I stopped and looked behind me. Alex wasn't in sight. The voices came at me from the left and I spun around to see who they were. It sounded as if they were just in front of me, but then the breeze kicked up and the noise was gone. I walked again and heard footsteps behind me. I looked back, but didn't see anyone.

I walked faster, thinking it had been a stupid idea to leave Alex. The people who had hurt Fred and Gordon had hidden in these rushes.

I heard voices again. This time right next to me, just through a patch of equisetum. My heart thumped as I came to a clearing and looked in the direction of the voices—and saw a bunch of emerald-feathered ducks. The wind had carried their communications and changed them enough to sound like people. Creepy, whispering, murderous people.

I breathed a sigh of relief, but didn't completely forget the feeling that someone could be hiding in the marsh. I glanced around, but the grasses obscured the view. It was time to go and face Alex. I turned to go back and stepped forward—straight through a board. My leg plunged into the water and I fell forward. My chest hit the side of the boardwalk, my head and shoulders dangled over the edge.

I opened my eyes and was face to face with a bloated dead body.

I screamed.

The face was only recognizable as such because it had a little hair on one end and it was connected to a shirt on the other.

I felt myself being yanked up and away.

***

I didn't remember my leg catching up on the broken boards I had plunged through, but Alex told me he was afraid he'd shredded my leg when he pulled me free. I told him the bloody gashes probably happened on the way in. I told him this at the hospital.

We soon learned the body was Harold Busby's. Once the story hit the news, a lot of theories floated around about how he'd died. Apparently, there were no visible signs of trauma. It was possible he'd had a heart attack while he was doing some bird watching. I think I heard something about them doing an autopsy to find out what really happened to him.

Most everything I know about my finding Harold Busby, I had repeated to me by other people. I don't remember much that happened or was said in the moments after seeing that ghastly image. Except for the image itself. That never leaves me.

CHAPTER TEN

Alex left for California a couple of days after the boardwalk incident, and wouldn't return until after he finished working in Boise. And he would have to miss K.C.'s wedding. He might have postponed the trip had I encouraged him to stay, but I may not have tried very hard to do that.

Maybe it was the trauma that made me do it, or maybe I'm just not a very good girlfriend. But I told him he should go take care of his business in California. And since he didn't think it was any of my business, there was no point in us talking about it anymore.

For once in my life, I actually appreciated my mother's overbearing nature. It provided a constant third wheel in my life. Adding my father to the mix gave me enough extra wheels for a stretch limo. There was no room for exploring feelings or talking things out and that was just what I needed. Well, maybe just what I wanted, whether it was good for me or not.

I'm sure Alex was in a whirlwind of emotions too. Unfortunately for both of us, he chose not to share any of the reasons for those emotions with me. I'd learned of those reasons from one of the reasons! And did she have to be such a good-looking and successful reason?

Despite all of my feelings of righteous indignation, I knew I hadn't handled the situation with Alex very well. In fact, in plain language, I had behaved like a moron.

The first day after he left, I still thought I'd just been protecting myself from heartache. After a few more days of letting things percolate, I was missing Alex terribly and thinking of all of the times where I could have just told him how I was feeling, or even asked him what was going on and talked things out.

Back to that whole hesitation thing again. I hesitated to look behind the curtain and find out what was happening and get his side of the story. Despite all the time I spent trying to convince myself that I trusted him, I hadn't come any closer to being less of a pathetic spinster. I'd be that one old lady in the neighborhood who would live and die alone because she wouldn't let anyone break her crusty old shell, let alone open the heart underneath it.

I buried myself in work to distract myself from thinking about what a jerk I was. I picked up the phone a few times—even dialed Alex's number—but never hit connect. I didn't think he would want to hear from me again. He was probably telling his family how he'd dodged a bullet.

Maybe in a couple of days I could gather the courage to call him and apologize. I would use Harold Busby's dead body as an excuse for having completely lost all of my faculties of reason and logic. It wasn't the apology that required me to gather courage—it was his response that I would need courage for.

Until I developed the emotional strength to call Alex and have him tell me where to go, I would make sure K.C.'s wedding would be organized and ready. The days were flying by and I didn't want anything to get in the way of K.C. and Fred's marital bliss or the world's most absolutely perfect wedding.

***

The bells on the front door of the shop chimed and Jenny McQueen came in. The dark shadows under her eyes said everything about the state of things in her life.

"Jenny, hi," I said. "What can I help you with today?"

"I just need to talk about the wedding plans and the flowers and..." her shoulders hunched and she looked at the floor.

I ushered her to the consultation table in the front corner of the store.

"I don't know what to do," Jenny said. "My mom's paid for all these flowers, and people are calling. All this time I've told people we would still be getting married, that Brock would be home soon." She put her head in her hands.

"He will be home soon," I said, though I had nothing to base the statement upon.

"What about the flowers you've ordered? And the tablecloths and everything. I know it's too late for a refund, and I don't care about that—I just feel bad that you've gone to all this work and put up with my mother."

I laughed internally. "Don't worry about me. Your mother came in the other day and we talked about doing some decorating with the fabric. I was under the impression you knew she was coming. I already talked to my suppliers and cancelled most of the flowers I ordered. I'll make some artificial arrangements with the flower money and the silk flowers your mother already bought."

Her face brightened at the news. "Normally I would be furious with my mother for coming without me, but now I have less to worry about. What is she having you decorate with that awful blue fabric, anyway?"

"Her fiancé's place. You think it's awful too—I mean, you don't like the blue?" I said.

She scowled and took a long time to answer. "No. I hate it. Mom's crazy about it. She's addicted to anything Egyptian. Bruce won't care about the blue either. I don't imagine he'll even notice the difference." She sighed. "I just played along because she was paying for it. If it were up to Brock and me, we wouldn't even have a big wedding with a reception." Her mouth drew into a tight line and her bottom lip trembled. "He asked me to elope the night before he disappeared. I wanted to so bad, but I couldn't do that to my mom. But I keep thinking how if we'd gotten married that night, he wouldn't have been anywhere near that bird refuge the morning he went missing."

"You can't think that way, Jenny. None of this is your fault. He'll come back soon and you guys can elope or have a huge wedding, whatever you like."

She stood up and wiped tears from her eyes. "Thanks, Quincy. I really appreciate your help." She walked over to the large flower cooler and perused for a few moments while gaining her composure.

"I'm going into the cooler, can I get you a cold water?" I said.

"Actually, can I go in with you? I want to look at your Phragmites."

"Sure. My what, now?"

She laughed, which lightened the mood. "Phragmites is a reed. You find it in marshes all over the world."

We went inside the cooler and I shouted over the noise of the interior fan, "I thought this was called Pampas Grass."

"They look similar, but they're different. You've got yourself a collection of Phragmites." We left the cooler and walked toward the front door. "It's interesting..." she glanced at the cooler window again. "Where did you get those?"

"Oh, don't worry, I didn't cut them from the refuge. I asked the next door land owner for permission to cut them from his ditch banks."

She looked at me apologetically. "I'm sorry, I didn't mean to imply you shouldn't have them. I just thought they looked a little different than the usual local varieties. I guess I'm kind of a Phragmites nerd. Actually, I geek out when it comes to reeds of all kinds. Weird—I know."

This made me laugh. "I think it's great you have something to be passionate about. Geek away. I've got plenty of extra in there if you want to take some home."

"Oh, could I? I want to look these up and see what they're doing here."

"Great, have at it," I said. She gathered a few stems and left after I told her to keep her chin up.

Witnessing Jenny's concern for Brock only made me feel even more foolish for being so awful to Alex. Here I had the perfect man and I'd let some tiny little communication problems force him away from me. Pathetic.

***

I heard a whistled version of "Get Happy" coming from the back of the shop. K.C. had returned from deliveries.

Daphne joined us in the back room. "Quincy, we just got this order in. They were hoping it could go out today. They're still on the phone. What should I tell them?"

I looked over the order. "Looks like it's about four blocks away from Kyle Mangum's house. K.C.'s about to leave, so I'll take it over while you're still here, Daphne."

"I'll go with you on the delivery," K.C. said. "No way I want to miss out on that scene."

I shook my head.

"What are you shaking your head at, missy?"

"Nothing." I couldn't keep from smiling. "I'll go put the order together and we can deliver it, then see if Kyle Mangum happens to be home, or his wife, since she wrote the rubber check. Ooh, since we'll be together, we can go look at the dress I picked out. You can give it the final approval."

"You and I both know that Danny gives the final approval on attire." She winked because she was teasing, but she was right.

The Mangums lived in a pale green post-war cottage on the southwest end of Hillside. A chain-link fence wrapped around the perimeter of the front and back yard. I called Kyle before we left and got no answer. I figured we could just swing by and see what happened.

We found the gate unlocked at the front yard. The front door was open too, with just the screen door keeping anyone from entering the house. I knocked on the screen and we stood there in silence for a few moments.

No one came to the door.

"Hmm. What should we do?" I said.

"Kyle? Lori?" K.C. shouted through the screen of the door.

I tapped my toe and looked at the ever-present dirt under my fingernails while waiting for a response. "We should go."

"Wait. Do you hear that?"

I leaned closer to the screen. "It sounds like talking—no—it's—is someone crying? A man is crying—I think."

"I smell something funny," K.C. said.

"Me too. Now someone is yelling."

"We should investigate," K.C. said.

"No way. We aren't cops. We can't just go into someone's house uninvited."

"Someone's life could be in danger, and besides, where's your sense of excitement?" K.C. said.

"I left it at the jailhouse the last time I was there. We should just call the police."

"It might be too late. Listen. The voices are gone. We've gotta go in!" K.C. pulled the screen door open and charged in.

I gritted my teeth, looked around for witnesses and seeing none, followed her in. I slammed into the back of her two feet inside the door.

"What the heck?" I whispered. "Whoa."

"Yeah, whoa," K.C. whispered back.

A thousand eyes stared at us from all around the room.

"I've never seen anything so strange in my life," K.C. said.

The room was packed from ceiling to floor with dolls. But they weren't just any kind of dolls. They were clown dolls. Clowns covered the couch, they sat on the TV, the coffee table, and on glass shelves on the walls. It was as if they levitated in row after endless row. One doll's giant clown feet on top of another doll's curly multi-colored freak hair. There were old dolls and new ones in what seemed like every possible baggy clown suit style and color. Some of them smiled and some had sad faces with tears on their cheeks. There were some crazed looking evil clowns and even scarier, some of them had teeth.

A faint wailing sound came from the back of the house. "Boss, we've got to go see. I think Kyle might be hurt."

"You're right," I said. "We've got to get out of this circus of the damned, anyway." I grabbed K.C.'s shirttail and followed her backwards with my back to hers so I could make sure none of the little monsters jumped out and sunk their teeth into our necks.

"What is the matter with you?" K.C. said.

I pushed a lump down my throat. "I don't like clowns."

"I gathered that. They're just dolls, you know."

"Are they—*just* dolls? Did you ever see *Circus Tent of Horrors*?"

"Can't say that I have," she said.

"Well, you don't want to."

We made our way into an orange Formica-covered kitchen. A strong chemical smell hit like a brick wall. My eyes teared and I couldn't help coughing. Small jars of paint lined up in precise rows covered the kitchen table. Paint brushes of various shapes and sizes stood bristles up in a wooden caddy, arranged from small to large, each brush hole labeled with numbers.

"Eck, that smell is horrible." K.C. held her sleeve up to cover her nose. "And what in God's green earth is on the counter?"

A kind of waffle iron lay open, but instead of waffle squares, the plates were flat around the edges with a hole in the center, like a half cantaloupe with the seeds scooped out. Little white masks surrounded the waffle iron, like ghost faces popping out of the countertop.

"They're doll faces!" I said, pinching my nose. I looked closer and realized they weren't just any doll faces, they were unpainted clown faces. "Now we know why she comes to the door with goggles and gloves on. She makes clown dolls."

"Ah, that makes sense." K.C. said.

The voice cried out again, coming from a door which led to the basement stairwell.

"Are we really sure about this?" I said.

"You can hear that noise, right?"

I sighed. "Yes, I hear it."

We rushed down the narrow stairwell. On the left was a closed door.

"Help!"

I opened the door and a gray tabby cat sprinted past my feet. We walked around a half-wall that partitioned a tiny laundry room into its own space. We saw no one. "Whaddya suppose made that sound?" K.C. said

"Help!" This time it came from behind us, upstairs.

I returned to the landing at the foot of the stairs. The gray tabby sat on its haunches, half-way up the stairs.

"Help!" the cat said.

"It can't be," K.C. said, as she joined me on the landing.

"Help," said the cat.

"Please tell me you heard that cat speaking English just now. I'm not hearing voices coming from a cat, am I?"

"I heard it too," I said.

The cat watched us from its seat on the step and blinked.

"Let's leave before someone comes home. Obviously no one is here," I said.

The cat got up and came down the steps. It sat on the bottom step. *"Help."* It hopped over my foot, turned back, looked at me. It walked a few steps, turned back and said, *"Help,"* over its shoulder.

I didn't move. The cat returned to my feet, hopped over them and then walked toward the laundry room. It stopped a few feet away and looked at me and then made the sound again.

"It wants us to follow," K.C. said.

"We can't follow it," I said. "We need to get out."

"What if the cat is trying to tell us something?"

"It's asking for help because it's creeped out by all those clown dolls."

"I think it just needs to use the loo." K.C. moved toward the back door next to the washing machine.

"What if it's an inside only cat?" I said.

"Help."

K.C. opened the door. "It'll come ba…"

The door hadn't opened to the back yard, as I had assumed it would. Instead, it opened to an addition with a narrow hall lit with a dim light bulb dangling from the ceiling. Music floated on the air from somewhere ahead.

The cat meowed again and looked up at us, then took a few steps into the hall. "I think this kitty is trying to lead us to someone," K.C. said.

"This is *not* a good idea. We are in so much trouble right now."

"Well then, since we're already in trouble, it won't hurt for us to investigate some more. I think this is a tool shed. I wonder if Kyle has had an accident and he needs help. The kitty is trying to get help and we are it."

"How would the cat know? The door was shut."

"Animals can sense things. Didn't you ever watch Lassie?"

I shook my head. K.C. was going in whether I accompanied her or not. "Just be careful."

She dug around in her purse and pulled out her stun gun. "I'm ready."

I looked at the ceiling while I pondered whether I would follow K.C. into the unknown, or go back upstairs and face the clowns alone. I shook my head, and then followed her through the hall.

K.C. stopped suddenly and I bumped into her.

"Quincy," she whispered.

She'd stopped at the opening of a small room. I stepped around her, instantly seeing why her voice had sounded so strange.

We stood in a dim, softly lit room. To our left was a bed covered with a lace bedspread, skirt and pillow shams.

On the right was an antique dressing table and matching bench, topped with a silk cushion. The walls were painted blush pink, which glowed with a yellow warmth from the many lamps scattered around the room. The music came from a small CD player on top of the chest of drawers, nestled next to a glass dome. Inside the dome was a dried flower bouquet. I realized it was the bride's bouquet I had made for the Mangum's wedding. I recognized the iridescent chartreuse satin ribbon. I had remarked at the time I made it how unusually pretty the ribbon was in the way it reflected different colors depending upon the angle in which it was held.

The music grew louder and I realized it was a classical piece on a continual replay loop. A multitude of photo frames covered the remaining space on the dresser. All the photos featured the same woman.

"I think we've walked into a shrine," K.C. said with an unusually understated reverence.

I examined the photos more carefully. Something about them told me I needed to pay attention. "We have to leave. Now." I grabbed K.C.'s shirt sleeve and yanked her toward me.

"What the…"

I shushed her before she could say any more and closed the shrine room door behind us. I had to hide any evidence of our presence and hoped we wouldn't be caught while still inside the house. The cat led our way out, always waiting until we were within a few feet before it continued. We passed through the evil clown room and stepped out onto the front porch. A wave of relief washed over me and I could breathe again. We were home free.

"Uh, oh," K.C. said.

A car pulled into the driveway next to the house and Kyle Mangum stepped out.

"Oh, crap," I said.

"He doesn't know we were inside," K.C. whispered.

She had a point. A great point. And I was comforted by the realization that the view of the porch from the driveway was partially obscured by a lattice-work screen, which supported a climbing rose bush.

As soon as I heard his car door open, I leaned out from our cover.

"Oh, Kyle! What a funny coincidence. We just got here too."

"Quincy, it's you. I thought that might be your van parked in front of my house." He approached the porch with the friendly face I had been so used to at my shop as he planned his wedding. He noticed K.C. on the porch and nodded hello. "We just had a birthday. It's not time for our anniversary roses yet is it?"

"Um, no. We actually came here about something else. It's a small thing really, and we can just figure something else out."

"What my boss is trying to say is that your check is made of rubber. It bounced like a kangaroo in the outback," K.C. said.

I glared at K.C. I would have told him, eventually.

Kyle laughed. He looked at me and said, "I'm so sorry about the check." He continued to laugh. "K.C., you're a hoot. You just made my day. Bounced like a kangaroo," he chuckled, "I'm going to have to use that one."

I laughed too, but didn't forget where we had just been. I watched carefully while Kyle interacted with K.C.

"Well, Quincy," Kyle said, "I owe you some money. I just spent some cash on my last errand," he pulled his wallet from his back pocket. "Let me see here. Not quite enough. I've got enough in the house. Why don't you come in and I'll get enough cash to cover the check and you can just give it back to me."

"Oh shoot." I thunked the heel of my hand against my forehead. "I can't believe it. I forgot the check. Tell you what, let's just leave it for now and next month you can pay for both. That way we won't have to come back and bother you. I'll just shred your returned check when I get back to the shop."

"Are you sure?" Kyle said.

"Yeah, are you sure?" K.C. said quietly, furrowing her brow.

"Positive. No biggie. Well, K.C., we'd better not forget the other flowers in the van. We didn't leave it running, so we need to get going."

"But Boss…"

I stepped in front of K.C. and motioned toward the van behind my back with one arm while waving goodbye to Kyle with the other. "Thanks so much, Kyle. We really love getting to send a new bouquet to your wife every month. We'll see you next time. Bye."

I rushed over to the driver's side and started Zombie Sue while K.C. paused with her open door saying goodbye to Kyle. He laughed at the K.C. show while he waved.

Eventually, she sat down and I hit the gas as she shut the door.

"What's the rush?" she shouted.

"We needed to get away from there," I said.

"I don't understand. We drove all the way to his house, went inside and left, and then you tell him you don't have his check. I saw you pick it up off your desk and put it in your bag, which is sitting right over there." She pointed behind my seat. "And why were you in such a rush to get out of the house anyway? I mean, I'm glad you did because Kyle pulled up as soon as we got out, but—ooh, did you get a psychic premonition?"

"No, I was psyched *out* by the creepiness of that bedroom, and the clown room and—every room of that house," I shuddered at the thought of all those eyes following our every move. "But I noticed something about those photos on the dresser downstairs."

"What about them? They were all of Mrs. Mangum. I admit it was a strange place for a bedroom, but maybe they keep cool down there in the basement."

"Didn't you find it strange that all the lamps were left on, as well as the music? I noticed it was the same music, just repeated over and over on a continuous loop. And where was she? She's always home when you deliver the flowers."

"Maybe she stepped out for more supplies?"

"Maybe. Anyway, the photos...they were all taken from the perspective of someone far off. She wasn't posing for any of them like you would in a family photo. If your husband was taking a picture of you, you would look at the camera at least once in a while. If you knew someone was taking a picture of you, you would look toward whoever was taking the picture. None of those photos showed any kind of recognition in the woman's face. They were all taken from afar. And they were all taken in different locations."

K.C. sucked in her breath. "You mean she was being watched?"

"Something like that. Maybe even stalked."

"But it's his wife…"

"I'm not so sure she is," I said.

"I'm so glad you got us out of there, Boss. No telling what we would have found next. Wait a minute—the woman in the photos is not the person who comes to the door—at least I don't think she is. The woman in the photo looks like she might be kind of tall and she's got dark hair. Lori Mangum is barely taller than me, has blonde hair, and is more round shaped than the woman in the pictures."

"Are you sure it's not her?"

"Well no, not a hundred percent sure, but fairly certain they're two different people. Do you suppose Lori knows about the shrine room?"

I shrugged, "Who knows? But you'd think in her own house she would know about a room with the lights on and the music playing all day." I suddenly realized I was sweating so much my hands were slippery on the steering wheel. I cranked the AC as high as it would go.

"What are you going to do about the check?"

"I'm going to call the police."

"Help!"

K.C. and I shrieked, and I pulled over to the side of the road. I had to make sure none of my vital organs had left my body.

We both looked back into the interior of the van. Kyle Mangum's cat was sitting in the middle of the floor, licking its front paws.

CHAPTER ELEVEN

"What do we do now?" K.C. said.

"We're not going back to that house. I guess we'll have to take it to animal control and see if the Mangums call to claim it."

She sighed. "I hate to do that. The poor thing. You know what happens to cats that go there. They say they try to find the owners and that they don't euthanize until they find a home for the animal, but I know for a fact it isn't true. I knew someone who worked there, and she told me the cats have the worst of it. If they don't get claimed and aren't adopted within two weeks, they're done. Curtains." She made a morbid slicing motion across her throat.

"*Help!*" the cat said.

"You said it, cat." She twisted to face the back of the van. "We can't just call you cat. What would be a fitting name for you?"

"You can't name it," I said. "Whenever I would name the cows on the farm, my mom would tell me it was a bad idea and that I was setting myself up for heartache."

"We need to figure something out. We can't just leave it in the van," she said.

"I don't know. We can't go back there, and I don't want to call him either. Alex has a friend who works for Hillside police. I'm going to call him and tell him what we saw today. That way it's in their hands. They can do something if they want to."

"What about the monthly deliveries?"

"I don't know what to do about that either. I'll just wait to see what Alex's friend says."

"Well, attached or not, we're not taking Shim to the pound."

"Shim?" I said.

"I don't know if it's a she or a him, so it's Shim for now. I'll get a closer look when we get back to the shop. Shim, you're coming home with me. Oh, now don't shake your head, Boss. Shim's got nowhere else to go."

Our little trip to the Mangum household had me completely rattled. Kyle had seemed so normal, so nice, when he came in to plan the wedding. I'd thought it to be odd the bride didn't come in or care about the flowers, but as Kyle had explained, this was a second marriage and she was busy working out of town a lot. At least I think that's what he told me. And how romantic was it that he had us send flowers every month on the date of their anniversary?

It didn't seem possible such a nice, thoughtful guy could live in such a weird home—and then there were those photos. Maybe he was a stalker, or worse. And where was his wife? Had she suddenly disappeared?

I knew I needed to report what we had seen to someone I could trust. First of all, we had snooped around that house uninvited. Big no-no. Secondly, I had no proof of anything except creepiness. Thirdly, the only crime that had been committed was a bounced check, which was hardly worth the police force's time. But I knew something weird was going on.

***

I was just polishing off a Bulgy Burger, tater tots with fry sauce, and a large Coke when I heard a knock on my back kitchen door.

I opened the door. "Hi, Dad. Come in."

"Not much of a meal," he said when he saw me cleaning the remnants of waxed wrapping and paper bags from the table.

"I guess not." Better eating had been one of Alex's influences on me. He loved to cook and I loved to eat. For now Bulgy Burger was my personal chef.

Dad turned a kitchen chair backwards and straddled the seat, resting his arms on top of the seatback. I laughed to myself, remembering Alex doing the same thing.

"Now that's better," Dad said.

"What is?"

"Your smile, lassie."

I felt my smile widen at the hand-me-down nickname from my father's Scottish parents.

"Better still," he said, then winked. "Hey, isn't your friend K.C. a bird watcher? Your mother and I went to breakfast at Skinny's today and we saw old Jack Conway. Said he was going out of town."

"Yeah, he's the one who lectured when I went with K.C.," I stood and walked over to the counter. "Ice cream?"

He nodded enthusiastically. "That's right, you told me about the bird he discovered. I wanted to catch up with him and ask about his world famous discovery, but he was in a blasted hurry. I barely got to wish him well. He grew up in this neighborhood, you know. Went to school with your aunt Rosie."

"Oh, really?" I tried to be interested, without much success. I needed more calories to stuff down the lonely feelings. I got two bowls out of the cupboard and pulled the chocolate chip ice cream out of the freezer. Dad came over and commandeered the scoop and told me I should sit.

He brought the bowls to the table and sat down. "I came over to see how your leg was healing. I expected a half-clad n'er do well to answer the door. Where is that beau of yours?"

I wasn't able to conjure a smile any longer. "He's still in California. He's got family stuff to take care of."

"Oh. I see." He knit his brows and looked at me with that gaze that always made me come clean when I was a kid. He never had to say anything. He would just look at me or Allie with the eye and the confessions would come spilling out like waterfalls. I don't think he ever gave the look to Sandy. She never lied to our parents, *allegedly*. Probably he never had to give it much to Allie, either. It was pretty much reserved for me, the middle child.

"There aren't many challenges that make it worth giving up on the right one, Quincy."

"How do you know? You've been back a few days. What if it doesn't take this time? I know how challenging Mom is."

He laughed, his deep bass voice rumbling tangible vibrations through the air. "She's my right one. I'm a stupid and stubborn man, my dear. It took a while for me to really see and know what I had let slip through my fingers." He held up two knotted, meaty hands with fingers calloused from playing the banjo.

"Really, is that walking stick of yours okay?"

I nodded. "It's fine. It looked worse than it really was when we were at the hospital."

"All right, then." He leaned over and kissed the top of my head. "You're my favorite girl, you know?"

I laughed. "You say that to all three of us."

"I really mean it, Quincy. And I think you've found a keeper in that one. It might be worth overcoming whatever challenge you're staring down right now."

"How do you know that? You've just met him."

He swallowed the last of his ice cream. "Mmmh, a man knows."

I raised my eyebrows in disbelief.

"Smirk all you want. He speaks the language."

"Oh geez, not the Mantown thing again."

"That's a new term to me, but it's just the thing. Mantown. Yes, your man and me, we speak the language of Mantown."

I rolled my eyes.

"I'll be on my way. By the way, don't let on to the lad that I approve of him in any way. Got to keep 'em scared."

"Dad, I don't think he's coming back."

"Oh, he'll be back, lass. His right one is here, so that's where he'll be. You'll see."

I closed and locked the door after he left, then got ready for bed. "Sorry Han," I said to the t-shirt in hand. "I'm sleeping with Starbuck tonight. Deal with it."

CHAPTER TWELVE

I flipped the open sign at three minutes after nine, which wasn't bad considering I woke up at eight thirty-two.

My new diet of grease and sugar had not been conducive to waking up any earlier in the mornings. Daphne was going to be a few minutes late, and Allie had asked for the morning off to square things away for a school project. So it was just me responsible for opening the store on time.

I rushed through the store turning on lights and the computer, then filled the can for watering the lush green plants filling the front of the store. Being alone in the shop had its advantages, and being able to talk to the plants while I gave them a shower was one of them. It definitely helped them to grow fuller and more deeply colored.

As I unpacked a box of vases in the front design room and put them on the shelf, I heard the doorbell chime. A walk-in customer this early in the morning would be a great start-off for the day.

No such luck. I looked down from my perch on the stepladder to see my mother dragging a giant garbage bag behind her.

"What's all this?" I said.

"Now what kind of a greeting is that for a customer? Good morning, Quinella."

The passive-aggressive use of my full name did not go unnoticed.

"I'm sorry. Good morning, dearest mother. Did you rest in the peaceful arms of blissful slumber last night?"

She huffed at my sarcasm and plunked her garbage bag on the design table. "Alright. You don't need to be that formal. And no, if what you were asking is did I sleep well, the answer is no." She busied herself pulling silk flowers out of the bag.

"Sorry you didn't sleep, mom. How come you're not sleeping?"

"Well," she blushed, "your father's been gone a long time…"

"Oh, geez." Let the uncontrollable shudders begin. "Um, Mom, could you hold on for one second—I just have to go and throw up now. Feel free to make something up next time. I don't want to hear about that. You're my parents for criminy sakes."

"You asked."

"So what are we doing with all these silk flowers from the 1980s?"

"Since your father and I are going to redo our vows, I thought we could use these for a bouquet. We don't really need any other flowers, and I didn't want these to go to waste." She pulled a smashed lily with fake plastic rain drops on the petals out of the bag and sneezed at the accompanying dust cloud.

My ever-practical mother had taken the science of frugality to the level of nuclear fusion. My mother was the Picasso of potatoes, the Manet of macaroni and the Renoir of repurposing. If it still had life in it, my mother could, and more importantly, *would* turn it into something else. Now, whether she *should* or not is an entirely different question.

"Mother, I'm afraid I cannot allow you to use those flowers for your bouquet. We can do silk, that's fine. But they have to have been produced within the last twelve months. Or," I raised the pitch of my voice and made an extra happy facial expression, "we could use real flowers."

"Real flowers are so expensive, though."

"Hmm," I stuck my fist under my chin and looked upward, "if only we knew someone who could give you some flowers for free. Someone who has their own flower shop…"

Mom tried to frown without much success. "Sarcastic as ever, just like your father." She smiled. "Thank you, dear. That's very thoughtful."

"It's the least I can do. Maybe I'll talk you into some other arrangements before we're through."

Daphne arrived and took over the morning's preparations while I helped my mother drag her bag of ragged silk flowers into the back.

"Your father tells me he came by for a visit yesterday. He said you were putting on a brave face about your leg. You have to take care of those wounds, Quincy. They have a high chance for infection."

"The leg is healing just fine. I'm following all the instructions, plus it wasn't as bad as it looked in the beginning."

She busied herself by rolling all the bolts of ribbon until the end of each rested exactly level with all the other bolts. I couldn't convince her it would all be ruined in a matter of minutes when I started making bows, so I let her do her never-an-idle-hand thing.

"I haven't heard you talk about your friend in a while," Mom said, facing the wall of ribbon.

"You mean Danny?"

"No, I mean your...er...Alex."

My Alex. She'd fumbled her words, but it was an interesting concept. I didn't think he was my Alex anymore.

"There isn't much to tell. He's in California with family."

"That's what your father said. He's worried about you, dear. I'm worried."

I laughed to myself, but it spilled out a little. "What do you have to worry about?"

"You and Alex, that's what. You really seemed to be hitting it off."

"Who says we're not?"

"Please, Quincy, we're not stupid. It's obvious something happened between the two of you."

I wasn't comfortable talking to anyone about the subject of Alex and our problems, but especially not my mother. And I wasn't sure what effect my father's return had had on the workings of my mother's spy network. Things were unsettled, and I wasn't about to give any sort of information to my mother that could be used against me.

By the time her cronies were finished, they would have turned me into an unwed, pregnant trollop who was left in the lurch by Alex, who went back home to marry his high school sweetheart. That was the mildest version I could imagine the Mormon Ladies Mafia—the MLM— would come up with.

"I would think you'd be glad to know Alex and I aren't together anymore. You're black sheep daughter isn't with the bad influence, non-member any longer. You should be throwing a party."

"Quincy! I'm not glad about that at all. And…and he's not…a bad influence. He's actually a very nice young man."

I think my eyebrows reached the top of my head. My father must have been putting some kind of drugs in the water at home.

"He is very nice." This was true.

"Your father seems to like him."

Also true.

"What is that smell?" my mother exclaimed.

Our seat in the back design room was far enough away from the front counter that I hoped Jacqueline DeMechante hadn't been able to hear my mother's less-than-tactful question. But it seemed no distance was great enough to prevent the olfactory assault from Jacqueline's perfume. She was indeed the customer Daphne was helping in the front of the store.

I held my finger up to my lips then pointed toward the front design area.

"What?" my mom power-whispered.

I whispered back, "It's Jacqueline DeMechante. I'm going to her boyfriend's place to measure for a decorating job."

"Oh, is this the job you're doing with the wedding money?"

I nodded slowly. "How did you know about that?"

"Allie told me. It's just terrible about that groom. Have they found anything out yet?"

"No, but K.C. says they keep questioning Fred, and she's worried they think he's involved as more than just a victim."

"Now, why isn't Alex taking care of all of this? I'm sure he could vouch for Fred."

All I could do was sigh. Alex wasn't here, for starters. Also, after countless explanations, my mother still couldn't understand that Alex wasn't actually an officer with Hillside police, he was a member of the state police, and had been acting undercover as a city officer when we met. I decided not to answer.

"Boy, she's swimming in that perfume today," I said.

"So this is the woman you've been working for?"

"Yes. I planned on leaving as soon as Daphne got here to go to the condo and take measurements."

"Ooh, Quincy, I have a great idea."

Here it comes.

"I'm not doing anything especially important today, and your father is messing around with his banjo. Why don't I come with you to the condo and help?"

Whenever my mother says the word *help* in that context, she should be required to use air quotes at the same time. There would be no real help. There would be snooping and mental cataloguing. Then, during the refreshment portion her Daughters of the Utah Pioneers or

DUP meeting, otherwise known as the MLM intel briefing, she would give her report.

"I don't know, Mom. I wonder if Jacqueline would want another person there. You know, privacy issues and all."

"Well she's here, right?" She stood and made it to the door before saying, "Let's just ask her."

Grrr.

Jacqueline actually loved the idea the way my mother presented it. Go figure.

***

I laughed to myself as I punched in the keycode to enter the parking garage to Bruce Tanner's condo building. Mom stood next to me, propping up the portable step-ladder I usually kept in the van.

"What's that for?" Mom said.

"What?"

"The look on your face. What's so funny?"

"I was just thinking how easily Jacqueline gave out the code to get into Bruce's condo. She doesn't trust me enough to handle her Lapis or Nile blue and she micromanages the air out of the room, yet she'll give me the code to a private home as easily as they hand out free samples at the grocery store."

"People have their quirks, that's for sure," Mom said.

We took the elevator instead of the stairs to Bruce's floor, since we had brought a portable step-ladder with us. His condo was all the way at the end of a beautifully decorated hallway. Earth tone paint and pictures of native Utah rock carvings made me question the need for this decorating job if the condo interior matched the path to the front door.

I punched in another code on his door, nervous at my capabilities as a decorator. I wondered if I was in way over my head. Of course, I wasn't the one who would be doing the interior designing itself. Allie—the interior design major—was in charge of that portion. I suppose I just felt nervous on behalf of everyone, since my shop's reputation was on the line. Once I opened the door I was relieved of all insecurities. Well, not all of them, just the ones related to this particular design job.

Austere would have been a kind word to describe Bruce's condo. Dump is what came to mind.

I heard a quiet groan from behind me. "He must travel—a lot."

"This is going to require a lot more than just the wedding money," I said. Admittedly, I did not have a finely furnished home. All the furniture and appliances had either been given to me or I'd found them at the second-hand store. All my artwork consisted of cheaply framed movie posters or prints from the clearance racks at Target. But Bruce Tanner had me beat by a long shot.

The living room contained a Santa Fe motif couch and a TV on a spindly faux-oak coffee table. The pass-through to the kitchen revealed nothing but a stainless steel fridge, which must have come with the condo, because it was the fanciest item in the place and it fit perfectly in the space carved out of the cabinets. A diminutive round table stood in the corner of the kitchen, with two clear plastic-backed swivel chairs which churned up memories of my Aunt Sally's kitchen in the late eighties.

The same story was retold in the main bedroom and the spare bedroom-turned-office. Despite the sparseness of any real décor, the office did show some signs of practical use, with a computer and printer atop a fairly large modern metal desk and rolling chair, flanked by two large filing cabinets.

And then there was the familiar fragrance of Jacqueline's perfume embedded in the gray- white paint covering every wall. I joined my mom in the occasional cough when we would enter a particularly strong Jacquie Zone.

"Wouldn't it be lovely to make this into a real office?" Mom said.

"Anything would help. I wonder if Bruce or Jacqueline will really go for it, or if they'll just want us to put up a few curtains and a table and lamp here and there."

I measured the window while my mother walked around taking notes on the small spiral-bound book she'd always kept in her purse.

"At least there's a little personality in here," she said. "He must spend most of his time at home in this room. Look at these photos on the desk." She picked up a framed five-by-seven from the edge of the desk. "He must be a real golfer. All of these pictures look like they were taken at golf courses. What company did you say Bruce worked for?"

"All-something," I said as I stepped down from the portable stepladder. "His company makes metals or things out of metal—something like that."

"Allmecore?" Mom said.

"Yeah, that's it. How'd you know?"

"It's in the picture."

"Mom, I don't think we should be looking at the stuff on his de...isn't that Clint Wheeler standing next to Bruce?" I said.

"I think so. I haven't seen him for years—since your dad worked with Grandpa McKay on the farm."

The photo showed a grinning and sunburned Bruce Tanner, holding up a trophy topped with a miniature gold man swinging a golf club. Clint Wheeler stood on one side while Jacqueline shark-stared at the camera on Bruce's other side. A banner above them read "Allmecore Metal Division Annual Golf Tournament."

"Since when do dairy farmers have time to golf?" I said.

"Maybe he has someone to work the farm like your grandpa had his boys."

It seemed strange to me that a local dairy farmer would even know someone like Bruce Tanner, who had only recently moved to our area. Jenny had told me her mother and Bruce had moved here when his company won a government contract with the Air Force Base, which hadn't been that long ago

"Oh!" Mom's shout echoed off of the walls of the nearly empty room. The echo startled her, causing her to fumble the photo. The corner of the wooden frame hit the hardwood floor, bounced, then tumbled over. The glass remained intact. We looked at each other, both of us with our hands covering our cheeks in a classic "Oh-no" pose.

We laughed at the mirror image of red cheeks shining through the spaces between our fingers.

"I didn't mean to say that so loud," she said, and bent to pick up the picture. "I was just going to say this reminds me of something Colleen Schofield told me about."

Colleen Schofield went to DUP meetings with my mother. She had a sharp tongue and a keen ear for stories that would make the neighborhood gossip round up. I think she'd just made the rank of captain in Mom's underground corp.

"She's a big golfer, you know. President of the ladies golf association and that. She was so angry one time telling us about the expansion of the Near Lake Golf Course. They were having fundraising tournaments and things like that to help fund the expansion. But when that Jack Conway discovered his new bird, the Feds got involved."

We had finished our work and it felt awkward to stand there and chat in someone else's home. I folded the ladder and carried it to the door to get her moving, but I couldn't resist the carrot my mother had left dangling.

"What Feds? Who are the Feds?"

"I don't know, just the Feds was all Colleen said. I assumed she meant the FBI. I think they've got Jack under surveillance. That's probably why your father and I saw him leaving town in such a hurry the other day."

I stepped aside so she could open the front door. "Jack supposedly found a bird that they thought was extinct," I said. "It was a protected species before they lost track of it." I'd actually absorbed something other than regret from that terrible night of the lecture and the Samantha sighting. "Maybe it's the Fish and Wildlife department she's talking about. K.C. and Fred told me the golf course wasn't going anywhere near the marsh. It's federally protected land."

She shrugged. "Well I'm not sure. A golf course was being expanded somewhere, but then it stopped. Who knows? Colleen might have been blaming one group for the wrong thing. It wouldn't be the first time."

No, it definitely wouldn't be the first time one of the MLM ladies confused their gossip with one of their own projects. Hopefully this time wasn't one of them.

After making sure we'd picked up everything we'd brought with us, we left the condo and made our way down the plush hallway. My mother noted the beautiful colors in the hall and actually made a joke about the Nile and Lapis we would have to use in Bruce's condo if Jacqueline had any say—which she did. For all my mother's annoying qualities, she had a few endearing ones as well. And she was talented in many areas too. She'd made very accurate sketches of each room, and had already made some notes about improvements we could make to the entire space.

We'd actually had a good time together. There was no talk of church, marriage, or Alex. It felt as if we had really accomplished something.

On the ride back to the shop, I ran through a mental list of my many relatives. There had to be at least one who could give some information on a proposed and nixed golf course. Also, maybe Fred could tell me if Jack Conway really was under federal investigation. And if so, why. I needed to find out the real benefits to sighting the Inland False Booby. Was there something to it besides notoriety, fame, and fortune? Perhaps the temptation to see something that wasn't truly there was too great. Was there really a Booby flying around out there in the marsh?

CHAPTER THIRTEEN

We returned to the shop to find Daphne and Allie trying to console a tearful K.C. She told us how the investigation of Harold Busby's death had been declared a murder, and that they were ratcheting up their investigation of Fred as a suspect.

"Why would they suspect Fred of anything?" I asked.

"One of the detectives says his story doesn't add up. It's ridiculous," K.C. said. "We've got to figure out what really happened before they blame it all on Fred. You've solved a murder case, Boss. Help me to solve this one, so they don't ruin our wedding…and our lives." She returned to tearful sobbing.

I had only solved the murder of my competitor by being in the right place—or the wrong place—depending upon how you looked at it. "I would love to help you, K.C., but I'm probably not the most helpful person for you."

"Nonsense," my mother said. "Quincy, you have a problem with selling yourself short. You always have. You made it possible for those crimes to be solved with your quick thinking. Now, I bet if we put our heads together, we can come up with some leads."

The last thing we needed was for my mother to become part of this investigation. There, now I was saying it too. *There was no investigation.*

Despite my objections, the rest of the "team" had already started brainstorming.

K.C. stood behind the false wall separating the customer counter from the design table. She used a marker to point at the dry erase board, where she had composed a list of bullet points. "This all started the night of the lecture. Everything was fine until then. Brock went missing and Fred and Gordon were hurt the very next morning after Jack Conway gave the lecture about the bird."

I couldn't resist protesting. "That doesn't prove anything. The crimes both happened at the marsh. That's all."

"It's kind of weird that two major crimes happen in a short amount of time at the bird refuge," Allie said. "Maybe there is a connection. What is it about that bird discovery that would cause someone to kill Harold Busby?"

"Harold was always blowing the whistle on something," K.C. said. "Quincy, do you remember what I told you about the Ivory Billed Woodpecker?"

I asked K.C. to explain the murderous story to the rest of the group.

"I could possibly understand why Jack Conway would murder Harold. Because Harold said he could prove Mr. Conway wrong," Daphne said. "But why would Mr. Conway want to kidnap Brock and injure Fred and his friend?"

"He made a mistake. He thought he'd killed them both too. Thank the Big Guy upstairs he made that mistake," K.C. said, pointing heavenward.

"This Brock works at the marsh, and he probably knew Jack was lying about the extinct bird. Maybe Conway found out about the meeting somehow and was afraid Brock would tell on him to Fred and Gordon." My mother looked very proud of herself. "Oh, and I almost forgot! Angus and I saw Jack Conway the other day." She looked at me. "Your father says it sounded like Jack was trying to get out of town in a hurry. He probably felt the heat on his heels."

"The Heat?" I said. "You mean the Po-Po, right?"

Mom nodded her head slowly. "I think that's right. Whatever your father said. I took it to mean Jack's feet had been put to the fire."

"You're pretty close, Mom," Allie said. "The Heat is a slang term for the cops. Dad must have thought he was being *hip*."

"Let's get back to business," K.C. said. "We were talking about the meeting. And Jack Conway fleeing the police. Too bad the meeting wasn't really about Jack." K.C. looked sideways at me.

I opened my mouth in surprise. "So you do know what the meeting was about? Have you always known?"

K.C.'s eyes lit up. "I wouldn't keep news like that from you, Boss. Fred just told me last night. I finally got it out of him."

"How'd you do that? I thought there was no way he would ever tell us," I said.

She ran her hands down her sides. "I used my feminine wiles," she said in a spot-on Mae West impersonation. "He told me while we were…"

"We get it!" I cut her off before any detail slipped out. "*Anyway*, what did he tell you about the meeting?"

"Brock was there to tell them about some polluting that he knew about. Fred had been tipped off by Harold Busby, of course, that Brock knew about the polluting that had been going on in the marsh. So Fred contacted Gordon, who is Brock's boss."

"So," my mother said, "Harold Busby somehow knew that Brock knew about polluting going on at the marsh, and Harold told Fred about it. Why tell Fred? And why would he need to tell on Brock about it?"

"I forgot one thing," K.C. said. She wrote the word "bribery" on the dry erase board and underlined it. "According to Harold, he knew that Brock was accepting bribes to look the other way."

"How did he know?" Daphne and Allie said in unison, then giggled.

"An anonymous tip. Harold received an anonymous tip that Brock was accepting bribes not to report the polluting of the marsh. Harold probably told Fred because he and Fred go way back. And he was such a tattle-tell that Gordon was probably sick of hearing from him. Harold knew that Fred would be a better listener."

The unmistakable sound of a banjo blasted out of my mother's purse. She dug through the enormous bag like a badger digging its den.

"How did she get that ring tone?" I said. My mother was barely able to answer her phone, let alone download a custom ring tone.

"I put it on there for her," Allie said.

After seemingly endless digging, the cell phone emerged. "It's your father," Mom said. She retreated to the back room to take the call.

"We should all get back to work, anyway." I said.

K.C. tapped her marker on the table like a gavel. "Meeting adjourned."

"There are more Halloween decorations in the basement," Allie said. "I was thinking me and Daphne could work on that today."

They left and went downstairs. K.C. stood staring at the dry erase board.

"What is it, K.C.?" I said.

"There's something I didn't tell the other gals. I figured we would get to it, but—it's about our polluter—it's someone we know. It's Clint Wheeler. Harold told Fred that Clint Wheeler has been polluting the marsh with his farm waste, and that Brock found out about it. Instead of turning Clint in, Brock was taking money from Clint to keep quiet."

"That nice old farmer is committing federal crimes on his farm? You know, it seems really suspicious to me that Harold Busby knew all of this information from an anonymous tip. I don't know what to make of everything, but it doesn't all line up to me. Including Jack Conway trying to kill Fred and Gordon. You don't really think he did do you?"

K.C. screwed up her mouth, then let out a heavy sigh. "No, I don't think Jack did anything. I'm just mad as a hornet about the sheriff investigating Fred for Harold's murder. I'm willing to consider any other possibility." She put the marker away and erased the bullet points from the board, then paused. "I know you don't want to get into trouble, but I can't stand to have anyone suspect Fred for something this terrible. I have to find out what's really happened, and I could use some help. Whaddya say? Can you put on your detective cap with me? Just until we find a clue—then we'll hang up our investigative hats forever."

I couldn't stand hearing the hurt and worry in K.C.'s voice. And what did I have to lose? Now that Alex was gone, I didn't have anything else going on in my life. I didn't have any hobbies. I didn't think we would accomplish anything anyway, but it would make K.C. feel better to know we were trying.

"Okay," I said. "I think we should go talk to Clint Wheeler and see what's really going on. My grandpa was a dairy farmer, and Clint says he has a lady friend who needs flowers. We'll go down to talk to him about flowers, and then we can slip in a little word about my grandpa and get him talking about farming. Then maybe we can work the marsh into the conversation somehow. Allie and Daphne can take care of the shop."

"What about your mom? I don't think we should tell her about Clint. She knows who he is, and if Harold was wrong, I'd hate for Clint's reputation to be ruined through gossip..." she looked over the top of her glasses. "Not that I'm accusing anyone of being a gossip—you know."

Despite my mother's good intentions, knowing about general polluting was one thing, but having a name attached to it? That would be far too tempting for her to resist sharing with the MLM.

"I've got to run, dear." Mom startled us as she walked through the door. "Your father is trying to cook. We'll continue the investigation later."

She rushed toward the front door then turned back. "Oh, and K.C., thank you! I haven't had so much fun in a long time. Let's do this again soon."

Heaven help us all.

CHAPTER FOURTEEN

"We should take Zombie Sue to the farm," I said as K.C. hung up her smiley face apron.

"Don't you want to take the fun car?" she said.

"It's not that I don't want to take it..." Yes it was. I didn't want to take her flashy car while we went to snoop around Clint Wheeler's farm. "I'm worried about getting it dirty, down there with the dirt roads and everything."

K.C.'s shoulders slumped slightly and her smile disappeared. "I suppose you're right. I don't want to get my new baby all muddy."

We walked outside. It was sunny and clear and the perfect September day. Summertime in northern Utah meant hot dry heat with many days over one hundred degrees. But in the fall, the days were in the nineties and eighties and the nights were cool but not freezing.

"Oh, what a fantastic day!" K.C said.

We climbed into the van and I turned the key. "Crap. I forgot to buy gas. We're on empty. We'll have to stop and fill up."

"There's no gas station on the way there. Besides, we don't have time to stop. Let's just take my car."

"Don't you think it's a little…noticeable?" I said.

K.C. looked at me with a straight face. "I suppose you're right. It is kind of flashy."

"*Kind of?*" I said.

"Okay, it's very flashy. That's what I like about it. Anyway, we're already wasting time talking. How about I park somewhere we won't be seen. Not that we're doing anything bad, anyway. We're just going to talk to Clint." She smiled and gave me a look.

I knew that look. It meant she intended to do everything *but* talk to Clint.

"Okay, but we're just going to talk to Clint Wheeler, right?"

"Of course," she said as she walked back toward the shop to get her keys.

When she came back outside, K.C. wrapped a red silk scarf around her head and tied a knot just under her chin.

"Couldn't be better weather to use this rag-top like we're supposed to," she said. I helped her put the convertible top down. K.C. settled into her seat and slid on some slick, pink driving gloves. "Ready to roll?"

I wasn't, really. I had a sick feeling about fishing for information from someone I hardly knew, especially when the illegal activities we suspected him of were severely punishable. If he really was involved, it could be dangerous to bring up certain subjects.

"Ready as I'll ever be," I said without much enthusiasm.

"Good. Hold on to your hootenanny!" Tires squealed, smoke appeared, and Newton's laws of physics were proven as she peeled out of our parking lot.

We approached Clint Wheeler's place in record time and K.C. pulled off to the side of the road, next to a grouping of giant elms.

"You were right about being inconspicuous," she said as she untied her headscarf. "It's maybe not such a bad idea. The barn's right there, just a few extra steps."

"Okay, we're just here to talk. Right?"

"Right. But it doesn't hurt to use good criminal detection techniques," she said. "You never know when those skills might come in handy, so it's good to practice."

I sighed. I was getting sicker to my stomach by the minute, and it wasn't just from the bumpy rocket trip we had taken on the way to the farm. I should've known a fact-finding mission with K.C. would never be a simple matter of having a conversation with someone.

I didn't want to become proficient at investigating crimes. The only reason I was involved in this investigation was that she and Fred were my friends.

We walked the twenty-five yards to the building connected to Clint's office and K.C. knocked on the door. There was no answer.

"He could be anywhere on this farm. Let's head over to that west side, behind those sheds. I think I hear a motor running. Maybe he's working on something over there," I said.

We walked down a dirt-packed drive running between the open pens where the cows stayed when they weren't being milked, and a tall shelter full of hay bales. The cows stood in the shade made by the shelter. Their eyes followed us as we passed, and occasionally a tail would twitch.

Beyond the cow pens were some empty corrals made from metal fencing. Beyond those, in one corner of a small pen, were a group of large pink pigs with black spots. The pigs made loud squeals and grunts and didn't seem like they got along very well. As we passed the pig pen my eyes watered and I clamped my hand over my nose.

"Uhn, nat smelws awpul," K.C. said through her pinched nose.

I merely nodded, not wanting to take in the extra breath required for speaking. We reached the end of the packed dirt, a few feet away from the pigs, where some ancient, rusty equipment rested in piles, including giant black tractor tires that would probably have come up to my shoulder if turned upright.

"I hear something, like a motor. Let's just see what's making that noise. Maybe we'll find Clint here or maybe not, but I'm getting curious," K.C. said.

"Are you sure?" I said.

"Don't be such a worry wart. We're just looking for Clint."

I sighed but didn't say anything, knowing it wouldn't deter her.

A narrow path that had been stomped hard over the years led into a cluster of Russian olive trees. Russian olives were almost always found near a water source. K.C. led the way under the thorn laden gray-leaved branches.

"Would you looky here," K.C. said.

A black pipe ran parallel to the path of the stream at our feet. A short walk through mushy grass on the shallow ditch banks led to a large pond encircled by reeds and grasses at least six feet high, much like the rest of the surrounding marsh. Now that I knew what they were, I noticed the prevalence of Phragmites.

"It stinks to high heaven out here. What's in this water?" K.C. said.

"This isn't regular pond stink," I said. "Look at that!" I pointed to a spot where the end of the black pipe hooked into a miniature pump house. That's where the mechanical noise came from. It looked like the emergency generator my dad kept in the garage.

A yellow-green skin covered the thick, unmoving water. The marsh connected to the pond on the side opposite from where we stood.

"I think I know what's going on here," K.C. said. "Let's follow this pipe to the source."

We followed the pipe in the opposite direction, losing our footing and occasionally slipping into the stream. My cross-trainers and socks were totally soaked.

The pipe ended at a sort of tank, nearly buried by tractor tires. The tank appeared to collect waste from the milking barn.

I crouched down to tie the laces on one of my shoes, but thought better of it when I saw them up close, covered in wet, green, slime. I'd risk tripping rather than touch them. "So here's what I don't understand. At my grandpa's dairy farm, the cows would stand in the milking barn, and while the machines did the milking, the cows stood there and ate and do what cows do…"

"You mean what cows *doo-doo*?" K.C. said.

"Yeah, exactly. Anyway, my uncles would hose down the cement after the cows left the barn, and all the muck would go down these slotted grates in the floor, into drains that flowed to a ditch that led to a pond. Then, what was left in the pond was spread over the fields for fertilizer."

"I don't think it's..." K.C.'s eyes panned from left to right, and she lowered her voice, "I don't think it's legal to dump anything, including cow manure into the marsh. In fact, I don't think—*I know*. We've got to sneak outta here and make sure neither Clint nor any of his farm hands see us or our gooses are cooked."

Now didn't seem the appropriate time to point out the proper plural form of goose. And she was right, our geese would be cooked if we were caught snooping around the illegal manure hose.

We crept along the side of the milking barn until we reached the front. Once in front of the building, we wouldn't be seen from the back, because of the grove of thick Russian olive trees near the stream we had just left. But if anyone drove up to the front of the property, we were toast.

The grain barn stood about fifty yards across the lot from the milk house. Fifty yards and the length of a barn and we were home free. Once at the end of the grain barn, we could cut through the elm trees to K.C.'s hot rod. I paused at the end of the milk house and peeked around the corner. K.C. crouched next to me.

"Okay, the coast is clear. We're going to run to the opposite corner of that building." I gave my head a short jerk toward Clint's office. "Ready?"

"Wait. Don't you think we should just walk? It will look like we're just going from building to building looking for someone if we happen to be seen. We can just act casual, like we're just stopping by for a chat. If we see

Clint, I'll just tell him we wanted to make sure he knew he was invited to my wedding."

"Yeah, alright. Good idea," I said. "Let's go—casually."

K.C. might have overplayed the casual act just a bit. She didn't walk, she sauntered and whistled like the guilty party in an old Bugs Bunny cartoon.

"Just walk normally," I whispered.

"I am. I whistle when I walk. Maybe I should call out Clint's name, so it looks like we're really looking for him."

"No, I don't think—"

"Clint. Oh, Clint, are you here?"

Oh boy.

As we approached the front of the grain barn, my cell phone rang, and then I heard the rumble of a diesel engine starting up.

"Crap," I said. I stopped and pulled the phone out of my back pocket. "Oh no, not now."

"What? Who is it?" K.C. said.

"It's Alex."

"Boss, that's fantastic. Why wouldn't you want to talk to him? Here, give me your phone." She grabbed for the phone and I extended my arm just out of her reach.

"What are you doing?" I asked.

"I'm going to answer it for you. If you won't use your brain and talk to him, I'll have to do it for you."

I continued pulling the phone away from her while she tried to grab it away from me. We spun in a circle doing our phone dance. As we waltzed back around to where we'd originally been standing, a front loader with its bucket extended in the air rounded the corner of the building.

K.C. got ahold of my phone. "Gotcha. This is gonna hurt me a lot less than it will hurt you, Boss. But it's for your own good. You'll thank me later."

"No, K.C. He'll want to know where we are. Let's just get in the car. I'll call him then." I tried to snatch the phone. As we played tug-of-war there was a loud mechanical groan.

We looked up. "Shiiit!" We both exclaimed, as brown splatters rained down from the sky.

I lay stunned for a moment, and realized I was pinned to the ground under a tractor load of cow dung.

The sound of the tractor grew faint and the sound of K.C. swearing grew loud, even though muffled by the manure.

My phone, still in hand, vibrated with a message.

I strained against the aromatic and disgusting bonds that held me until I got one arm free. I used it to swim out until my head and shoulders emerged from the massive, steaming pile. Okay, so maybe it wasn't steaming, but it was warm enough. K.C.'s head popped out of the manure mound like a particular rodent on Groundhog Day. We looked at each other for a long few seconds, then both of us broke out in mad laughter.

"K.C., do you smell that?"

She bunched up her nose and narrowed her eyes. "I may be hard o' hearing, but I ain't hard o' smellin'! Are you daft? Did the pucky pile-on make you ding your gourd on the ground?"

"No, I don't mean that. Of course I smell the manure. I'm talking about the smell above that. I noticed it right before the tractor came, as I looked down at my phone."

"I don't know what you're talking about."

"It's the perfume! It's Jacqueline's perfume. That stuff is like turpentine, it cuts through anything."

"Jacqueline or Clint, it doesn't matter. We'd better skedaddle. Someone didn't like us being here and now we're sitting ducks," K.C. said.

We dug ourselves out of the pile and ran to the grove of trees which blocked the car from view.

We crouched on the passenger side of the car. "I don't think anyone followed us," I said.

"*Someone* knew we were here. That weren't no accident. But I swear no one followed us down this road. If it was Clint, I don't know how he saw us. We were blocked by trees and marsh grass on the one side. Oh, I don't know. I'm never going to get the smell out. My clothes, my hair. My hair is going to smell like cow pucky at my wedding!"

I pushed the latch on the outside of the car door.

"Wait!" K.C. said. "We can't—we—just—can't sit on this upholstery in these clothes."

"We've got to leave!" I said in as much of a whisper as possible when shouting.

K.C. began to cry.

"K.C., I'm sorry, but we have to go before Jacqueline comes back for us."

"Why did she do this? Was it because we were rude? Did she hate your ideas for decorating the apartment?"

"I'll explain in the car. Let's just go!"

"We can't get cow pies in my car. Do you know how much I paid for this baby? I can't take any more stress. I can't! We'll have to walk."

"You know we can't walk. What if Jacqueline comes back? Who knows what she'll do?"

K.C. paused for a moment and looked at the ground. "Well, there's only one way to do this, then."

"You don't mean…"

"Yes I do."

"No freaking way, K.C.!"

"Strip, sister! Down to your skivvies. If I can do it, you can do it too. We're out here in the boonies—no one will see us."

"Until we get into town. Then what?"

A diesel engine started up in the distance, and then the sound of a shot or an engine backfire blasted out.

We looked at each other for a second, then turned our backs to each other and stripped.

Why hadn't I obeyed my mother's frequent admonishments about wearing good underwear *"because you just never know?"* My underwear wasn't dirty, of course—at least it wasn't when I arrived at the farm. However, it wouldn't ever be confused with someone's finery. And my panties just may or may not have been on inside out.

"Throw everything in the trunk and let's go," K.C. said.

I did as I was told and looked at the ground on the way back to the car door. I located the latch by feel and got in without looking up. I slid so low to the floor, my knees were touching my ears.

"What were you going to tell me about Jacqueline? Why did she do this?"

"I'm not a hundred percent sure it was her perfume I smelled. Maybe I was just relating one unpleasant smell with another, but I have an idea why she might want to scare us off."

"Oh, dear, you may as well get up off the floor. No one can see us, and besides, you look just fine. Although, you should really look into updating your style." The car hit a bump in the road and my knees slammed against the glove box.

"Whoopie. That was a humdinger. Sorry about that," she shouted. "You handled that bump better than I did, though. And at least you're *wearing* underwear."

"What?" I couldn't help but look up.

"Ha! Made you look."

She wasn't completely nude, praises be to Spanx. Wow, they really did come in all shapes and sizes. She also wore a red and black lace bra/containment system. There was so much lace. A LOT of lace. I mean like a full bolt of lace.

I had to look at the glove box in front of my nose in order not to be distracted by the sight in the driver's seat. "Jenny came into the store the other day and told me about Phragmites. I thought they were interesting, so I did an Internet search and found out that there is a variety called Egyptian Phragmites that is not a legal plant in the United States."

"You'll have to speak up. We're going to be hitting city traffic soon."

The thought of reaching town made me nauseous, but I held it all down because we couldn't dirty K.C.'s upholstery.

I shouted, "It's illegal to import Egyptian Phragmites into the U.S. because the plant is invasive. It's used by companies to help keep the pollutants in holding ponds and from being detected by authorities. Egyptian Phragmites surrounded that pond we just saw. Jacqueline is an Egyptian specialist, so I think she's the connection."

"Why would she be working with Clint?"

"I don't know."

"Uh-oh."

"What? Uh-oh, what?" I said, panic rising in my stomach.

"Guess I was speeding," K.C. said.

I looked up at her just as she was turning the wheel to the right. The car slowed down, then stopped.

"No. We're getting pulled over?"

"Sorry, kid. Don't worry, I'll sweet talk us out of this."

Yeah, a plus-sized grandma in Spandex and lace from ankle to chest and me in my granny panties and a bra whose last pliable strand of elastic said goodbye during the *Seinfeld* finale. I'm sure the officer would find it all to be pretty sweet.

"Hello ma'am. Do you, um, wow. D—do you know why I pulled you over?"

"Officer," K.C. replied. "Beautiful day for a drive, dontcha think?"

He cleared his throat.

"Have we done something wrong?" K.C. asked in a saccharin voice.

I made the mistake of looking up.

"Quincy McKay, is that you?" the officer said.

"Oh, uh, hi, Chad." I gave a little finger wave. Did I mention being sick to my stomach? Chad Fullerton had been the star quarterback of our high school football team.

He was a senior when I was a sophomore and I, like most other girls, had a huge crush on him.

"What are you—are you okay? You're all crammed under the dashboard."

"I'm fine...just fine here...out driving around—how's your sister?" The embarrassment was physically painful. My cheeks were about to incinerate—the one's on my face, that is.

"She's fine. What's going on?"

"Oh, well, that's what I was just going to tell you officer," K.C. said. "Boy, is my face red or what?"

The look of disbelief on Chad's face grew even more intense. "Something's definitely red," he quipped, staring at the red and black menace. "You were going sixty-five on Bluff Road in a thirty zone. And we got a call about trespassing on Wheeler's farm. The description of the car fits this one..."

"How did they describe the trespassers, hmmm? I'm sure they described someone wearing clothes, so it's obviously not us, dear."

"K.C.!" I hissed.

"No, they definitely didn't describe—this. Where are your clothes, ma'am?"

I couldn't let K.C. say anything about the trunk. She had an arsenal in there, and I wasn't sure which parts of it, if any, were legal.

"Chad, I know this looks bad," I looked down at myself, then at K.C. "*Really* bad. But if you just let us explain, we can clear this all up. I mean, obviously we were hoping not to be seen like this, and K.C.—um Ms.

Clackerton here, was just trying to get home as fast as possible..."

"Her boyfriend is a cop..." K.C. threw in.

New realms of hell had just been discovered.

Chad's left eyebrow arched. That must be something they learn in the police academy. Alex was proficient in the suspicious eyebrow raise. "Yeah, Cooper, right? With the state police? Does he know you're doing—whatever it is that you're doing—right now?"

"Listen, sonny. She doesn't need permission from her boyfriend to do anything, especially not because he's a cop. You cops just think because you wear a badge you're rulers of the roost. My fiancé didn't do anything, and yet you cops..."

"K.C.!" I reached my hands out in the universal stop sign hand gesture, then looked down and realized what Chad could see. I crossed my arms over my chest and stuck my hands under my armpits. "Chad, she's under a lot of stress right now. She is so sorry, and didn't mean to be so disrespectful. We were just—cutting some greenery from the ditch banks down at Clint Wheeler's farm and we slipped and fell in the mud. K.C. just bought this car and we didn't want to dirty up the custom upholstery. That's all."

"Smells like you fell in more than just mud."

"Okay, okay," K.C. said, "you got us. Someone dumped a whole front loader full of cow pies on top of us and our clothes are in the trunk. Go ahead and look."

The old car had a separate key that unlocked the trunk, which was on the same key ring as the one in the ignition, so K.C. had to get out to unlock the trunk. The last thing I remember Chad saying before we were put in the back of his police car was, "Do you have a concealed permit for this weapon?" I don't remember K.C.'s response, but I'm pretty sure it wasn't the right one.

***

"Hi, Kathy." To keep from fanning the fragrance, I avoided waiving at my former classmate, who was the dispatcher for Hillside police.

"Hey, Quincy," she said, her voice full of question.

While we waited for my lawyer to fix things, we had to sit in the holding cell because of—well, the smell, of course. Kathy had managed to rustle up a couple rolls of paper towels from the supply closet for us to cover up with while we waited for my lawyer to take care of everything. "Do you want me to call him for you?" Kathy asked.

All I could do was nod.

"Him who?" K.C. said.

"You'll see." As I sat and contemplated our mess, a uniformed police officer approached.

"Quincy? Is that you?" he said.

I looked up. It was John Davies. I'd contacted him about the bounced check from Lori Mangum.

"It's *me*," I said sheepishly.

"I've got some news for you about that—um—bounced check you gave us." He did an award winning performance, keeping a straight face the whole time.

"Are we fugitives allowed to talk about other cases?" K.C. asked.

John smiled as if he was enjoying himself a great deal. "I suppose you are. Captive audience and all that—no pun intended."

K.C. managed a laugh, but I was too embarrassed to speak.

"So, that check you gave me," John continued.

I nodded, "Mh hmm?"

"Turns out it comes from the bank account of a deceased person."

"What?" I said, suddenly able to speak.

"Can you tell me the name of the person who gave you the check, again?"

"Why, it was Lori Mangum," K.C. said.

"What is your name ma'am?" he asked my cellmate.

"I'm Karma Clackerton, Quincy's delivery driver. Mrs. Mangum handed me the check at the door."

I nodded in affirmation.

"What is Lori Mangum's address? Is it the same as the one on the check?"

"I think so," I said. I described how to get to the Mangum's house, and John said he would let me know what he found out. As he walked away, he expelled the laughter he'd been holding in.

"Oh—my—*hell!*"

I looked up and saw Danny walking toward us.

"Aren't you a sight for sore eyes, sweetie-pie," K.C. said.

He shook his index finger at her. "Ethel, you two have lots a 'splainin' to do." He set down two canvas bags with his shop logo printed on the sides, then stood with hands on hips, mouth taut.

"Can you take us home?" I said, the weariness seeping through my voice.

"What happened?" he asked. "Kathy Green called me to come and get you but didn't give me any details. She just told me to come and to bring something to cover you with. I brought these aprons from the shop. It was all I could think of in a pinch."

"They're just perfect," K.C. said.

He approached as the door of the cell was unlocked and we stepped out.

"Tell me what happened."

"We had a little—mishap," I said.

He stepped too close then recoiled. A sort of high-pitched squeal came out of his mouth. "What kind of mishap, what do you—oh blessed saints! What is in your hair?" He sucked in an audible wheeze. "That smell, what is that smell?"

"I'll explain later, but my paper towel dress is unraveling," I said.

K.C. and I walked out of the public restroom wearing our aprons. There are only so many ways you can adjust a loop and two ribbon ties to try and maximize coverage.

Danny clutched his chest. "Sweet Georgia Brown, what are you wearing?"

I looked at him knowingly, agreeing with his assessment of K.C.'s giant black and in-your-face-red brassiere.

"Quincy, hon, we have got to go shopping. Those panties are only appropriate for my sweet grandmother, who is long dead. I mean, really. What is your boy Alex going to do when he sees those—those *things*—you call undergarments? And that bra." He put his palms on either side of his face. "You may as well cinch an old dishtowel around your breasts for as much support as you're getting from that abomination. Tsk, tsk, tsk, disgraceful."

"Can we just go home, please?" I said.

"Oh, I'm sorry, Roxie. Just giving you a little tough love. Um, one more thing, ladies. Could I just ask that you not let those lovely locks touch the inside of my SUV? I just had the car detailed. Thanks-sa-much."

***

Danny dropped me at home and I asked him to pull as far into the driveway as possible. I just might be hidden from my neighbors' view if I ran to the back door.

My cell phone had been in my pants pocket, which had been thrown into K.C.'s trunk. Once I got my clothes back, I found that just as I had feared, there were plenty of missed calls on my phone display.

Alex Cell. The call I missed at the farm. I'd come back and listen to this one first.

Mom Home. This came in about the same time we were driving back from the farm. I'd skip this one.

Mom Home. This probably came while we were driving to the police station. Skip.

Mom Home. This was only thirty seconds after the last one. Skip.

Mom Cell. This happened while I spoke with Officer Davies. Delete without listening.

Mom Cell. This happened only ten seconds after the last call. Delete for sure.

Shop Phone. Mom had taken matters into her hands and driven to my shop. Good. Now Allie and Daphne had heard the MLM's version of events. I'd have to listen in the highly unlikely possibility it wasn't Mom who called from the shop.

Alex Cell. What was this? It had probably happened while I was changing my clothes at the station. Move this one to the front of the line. I put the phone to my ear and before I could listen, I became nauseated at my own stench.

The verdict on whether Alex missed me or wanted to end it completely would have to wait. I was just glad he hadn't been around to find out about the whole almost-naked-convertible-driving-spree-thing.

I showered, shampooed, and rinsed three times. After that, I scrubbed every inch of the claw-foot tub, then filled it with steaming water and herbal bath oil that was supposed to calm frazzled nerves. My nerves definitely qualified for frazzled.

Once settled in the tub, I took a few cleansing breaths and grabbed the phone. Another missed call from Alex.

The herbs and the hot water had already kicked in, but despite my uber relaxed state, I was giddy with the anticipation of hearing his voice. I played back his second message.

"Quincy...call me back." No pet name, no pleasantries? Still, the deep smooth tones of his voice did not disappoint. After the embarrassing and scary afternoon I'd just had, at least I could find some comfort with Alex, even though we hadn't been on the best terms when he left.

I called back, barely able to contain myself. I was afraid I'd break into happy tears or laughter as soon as he said hello.

"Hi!" I said.

"What the hell is going on over there?"

"Are you referring to the shop?" I said, then made a weak laugh.

"I've been trying to take off your clothes for a month with no luck, but the entire Hillside PD gets to see you naked without even buying you a drink first?"

The tears came, but they weren't happy tears.

"It was all out of my control. First the crazy clowns and the Shim cat, and then the farm and the manure bath and K.C.'s Spanx. And it all smells like Jacqueline's perfume."

"Babe, slow down. You're taking a manure bath?"

"No, I'm taking a regular bath now. I had to wash the manure out first."

"So—you're in the tub—now?" His voice had a new ring to it.

"Too bad you're in California."

"Yeah…too bad." There was a long pause. "Do I want to know what really happened today?"

"Well…"

"Were you naked?"

"No…" I paused to think of the best way to describe the unfortunate state of my undress at the station, "…not completely."

Heavy sigh from the phone.

"We were covered in manure and K.C. wouldn't let us sit in her new car. It was either comply or walk home. No one would have seen us if K.C. hadn't been speeding."

"Should I be worried about you?" he said.

"No." *Yes...maybe?* "It was a total accident at the farm. We just went to talk to the farmer—and—walked under a front loader dropping a load of manure."

"Sounds like a load of manure," he said.

"I still had my underwear on. And Danny says it wasn't anything special to see, anyway."

An unhappy groan came through the receiver loud and clear. "How's the cut on your leg?"

"It's fine. Really. It looked a lot worse than it was."

"Are you still mad at me for giving it to you?"

"I'm not mad at you for that. It wasn't your fault. It happened on the way in."

Another heavy sigh. "Then why were you so mad at me? I would have stayed there with you."

The thought of him being there with me at that moment was enough to cause an engine overheat. But I had to focus. "How's your relative?"

"Nice subject change, Miss McKay. It's great news, though. Kev's checked into a really good treatment facility and I think he'll get better there."

"Wait. Are we...talking about the same...relative?"

"He's the reason I came out here. We had an intervention. I tried to tell you about it that day at the marsh, but you walked away and then you fell and I cut your leg pulling you out."

Oh.

"You didn't cut my leg. And what's an intervention? And who are we talking about?"

"My cousin, Kevin. He has a drug problem. An intervention is where people who care about a person with an addiction problem meet with that person through the help of a facilitator. It's kind of an orchestrated confrontation." His voice took on a somber tone. "Kev and I grew up together. We were practically brothers. Everyone thought we were twins. We were really close until...well anyway, I wanted to be here for him."

We would have to delve into that specific "until" another time. "I'm so sorry about your cousin. I hope he recovers. I had no idea you were talking about an adult relative. When you said it involved Samantha and that it was private, I guess I got...jealous." I was starting to prune up in the tub and the tears that welled up once again didn't help any. "I miss you so much." I began to sob. "I don't know what you're going to do about your little boy, but I hope there's some way we can still be together."

Hysterical laughter exploded out of the receiving end of the phone. "What—are you—talking about?"

"Your little boy. Samantha showed me and K.C. his picture."

"Phew. You had me sweating there for a second. I thought I was learning about another offspring."

"Another?"

"Quincy?"

"What?"

"I like you."

I thought about that for a moment. Did he mean like, or *like*? And did it really matter, since he had another kid he hadn't told me about?

"You know why I like you?"

"No, not at all."

"Because you're gullible. It's sweet."

"But Samantha…"

"She likes pushing your buttons. Sam and Kevin are a couple. Kevin is Matthew's father."

"Matthew is…"

"Yeah."

"But he looks just like you."

"I know. So does his dad."

"Alex?"

"Yeah, babe?"

"I like you too."

Alex said he could hear my teeth chattering through the phone, so we decided it was time to wrap it up.

"Come back soon, okay?" I said.

"On one condition." His voice had taken on a seductive tone. "Will you show me what Hillside PD got to see when I get home?"

"Oh, I don't know if Danny will allow that. It depends on his schedule."

"Huh?"

"Goodbye, Alex."

CHAPTER FIFTEEN

K.C.'s wedding was a mere three days away. Now that Alex and I were straightened out, I could completely focus on the event...just as soon as I dealt with my mother's wrath about the joyride and the jail visit.

I'd decided the night before not to delete my mother's messages. It was better to face her battery of complaints in a recording before I actually spoke to her. Plus, I was still on a high from my talk with Alex. I knew her mafia informants could have told her any version of the story, so I geared up to get an earful.

Yes, her daughter was in a car with the top down and only wearing her underwear in said car as it drove through town, far exceeding the posted speed limit. And yes, her daughter was taken to the police department in said underwear, but left with the additional coverage of two small aprons, having given K.C. the extra one to accommodate her larger girth. The MLM comrades couldn't make this stuff up any worse than it already was.

Turns out my mother hadn't heard about any of the wild nature ride. She'd called to see if I wanted to come with her to look for a dress for her new wedding ceremony. She'd already gone to my shop to pick up Allie, and called from there for one last try at an invitation.

So, my mother and the rest of my family didn't know about our ride for some strange reason. I wasn't about to let them learn about it if I could help it.

I met early that morning with Danny, K.C., and Fred to go over the action plan for the day of the event. We hadn't heard anything new about the Sherriff's investigation of Fred. We didn't know if that was good or bad, but Fred told us as far as he was concerned, no news was good news. We were to carry on as if none of that "pish-posh" had ever happened.

We planned a final walk-through for that afternoon. Danny, K.C., and I would go to the marsh and do a quick run-through of our delivery plan. Parking would be an issue with all of the guests arriving on the wedding day. We needed to make sure the crew was in and out without issue and without any guests seeing any of the behind the scenes dirty work.

I pulled K.C. and Danny aside when Fred left for work and reminded them of how we didn't want to share our little run-in with the law with my family, or with anyone else, for that matter.

I looked at K.C. "I know you've probably already told Fred about everything, but," I pointed at Danny and K.C. and myself in a circular motion, "we don't need to share any of yesterday's unpleasantness with anyone, right?"

"I wouldn't share that story for any reason," Danny said. "I get nauseous just thinking about what I saw. And smelled. Qu'elle horreur."

I made a face at him and turned to K.C.

"Oh, I didn't tell Fred anything," she said. "Danny here dropped me at my place so I could clean up before he took me to get my car. Then I drove over to Fred's. I don't want him to worry about one more thing. He's keeping a brave face about everything and I'm concerned that our little problem at the farm would just throw him right over the edge."

***

The third day before a wedding can be kind of strange. Depending upon the scope of the event, it can be a super busy day or it can be a limbo day. All of our containers, ribbon, linens, and supplies were cleaned, polished, and accounted for. All of our fresh flowers and branches were in-store, having been processed by removing leaves that would fall below the waterline in the buckets and trimming the bottoms of the stems with sharp clippers and knives. Now all the flowers sat comfy in the cooler, at a perfect forty-one degrees Fahrenheit. In the countdown to event day, the centerpieces and other decorations were scheduled for production on day two. The more delicate personal flowers, like the bride's bouquet, would wait until day one, as late as possible.

My whole family was pitching in to help with K.C.'s wedding. My dad would be taking care of transporting the rented tables and chairs for the ceremony. He would also use his old pickup truck to move the beautiful arbor Danny and I had designed and put together using white quaking aspen poles. K.C. and Fred would stand with the officiant under the arbor, which would be adorned with birch and willow branches, ribbon, and flowers in the range of autumn colors.

My mother stopped by the shop to see where she could help, and since most things were on schedule for the wedding and Daphne and K.C. had daily deliveries taken care of, I asked her if she could help me pick up lunch for everyone.

The consensus had been Skinny's, but I made the excuse that K.C.'s favorite was a nice Bulgy Burger, ranch style. No need for me or K.C. to share the shame of our Skinny's probation. It would be tantamount to wearing a red "A" on our shirts.

I drove over to Bulgy Burger with my mother. This time, I pulled into the parking lot, deciding to order and pick up the food inside the restaurant. In another attempt at changing my routine, I was going to order chicken strips for myself, with barbeque, no—make that sweet and sour sauce—and onion rings with ketchup, not fry sauce. Why was this change-up so important? In the larger scheme of life, it wasn't. It simply gave me great satisfaction to prove Burger Guy wrong.

Mom took a call on her cell phone from one of her friends. My heart jumped up in my chest—worried she was about to receive the news about our wild ride. I paused long enough to hear Mom's replies but they didn't seem to bear any anger toward me. Later, I learned it was an intelligence report about someone being seen at the grocery store with curlers in her hair at five that morning. *Imagine!*

She waved me out of the car, indicating with exaggerated mouthing that she would stay inside.

I stepped out of Zombie Sue and the hair on the back of my neck stood up. My nerves tingled. I looked over my shoulder to the left, and saw no one. Nobody to my right either—but it felt like I was being watched.

I entered and walked up to the bright red counter at Bulgy Burger to place my order. The same kid from the drive-through was at the cash register this time. I looked him in the eye and before he could say anything, I said, "I'll have chicken strips—"

"With sweet and sour," he said.

I suppressed a scowl. "I need a side of onion rings—"

"Ketchup?" He had a you-know-what-eating grin on his face, so I called an audible.

"*No,* fry sauce." I gave him my "so there," face.

"Sorry, we're out."

"Do you have ketchup?"

"Yes, I told—"

"Do you have mayonnaise?"

"Yeah," he said.

"Well then, you have fry sauce."

"You're missing the secret ingredient," he said, the same certain grin back on his face.

"What's that?"

"If I told you, it wouldn't be a secret anymore."

I didn't suppress the scowl this time. I placed the rest of the order for everyone else. When the food was ready, I took the bag and left, pretending not to notice the strange looks from the other customers as I grumbled to myself on the way out. They just didn't understand. I was trying to make some changes in my life. I refused to be known as just the Bulgy-Burger-with-Fries-Girl.

When I got back in the van, Mom was still on her call, and then my cell phone rang. It was Jacqueline DeMechante's number. I took in a sharp breath and felt my guts drop to the bottom of the seat.

I didn't want to panic and let her know I was scared of her. This woman was bat-crazy and I didn't want to antagonize her any further, so I thought it best I answer the phone. I also couldn't do anything to make my mother suspicious. She would start digging, and when she got that information shovel into the ground, all secrets came to the surface.

I couldn't understand how she'd remained out of the loop for this long. Unless there'd been a major catastrophe to distract the MLM when K.C. and I were being hauled in to the police station. But I did know that if she found out about that car ride or the cow pie pile-on, I would never be able to take off the disappointing daughter tiara.

"Hello." I tried to answer the phone without letting my voice shake.

"Yes, Quincy, this is Jacqueline. I was just wondering if you would be available to meet at Bruce's place this evening. I've got something urgent to speak with you about, and I think Bruce should be there too."

I thought for a moment, then cut my eyes to my mother who sat very still in her seat, trying—but failing—to disguise her eagerness to overhear the conversation.

"Is this about the decorating job?" I asked, then immediately felt my mom's excitement reverberating from her side of the car.

"Well, yes, in a roundabout way," Jacqueline said.

"I have a meeting this afternoon, but I could probably come after that," I said.

"Alright. Seven o'clock?" she said.

"Yes, that sounds fine."

Wow. That was one cold snake of a woman. She didn't flinch. There was no hint in her voice that she had tried to seriously injure me and K.C.

My plan was to call the police and tell them everything that had really happened. Then, I would go to Bruce's condo with the police in tow and they could arrest her on the spot.

There was only one flaw with that plan. Well, only one primary flaw.

That plan assumed I could prove that a woman who no one would ever suspect of going near a farm, let alone a tractor, would climb on top of it, and know how to use it, and attempt to kill a florist and a delivery driver. Oh, and the only proof I had was that I thought I had smelled some perfume over the top of a full load of fresh, fragrant manure.

Ideas, anyone?

"Was that about the decorating job that I'm helping with?" Mom asked.

"Um, yeah…she wants to meet at the condo."

"Really?" My mother looked as if she was just about to explode with glee. "Oh, Quincy, I just loved going and helping you with those measurements. When we left there, I felt like…a professional. Or maybe just a successful woman. I had actually been good at something. It was thrilling."

"Mom, you're good at lots of things. You *are* a successful woman. You've raised us three, some of the time on your own, and we're all still alive. You took care of Grandma McKay until she died. You taught me how to...well...you taught Allie and Sandy how to cook. You have a beautiful home."

Mom's face grew rosy and she looked at the floor. "Oh, we'd better go...this food is getting cold."

I put Zombie Sue in reverse and looked at either side mirror to back out.

"Quincy?"

"Yeah, Mom," I said, still looking at the side mirror.

"Thank you." I smiled as I put the van in drive. "Would you like to come with me to...?"

What, was I insane? I had almost asked Mom to come to the meeting. She'd given me the puppy dog eyes. I wanted so much to make her feel good, and then she threw the puppy dog eyes.

I cleared my throat. "The meeting with Jacqueline is just...about some paperwork. It'll be really boring. But I was wondering..." *Think of something, Quincy, or she'll start asking questions!* "If you'd like to come to a walk-through for K.C.'s wedding this afternoon?"

"I would love to," she said. "I'll call your father and tell him he's on his own for dinner."

CHAPTER SIXTEEN

After lunch, Mom went home to take care of a few things and give instructions to my father for the dinner she'd already started. Most likely there was a roast in the slow cooker and all he would have to do is turn it off when the timer dinged. Somehow life always boils down to just managing the spaces in between meals, doesn't it?

Now, I just needed to get through the meeting with Danny and K.C., and keep up my nerve until it was time to face the cow dung hit-woman.

I needed some police help for the soiree with Jacqueline and Bruce later that evening. I couldn't go into her lair alone. It was time to call in for back-up.

Eventually, I would have to come completely clean to Alex about The Manure Incident, but it didn't feel like now was the time. Nor, maybe, would it ever. So, his police presence—despite how much it was missed for non-law enforcement reasons—was out for now. And it happened to work out really conveniently that he was out of town, anyway.

I called John Davies, who was polite to me and K.C. despite seeing us wrapped up in paper towels in the city jail.

I told him why he had seen me in that condition and who I thought had done it and why I had no solid proof. He sounded skeptical at first, but said that my instincts had been good on the Mangum case (I left out the part about it really being K.C.'s creepy crawly senses). He agreed to go with me to the meeting in plain clothes. I would say he was my brother and we were on our way to a family party or something, then we could get Jacqueline talking. She would incriminate herself or I would confront her. I was sure John would provide a bit of "blue courage" to back up my accusations. Hopefully after tonight this would all be over.

I figured John was the one who'd alerted Alex about our jail stay, so I mentioned that maybe Alex would be too busy with his family to worry about my meeting with Jacqueline. John read between the lines and he reluctantly agreed not to leak anything this time.

After the call, Allie and I went downstairs to the basement storage area, otherwise known as the dungeon. Old wedding props, unwanted containers, ribbon, holiday decorations, and ancient window displays sat in the dungeon in undiscernible piles, some reaching all the way to the ceiling. Since we had a couple of hours to kill, we thought we could begin the process of sorting and digging out.

An hour later—or maybe a lifetime, it's impossible to comprehend time in the dungeon—Daphne came downstairs. "Quincy, there's someone here to see you. It's that bride you've been meeting with—Jenny, I think?"

As we walked into the design room and toward the front counter, Daphne reminded me her shift was over. "Oh, and your mom called. She wanted me to tell you not to forget the meeting with Jacqueline after you go to the marsh," she said on her way out.

Mother! Stop trying to be my mother all the time!

Jenny stood at the cooler perusing the different arrangements on display. Her head snapped up at the mention of Jacqueline's name.

"Jenny, hi," I said, wondering how to keep it all together, knowing what her mother had done. "What's going on? Is everything okay?"

Her face lit up with a huge smile. "I have great news. Brock just called me from Ohio. He said he's okay."

I felt an immediate sense of relief and elation for Jenny. "What do you mean? He got away from his kidnappers?"

Her face flushed and she wrung her hands. "Well…he wasn't actually…kidnapped," she said. "I'm so embarrassed." She looked at the floor.

"What happened?"

"It's just that…well, you know what it's like to try and please my mother. I guess he just got so scared with the wedding coming. He felt…trapped. He said he knew he would never be able to live up to her expectations and the more he thought about it, the worse he felt. He just had to get out of here. So…" her voice grew soft, "he, um, staged the kidnapping."

My mind went blank. I couldn't comprehend what I had just heard. I could totally understand feeling unable to live up to Jacqueline's expectations, but that didn't explain why Fred and Gordon got hurt.

It's not as if I knew Brock well from the few meetings we'd had to plan the wedding, but I just didn't see him as someone capable of hurting the two men simply because he didn't want to get married. But then, I'd probably been wrong about him taking the bribe money too.

"So, he bashed Fred and Gordon's heads in and left them for dead because he didn't want to put up with your mother?"

"Oh, no! Brock didn't do that. He had some friends come and pretend to be kidnappers. He said he'd told them it needed to look and sound real, but I guess they took it too far. He didn't realize they'd actually hurt anyone until I told him. He felt so bad about it, Quincy. I feel terrible about it too."

"Sounds pretty extreme just to get rid of a future mother-in-law," I said. Although I understood how Jacqueline could drive someone to extremes. Brock's story didn't make complete sense. He didn't know his friends wacked Gordon and Fred on their heads hard enough to put them in the hospital? Of course, I didn't know the exact details. Maybe it was just Jenny's retelling of the story that made it hard to believe.

"It's too bad Brock didn't feel like he could measure up to your mom's standards," I said. "*That* I understand. Boy, do I understand."

She smiled and nodded empathetically.

"At least they're both doing better now—I mean, Fred and Gordon," I said.

"Yes, we're both so relieved," she said.

"What will you do now? I guess you've contacted the police?"

She looked at me blankly. "Oh—yes. Well, I told him to call and tell them the whole story as soon as we hung up."

"Oh, good. K.C. will be so happy. I'm meeting with her soon. I can't wait to tell her. Does your mother know he called you?"

"No, I haven't told her yet. I've been waiting for the right time. We're not getting along too well ourselves right now. I honestly think I will go to Pennsylvania to meet Brock and not tell anyone." She glanced around the shop. "Actually, I was hoping you wouldn't tell anyone what I told you. At least not until I leave tonight."

"Jenny, I don't know what to say. Why are you telling me about this if you don't want me to share the news with K.C.?"

"I just wanted to let you know that Brock's okay. You're the only one who showed any concern that he was gone. My mother just acted like she was glad he was out of the way." Her eyes welled with tears. "You're the only person in Hillside that's been a friend to me. I don't have any other friends. I have to pretend to get along with my mother, and until today, Brock was gone."

I took a box of tissues from the consultation area and handed it to her. I'd had no idea how lonely she was. Every time I'd met with her she seemed extremely friendly and happy. I guess she was a good actress.

She cleared her throat and dabbed at her eyes. "I feel so silly. And I want you to know, I'm really sorry about your driver's boyfriend and Gordon. Brock never wanted to hurt them."

"I'm sure he didn't." I sighed. "You don't need to worry about me telling anyone. I'm sure the police have already contacted Fred and Gordon if Brock called them."

"Thank you. I got worried when the girl that just left said you had an appointment with my mother tonight."

Ugh. The appointment where I was going to have her mother arrested, if possible. Maybe it was a good thing Jenny would be on her way to be with Brock. She deserved a break from all the stress for at least one night.

"It's just a numbers meeting. I think I'll just reschedule, anyway. With K.C.'s wedding coming up so soon, I think that might be best. So what will you do next?"

"I'm flying to meet up with him, and after we elope, we'll try to find jobs while we stay with some of his family." Now wasn't the time to remind her that Brock and possibly she would soon be spending time in jail.

"That will be great for you guys. I'm so glad you came in to tell me."

"I am too. I just wanted to say goodbye and thank you for all that you've done for me and Brock and for putting up with my mother."

"It was my pleasure. Good luck to both of you."

She left and I sat down at my desk to write down some thoughts about what I knew, given this new bombshell. Brock's hands weren't clean, but he and the police and probably Gordon's lawyers could work all that out. It wasn't my concern any longer. Apparently Brock wasn't the cleverest of boys, and he and Jenny most likely had a rough life ahead with all the trouble he was in. But at least they had each other to get through it. And thankfully, everyone had come out of the false kidnapping alive. Now all I had to worry about was Jacqueline.

I wished I had never agreed to take on Brock and Jenny's wedding. What had first started as a sweet love story had turned into a nightmare for everyone involved, including me, K.C. and especially Fred and Gordon.

Tonight I would go to Bruce's condo, get Jacqueline to say something incriminating to the police, and be done with them forever. Before I left the shop, I would do an Internet search and arm myself with as much information as possible about Jacqueline and Bruce and everything I knew they were involved with. If Jacqueline wouldn't admit what she'd done to us at the farm, I would bring up any dirt I could possibly have found to try and get a reaction. K.C. and I had found some hidden secrets at the farm the day she attacked us. But what was her connection to Clint Wheeler and his dairy farm?

Hopefully, after tonight, we could all move on with our lives and finish at least one happily ever after story with K.C. and Fred's wedding.

CHAPTER SEVENTEEN

"Where is everyone?" Mom asked.

We stood in the parking lot at the bird refuge for the walk-through appointment with K.C. and Danny. We'd parked next to their cars, which were among four other vehicles in the lot. K.C.'s electric-blue rocket stood out in stark contrast to Danny's Suburban, which he called the MAV—short for Mormon Assault Vehicle. There was also a Subaru wagon with a wire pet divider in the back, a minivan full of child-safety seats, a beat up silver pick-up truck, and a cute little mini SUV.

"They should be here. I'll call Danny." I reached to my back pocket, but found nothing. I checked my seat in the van and then realized I'd left my phone on the desk at work.

"I forgot my cell," I said. "They're probably already inside the building." We walked along the asphalt path leading to the visitor center entrance. I tried the front door. It was locked. "Maybe they walked around back." We made our way around and found no one.

"Is there anywhere else they would be?" Mom said.

"I guess they could be looking around. Danny mentioned wanting to put some small decorations along the boardwalk and on the tower, just to make that less of a bad memory for Fred."

We walked down the main boardwalk, the same place Alex and I had walked when we had our major...misunderstanding. The reeds and grasses loomed above our heads and danced as the breeze occasionally disturbed them.

A frazzled mom pushing a stroller containing a few-months-old baby, and loosely followed by four other little kids passed by. The older girl, probably about six or seven, tried to help wrangle her little sister and two younger boys, who looked like identical twins, down the boardwalk. One of the boys ventured to the side of the walk and kneeled at the edge.

"Fishies!" he said and reached down in an attempt to touch those "fishies."

Mom stopped and made sure the boy didn't fall in. He looked up at her and ran over to his mother's leg. Mom laughed. "Looks like you've got your hands full," she said.

"Wyatt, say thank you to the nice lady," the mother said.

The little boy maintained his fierce frown then buried his head against his mother's leg.

"I'm sorry," the woman said. "He's going through such a stage right now."

"Don't you worry about it. I know how difficult it is with small children, but five? I don't know how you manage. I only had three and I was exhausted all the time." Mom waived at the baby who looked up from the stroller with great interest. "You're brave to come out here on your own with such an active brood."

The woman laughed. "I think I must be crazy at times, but we come out here and walk two or three times a week, huh kids?" Three little heads bobbed in agreement, while one tucked deeper into his mom's thigh.

"Let us help you back to your car," I said.

"You're so sweet to offer but..." I could tell she really wanted the help, despite the tone of voice suggesting she'd turn down the offer.

"What a great idea," Mom said. "Let us lighten your load for just a minute."

"Actually, that sounds great," the woman said.

I raced the kids back to the parking lot, assuming they belonged to the mini-van. We folded up the stroller while she buckled each child in, despite their squirming and protestations.

"Phew," Mom sighed as they drove away.

I checked the doors of the visitor center one more time and they were still locked. We returned to the boardwalk to search for K.C. and Danny.

My mother sighed. "It sure would be nice to have little feet running around the house again. Your father and I were just talking about it—"

"Oh my gosh, Mom. You and Dad aren't thinking you're going to have more kids...are you? Shouldn't you get married first?"

"Very funny, Quincy. Don't be ridiculous. We were talking about grandchildren. How it's about time we had some."

"Um...I thought I might get married before I had kids, but if that's what you want I'm sure Alex would agree we could work on that..." I hadn't really teased my mother in quite a while and she was due.

She did a sharp intake of breath. "Quinella McKay, don't tell me that you and Alex..." she covered her mouth with her hands. "I meant after you get married. I meant Sandy, or Allie, once she finds someone."

I pursed my lips, trying to fight back the smile, but failed. "Mom...calm down. I was just joking."

"Oh, Quincy!" She shook her head. "You're terrible. You're a horrible tease...just like your father."

I had to suppress the giggles as we continued walking down the path. Mom stopped and glanced around. "Where are they? It's going to be dark before we know it."

I craned my neck, stretching to see past the plants blocking our view. And then I heard something. It was Danny's high pitched laugh. The voice seemed to travel. "I hear Danny. I'll go catch up to them before they move too far." I ran in the direction of the voice and then I heard another. It had to be them. We'd probably just been walking in circles, looking for each other.

I reached another branching off of the boardwalk where I thought their voices had come from and stopped to listen. Nobody there. All that running for nothing.

The voices started up again, and I remembered how the wind distorted the sound of the birds calling to each other. The birds had fooled me again. I turned to see if my mother had reached me yet, but she was nowhere near. The wind stopped, replaced by stark silence. I called out for my mom.

She couldn't be that far away. I listened and again—there was nothing.

"Mom! Can you hear me?"

Nothing.

Maybe I'd gone further than I realized. Or maybe she couldn't hear me because the plants were too dense. I retreated back to the place where I'd left her. She was gone. I let out a groan of frustration. We were like clowns, running circles around the tiny car at the circus. That thought made me think of the clown dolls at Kyle Mangum's house and I glanced around, feeling the gaze of thousands of painted clown eyes peering through the cattails, just like in a scene from *Circus Tent of Horrors*.

I continued down the path my mother must have taken with a quicker pace to my step. This non-meeting had been a complete waste of time. I grumbled to myself, angry that Danny and K.C. had completely changed the plan without letting anyone else know.

As I walked, the boardwalk widened and the plants thinned out. I could see the top half of the observation tower ahead. On this loop of walkway was a circular group of signs on wooden legs, topped with miniature shingled roofs. The roofs kept the weather off the information posters, which displayed pictures of the bird species common to the marsh on one side and pictures of native plants on the other.

There were eight signs, all arranged at different angles, each one taller than me. It looked like Stonehenge, but with wooden signs instead of rocks. The corner of the sign nearest the boardwalk caught my eye. The threads of some leftover tie-down from a long-gone sign or poster twitched in the breeze. I grumbled to myself some more. Different groups used the boardwalk system at the marsh for various events, like trail-runs or educational field trips. I could understand the need to tie up a poster, or mark the path of a race, but I didn't understand why they couldn't clean up after themselves when they were finished.

I set my gaze on the tower but something stuck in my mind. I turned back to take another look. It was blue satin fabric. But it wasn't just any kind of blue. It was a kind of blue that only someone who had spent hours trying to find that specific color in ribbon and table and chair coverings would know. It was *Nile* blue fabric. Fabric that had been torn into strips and tied to the sign. The edges were frayed and slightly faded.

I hurried to the steps of the tower. It was still there. The sign post at the base of the tower was tied with a Nile blue piece of fabric, which danced on the breeze.

I'd seen this fabric when Alex and I had found Fred and Gordon lying unconscious inside the structure. It hadn't occurred to me then that I recognized the specific *color.*

I got a sick feeling. I had to find my mother. I ran down the path I'd just come from.

Waist-level information signs dotted the entire boardwalk trail system. The section I was on today had a Nile blue scrap tied to every third sign post. I hadn't seen the fabric when I was here with Alex because I'd taken a different path. I made the loop clear back to the "V" where Mom and I had separated. I stopped to catch my breath.

Hopefully my mother had already found K.C. and Danny. I would use one of their phones to call the sheriff's office, and tell them who had really assaulted Fred and

Gordon. Jacqueline was the only person who would have extra Nile blue cloth sitting around. She must have marked the path for the kidnappers.

Shadows were forming in the early twilight. I began to run again. I reached the point where I had fallen through the boards and noticed they'd been repaired. The horrible image of Harold Busby's bloated body flashed through my mind. I moved past that spot as quickly as I could manage.

The marsh boardwalks covered over a mile of walking distance, and I wasn't in the right kind of shape to keep up a running pace. So, once I'd put some distance between me and the spot that held such awful memories, I slowed down while my heart pounded. None of the signs I'd just passed had cloth markers on them.

It had saddened and surprised me to think that Brock staged his kidnapping. I'd completely misread his character. Now it appeared that his mother-in-law was in on it too. Jenny thought Brock was trying to get away from Jacqueline, but it looked as if he'd wanted an out from his impending marriage to her.

The trail of ribbon led directly to the tower. I knew that Jacqueline had miles of that fabric to use up, but how could anyone be stupid enough to use such a specific and recognizable cloth creating a *literal* trail of evidence? Maybe Brock had found her cache of Nile blue yardage and figured he would save a buck by not having to buy any twine for the markers he set for his "kidnappers." Either way, poor Jenny seemed to be surrounded by idiots.

I walked as fast as I could, but the stitch in my side slowed me down. I tried to link all the parts together. Thanks to Fred, I knew that Brock had been taking bribes from Clint Wheeler to look the other way about the polluting. When Gordon had called Brock for a meeting, Brock must have guessed that Harold Busby had told on him. I knew something was odd when Jacqueline stated with certainty the wedding wouldn't happen, and now it seemed obvious she'd had first-hand knowledge.

There was something else. Bruce's company did metal fabrication. I'd found out earlier on my Internet search that many of those types of companies had been charged with violating the Clean Water Act by dumping their by-products in protected waterways. Allmecore had been cited in several states. I didn't find anything for Utah, but "Birds of a feather..." as they say. Birds like Brock, Jacqueline, Bruce, and Clint were polluting the marsh, and they had to stop whoever threatened to reveal their "dirty" little secret. If found out, they would all go to prison.

It was getting harder to see the outlines of the boards under my feet. The cattails and foliage which towered above made it appear even darker than it already was. I decided I'd just go back to the car where my Mother was probably waiting for me, just like when I was a kid. We'd always had the rule that if we got separated at the grocery store or the mall, we were to go back to the car and meet each other there. It would be faster to back-track than to continue on the longer loop I was currently on. My mother had probably been waiting at the car for a long time, tapping her toe alongside K.C. and Danny.

I reversed direction and ran. I neared the tower once again, but I couldn't continue on to the parking lot—my lungs burned. I stopped at the foot of the tower steps to catch my breath and smelled a familiar scent.

CHAPTER EIGHTEEN

"Jacqueline?" I called out.

No answer.

"Jackie?"

I heard a thumping sound coming from the center core of the tower. I moved closer and the sound grew louder, accompanied by a muffled voice. I walked onto the ramp that led to the lower level of the tower. The voice came from a utility closet in the center column of the structure. It was a very familiar voice.

"Mom?" I yelled at the door.

"Quincy! Don't—"

Jacqueline's perfume overwhelmed me and I got lightheaded. I felt a thump on the bottom edge of my shoulder blade.

"Ow!" I said.

I turned, anticipating looking into shark-black eyes. Instead I had to look down to see Jenny.

"Jenny? Where's your moth—wait...why did you hit me? That kinda hurt. And why would you hit me *there*?"

"You're so stinking tall. I missed. So shoot me. Oh, how funny. I just made a pun." She held a gun up and wiggled it at me. "See? *I'm* the only one who can shoot right now."

"What do you need a gun for? What's going on? Why is my mom locked in the closet? And why do you—reek?" I couldn't hold back the gagging. Jenny literally must have bathed in the stuff.

"You like it? Yeah, me neither. The only person in this world who would wear this stuff is my mother."

"Then why are you wearing it?" I asked.

"Well, duh. If the only person who would ever wear this is my mother, then that's who you would suspect of locking you in the closet."

"But...you didn't...lock me in this closet," I said confused.

Jenny let out a short sigh. "Things didn't go as planned this time."

"This time?" I put my hands on my hips. "What other..." I sucked in an audible breath, which was a big mistake considering the perfume. "You dumped a bin fill of cow manure on me and K.C., didn't you? Why?"

"Hands up!" she said, pointing the gun at my chest. "I thought it would get rid of you."

Despite the dangerous position I was in, I couldn't help rolling my eyes at the cliché. She was holding a gun though, so I couldn't get too snippy with her. I'd gotten a "little-sister" vibe from her when we would meet for consultations and I thought I'd try to take advantage of that until I came up with a way out of the situation. I'd always felt like Jenny followed my lead and did everything I told her to when it came to wedding planning.

"What—you were going to kill me with stink? Your mom's perfume is more likely to do that. Why would you want to get rid of me, anyway? I've been your ally this whole time. When your mom was throwing her fits, who was the one to side with you?"

She set her jaw and I thought maybe I was reaching her.

"I just—I was following you at the farm and I didn't know what else to do. Clint leaves the keys in all the tractors, and that one had a load ready to go. You would've called the cops and I just needed to stop you somehow. You and your driver lady didn't move after I dumped it so I figured maybe it killed you."

"Then why did you come into my shop later to see me, if you thought I was dead?"

"I saw you drive past in the blue car."

The drive of shame. I closed my eyes and groaned. "Oh no, you didn't tell my mother did you?"

"What did you say, Quincy?" my mom asked from behind the door.

"Nothing," I yelled through the door. "How much did you see?" I whispered.

"*A lot.*" She did an exaggerated shudder.

Everyone's a comedian.

"Really—what did you need to stop me from doing?"

She shrugged, casually. "From telling someone about the Phragmites and the ponds."

I decided to play dumb. "What about the Phragmites? What do they have to do with anything?"

Jenny let out a huge sigh. "It wasn't supposed to be like this. Bruce told me all I had to do was get him those plants and I would get the money." She looked down for a moment but then snapped her eyes up at me and repositioned her gun. "Nobody knows what those Phragmites are. Everybody just thinks they're weeds out in the marsh. Except for you."

"I didn't know what they were until you told me," I said, shrugging.

She made a sputtering sound with her lips. "Yeah I got carried away. I'd actually found someone who thought I might know what I'm talking about and it went to my head. But I didn't think you'd go snooping around looking for proof to share with the police…or my mother."

"But I didn't. I had no idea those plants were illegal…" *Oops.* "I mean, I didn't know until recently. When you dumped the manure on us, we were just going to visit Clint about cutting some more of them."

"You're lying. I followed you that day. I saw you go over to the retention pond. You didn't even look for Clint. He was in the house. You're not a very good liar. And you eat at Bulgy Burger too much, by the way."

Geez, she really had been following me.

Her mouth twitched and she grimaced. She rolled her shoulders as if she was trying to loosen them up. I hoped she was getting uncomfortable holding her arms up to point the gun at me. If I kept her talking she might wear out.

"You know," she said, "I would be long gone, out of the country by now if you hadn't complicated everything."

"I don't understand," I said. "I didn't know you and Brock planned to move out of the country."

"*We* weren't moving. Just me. Not Brock, not Bruce, and *especially* not my mother." Her voice cracked and her eyes glossed. "For once in my life, I could make my own decisions and live how I wanted to."

"So you didn't really want to get married?" I asked.

"It's complicated. Besides, it's none of your business". She laughed under her breath and shook her head. "You've been involved in every single aspect of my life since we first came to you to do wedding flowers. How is that possible? First with Brock and the kidnapping, then after I find the most perfect, obscure plant that nobody in the freaking world knows about." She gestured with both hands, waving the gun in front of my face, "You've got it on display in your shop, taunting me with it."

"I cut those plants from the ditch banks," I said. "I didn't know they were anything special. And I didn't look them up on the computer until you told me what they really were." My arms were getting tired. I let them drop a few inches. "If it's any consolation, I really did think your mom imported the Phragmites, being such a fan of Egypt and all."

"Hands up!" She sharpened her stance. "What am I going to do with you?" She glanced around, as if weighing different options. I tried to think of anything to distract her.

"Isn't it going to be expensive to move out of the country? I guess you must have a job lined up somewhere." Okay, it wasn't the best distraction, but I was under duress.

"Phht, I'm not worried about that. Bruce is taking care of me." The thought of what that little tidbit meant was nauseating and confusing.

"Um…I thought…well…does Brock know about you and…Bruce?" Another visual to add to the nightmare collection popped into my head.

"Like I said, it's complicated." She sighed and backed up a step. She took a deep breath. "When I got my job with the BLM, Bruce approached me about helping him find some plants to hide the pollution in the holding ponds that his company uses to dump their bi-products. I told him I could go to federal prison if I was caught, but then he told me how much he would pay. It was almost enough to buy me a new life somewhere. When I found the Egyptian Phragmites, I knew it was perfect. I could protect myself by making it look like my mother, with her stupid *fascination* with Egypt, had ordered the plants. And I would be that much closer to getting the hell away from her and her control for good."

She screwed up her mouth and looked at me as if she was deciding whether to tell me anything more. "Man, this feels good! Thanks for listening."

"I kinda have to…you know with the gun and all."

"Oh, yeah. Well, anyways, I knew I needed more of an insurance policy if I was going to take on the risk of getting caught. So I fooled around with Bruce a few times while my mom was away on one of her trips. No big deal."

Eeuww.

"So now, I have bargaining power. If Bruce decides to tell on me for any reason, I can remind him that I can tell my mother that he cheated on her. And I'm screwing my mother in the process. Now there's a pun for you." She looked upward and made a face. "For some reason he doesn't think he could live without her. Maybe it's her trust fund—which she doesn't share with me, by the way."

I interrupted her rant. "What about Brock? Why would you even get engaged if you and Bruce were…?"

The wild spark that had lit her eyes throughout her confession disappeared. "That was…unexpected. I didn't plan on Brock."

"Did Brock know about your—*agreement* with Bruce?"

"You mean, did he know we had slept together? *No!*" She said it as if *I* was the crazy one.

"I meant—the money—the Phragmites and the retention ponds."

She bit her bottom lip and frowned. "Brock didn't know what I had done. I overheard him talking about meeting with his boss about something and I just knew it was Clint's pond. So I had to tell Bruce."

"Jenny. You have to tell me something. You don't need the gun. I'm not going to run off. Let's go sit on that bench over there."

She stared at me for a moment, then nodded and waved me in front of her with the gun. I sat down and waited for her to do the same. She eventually did and held the gun down to her side.

"Brock didn't call you, did he?"

She let out a heavy sigh, "No."

"Do you know where he is?"

"No. I told Bruce about Brock's meeting here at the tower, and he said he would take care of it. He sent some guys and that's all I know." Her voice carried a hint of sadness.

"So…you don't know what the meeting was really about?"

She stared at me for a moment with pursed lips then slowly shook her head.

"Aren't you worried about him? Did they hurt him, like they did Fred and Gordon?"

"I don't know." She finally sounded like the same Jenny I thought I had known before. "I worry about him every day. I think he's alive." I heard a sniffle and looked at her more closely. Was that a tear I saw leaking out of the corner of her eye?

"Why did you come in and make up the whole thing about him faking the kidnapping?'

She put a hand to her forehead then ran her fingers through her hair. "I don't know. I just thought it would make you stop trying to find things out. I just want everything to stop."

"Do you even love Brock?"

"Yes, of course."

I crossed my legs and leaned back to appear casual and non-threatening. "I'm not judging you about anything, but I just wonder why you got engaged if you were involved with Bruce?"

She cleared her throat a couple of times and wiped at her eyes with the back of her hand. "I thought getting married would fix everything. I would get out from under my mom's thumb. It seemed like a good idea, and Brock was so happy but…" she stared ahead for a long moment, "…once we started making the wedding plans and my mom just took over, I knew I was stuck. Even with Brock, she was still controlling my life. I kinda…freaked out. By the time we got to you for flowers I couldn't handle it anymore."

I'd seen that happen more than once during wedding season. Everything is unicorns and rainbows when a couple gets engaged. But when the actual wedding planning starts, families and money and payments all bring reality into sharp focus for the young couple. The reality stage is when many engagements are broken off. And with a control freak like Jacqueline in the mix, I could see why Jenny had snapped. Well...almost.

"Jenny, you need to make things right. If you still love Brock, you need to go to the police and tell them what happened."

"I can't. I don't want Bruce to get in trouble."

"But you said you love Brock," I said.

"I do," was her tearful reply.

"Then get out of here. Go. Forget about me. Call the police and tell them about Brock. You can help them find him. Please."

She stared at me for a couple of beats then stood up. She started to walk away, stopped and turned back. Her mouth moved as if to speak, but she didn't. She walked away.

It had actually worked. All those summer afternoons watching soap operas instead of playing outside had finally paid off. I'd reenacted a scene from my favorite soap, "Restless Lives," and I'd done it perfectly! I'd played the part of Loretta, who was talking to her best friend Cinnamon, who had just found out her first boyfriend Rick hadn't really died in the whaling accident off the coast of Florida, but she was already engaged to Phillip, who was away on a gold mining expedition in Venezuela. Cinnamon was also pregnant with Julio's baby, but that would have to wait for another episode. With my acting skills, Jenny never stood a chance.

I hurried over toward the closet, hit my shin on the corner of another bench and then found the door. I pulled on the handle, but the door wouldn't open.

"Hello! Who's there?" Mom's panicked voice cried out.

"There's something wrong," I said. "It won't open."

"You have to have the key, dummy." I jumped at Jenny's voice, which came from directly behind me.

"Um, did you call the cops?" I said hopefully.

"Move!"

I moved to the side and Jenny shined a flashlight on the doorknob. I thought about running then, but she had my mother. Jenny unlocked the door. "Oh, Quincy, you did it." The flashlight illuminated the relieved look on my mother's face.

"Mom it's not—"

"Oh shut up," Jenny said. "I'm sure she knows the difference between a petite size two holding a gun and her Amazon daughter." She told Mom to walk out, then handed her a flashlight and ordered us to walk single file toward the parking lot.

"What about Brock?" I said.

She laughed dismissively. "Quincy, you are so naïve."

"What are you going to do to us?" Mom said, her voice full of fear.

"Quiet, helmet hair."

Mom had asked a good question. I didn't believe Jenny knew what she was going to do with us. I got the impression she was making things up as she went and had been the whole time. My guess was that she'd had a complete mental breakdown. And the longer we spent with her, the longer she had to imagine things to do to us. I needed to think of something to get us out of the situation.

"You must think I'm pretty dumb, huh?" I said over my shoulder. Jenny didn't reply. I chuckled, "I mean, I really thought you were going to leave and call the police. How stupid was that?"

I heard a quiet laugh. "You are pretty stupid," Jenny said.

"Hey…" Mom said. I shushed her, even though it was touching to have her come to my defense.

"You do really love Brock, don't you? Life's not all about the money. You need family and relationships too," I said.

"Shut up, Quincy."

"Yes, shut up, Quincy. She's holding the gun," my mother quietly sing-songed from in front of me.

"It's just…I don't think it's too late. You could talk to the police and tell them how Bruce used you to help his company cover up the pollution. They could find Brock and you guys could get married and move away."

No response. If Jenny got us to the parking lot, I was afraid we would end up in the trunk of her car. Then she would take us to some remote part of the marsh and dump our bodies. K.C. and Danny were probably already sleeping with the fishes…well maybe not fish, but brine shrimp and whatever else lives in the marsh water. After working in the marsh as long as she had, Jenny likely knew places to dump bodies where they would never be found.

I thought about Alex and my dad and sisters as we marched on. What would happen if Jenny killed us? What about the shop and Aunt Rosie? I couldn't let Jenny hurt us.

Especially not my mom. Maybe I could lunge at Jenny and my mom could run away. Problem was, she probably wouldn't run away. She would stay and try to help me. Then we would both be toast. I had to think of something better.

As we walked, I occasionally heard the splashing of water and the sound of a ducks squawking. The breeze started up and at that time of the evening with the sun blocked out by plants, it was cold. We came to the Stonehenge of signs and I recognized a new, very familiar scent on the breeze. It was too dark to confirm anything by sight, but I knew who was wearing it. Not only was it familiar, it gave me the inspiration I had been searching for.

"Jenny, I need to tie my shoe," I said. "Please."

She sighed, "Hurry."

I bent down on one knee so that I was level with my mother's leg. I patted her on the foot and she pointed the flashlight at my shoe. I took hold of the flashlight and stood up, then spun around, shining the light into Jenny's eyes. She did exactly what I had hoped and instinctively put her hands up to block the light. I smacked her gun-arm on the wrist with the flashlight as hard as I could. I heard the gun clank on the boardwalk.

"Now, Danny!" I yelled.

A primal scream ripped through the air, the pitch high—even for Danny. I directed the beam at the scrum at our feet and pulled my mom out of the way. We backed away from the pile created by K.C. on top of Jenny with Danny barely grasping one of Jenny's feet. Jenny easily kicked out of Danny's grasp, but K.C. held on. They rolled around on the boardwalk. K.C. must've outweighed Jenny by...well...a lot.

Even with the flashlight it was difficult to see everything that was happening. There were lots of grunts and slapping noises, and then I heard K.C. shriek, "Not the face!" and there was a loud splash. I shined the light at K.C., who kneeled at the edge of the boardwalk. The flashlight beam illuminated a soaked Jenny, chest deep in marsh water.

K.C. panted, as if trying to catch her breath. "She had to go for the face. Three days before my wedding—and she goes for my face. Bad idea little sister. Bad idea."

Danny retrieved his phone from his MAV and called the sheriff while my mother held the gun pointed at Jenny and K.C. held the flashlight. I was more than slightly disturbed by the adamant way Mom volunteered to hold the gun. Danny took over flashlight duty so K.C. could call Fred, and I called Dad because Mom wouldn't loosen her grip on the gun until the sheriff's deputies arrived.

K.C. explained to the officers that Jenny had ambushed her and Danny inside the visitor center and made Danny tie up K.C. at gun point, and then Jenny had tied up Danny. Danny eventually wriggled free and untied K.C.

"She ain't no boy scout," Danny added. "Those were terrible knots."

Jenny had stolen Brock's keys to all the buildings on the marsh. That's why the building had been locked up when my mother and I arrived.

My father and Fred were waiting for us in the parking lot once the sheriff's deputies escorted us out. Mom rushed into Dad's open arms and he wrapped her up in a bear hug.

Memories of happy times together as a family filled my thoughts, and tears were rolling down my cheeks when Dad looked up and beckoned me over with an outstretched arm.

Once we were cleared to leave, Mom rode in the truck with Dad, leaving me to drive home alone. As I passed Clint Wheeler's farm, lights from the sheriff's vehicles bounced off of the barn walls and lit up the usually black western sky.

CHAPTER NINETEEN

The next day at Rosie's Posies was spent directing traffic and revisiting the events of the previous night. It would have been nice to stay home in bed after the traumatic evening, but it was time to make the centerpieces for K.C.'s wedding and prepare for the other decorations we would produce over the next two days.

I'd recruited as much help as I could. Allie and a couple of her fellow interior design students with some floral experience helped, along with Daphne, K.C., Danny and some of his staff members, and my mother.

"You know, it's really too bad Rosie isn't here to help," Mom said. "Where is she these days?"

"I think she's in Turkey, or Greece about now. Hard to say," I said. "She would have loved to do a wedding this big. I'll write to her and give her all the details when it's done. She doesn't do email, so I'll have to write it all out and mail it to the cruise company."

"You can do that?" Allie said.

"Those were the instructions she left. I guess they collect it for the passengers and forward it on."

"Make sure you tell her all about how you figured out Fred's case too," K.C. said. "She'll be proud of ya kid, just like all of us, right, Annette?"

"Absolutely," Mom said.

"It wasn't just me that figured it out, it was all of you."

Mad banjo music blasted through the air. "Oh, there goes my cell," Mom said. "It's your father."

I went back to work on our assembly line. The first person in the line put wet floral foam in the container and secured it with waterproof tape. The next person added an armature of curly willow in either horizontal or vertical orientation, and then passed it to the person who inserted green seeded eucalyptus and smilex vines. Then, two different designers worked at adding burgundy dahlias, orange safflower, brown sunflowers, burnt orange and milk chocolate brown roses, carnations, *Flame* mini calla lilies and celosia. Once all the flowers were arranged, brown hypericum or orange bittersweet was placed as a finishing touch.

Mom came over to the design table. "Your father will be here at noon with lunch for everyone. He just confirmed that he's on time. I told him to bring utensils and plates and napkins. You don't have those here do you? You really should keep those kinds of things on hand."

"Thanks, Mom," I said. We had plenty of those things on hand, but it was kind of comforting to have the old mom back, instead of the pistol-packin' mama from the night before.

"Quincy, tell us how you managed to escape yesterday. K.C. says you wrestled the gun away and knocked the lady out," Allie said.

"K.C. was being modest. I didn't really do anything. It was K.C. who tossed her into the water."

I'd been in and out of the design room when K.C. described the events of the previous night. She'd added her own "interpretations" to the story.

"I'm confused about something," Allie said. "Mom said you went to tie your shoe and that all of a sudden Danny and K.C. were there, like maybe you had a premonition."

"Yes, dear. How did you know they were there?" Mom asked.

"I smelled Danny's cologne, so I knew he must be nearby. I just figured I would do what I could to distract Jenny, and then hoped Danny would jump in." I shrugged. "It all kinda just worked out."

My cell rang and I went to a quieter section of the store to answer. The caller ID said Hillside Police and little sparks of excitement filled my chest until I remembered Alex didn't work for Hillside PD. Alex's phone had rung straight to voicemail both times I'd tried to call him about what had happened with Jenny.

After the call I returned to the workroom. "Who was that, honey?" Mom asked. Normally, I might have been ever so slightly annoyed at my mom's nosiness, but I wanted to share this news with everyone.

"That was Hillside police. It turns out we never saw Kyle Mangum's wife for a good reason. She's been dead for almost a year. And she wasn't really his wife."

K.C. placed her hands on her hips. "That can't be." She held her hand out as if giving an invisible bouquet to an invisible woman. "I handed flowers to her myself more than once."

I lifted a pointer finger. "The woman you were delivering flowers to at the house..."

"Yes," K.C. said expectantly.

"...wasn't a woman. It was Kyle."

"Well, slap me silly and call me Sally," K.C. said.

Allie cut her eyes to me, and mouthed "What?"

I laughed and gave a little shrug. "Kyle was pretending to be Lori when he came to the door. I guess Kyle and Lori met here, but she was from the Seattle area. Lori got sick, quit her job here and went back to Seattle. Apparently she never mentioned Kyle to her family, which only consisted of a distant cousin or two. They didn't know about him until Hillside police tried to contact Lori about the bounced check. Unfortunately, Lori passed away from her illness."

K.C. looked at me with teary eyes. "That poor girl. Dying with no family to speak of. How in the world did Kyle have her checkbook?" She dabbed at the corners of her eyes with the edge of her apron.

"He had more than her checkbook," I said. "Kyle somehow doctored all the paperwork that declared them married, and got his name on all her accounts. Then, he ordered flowers from me, wrote checks from their bank accounts, etcetera, to keep up the illusion that she lived here with him."

"So that bedroom we saw...?" K.C. said.

"Was a shrine, I guess."

"Wow. All those clown dolls were his?"

"I don't know. He's a doll maker and does gigs as a party clown. She was a doll hobbyist. That's how they met.

At some kind of clown conference." I felt a sudden chill and rubbed my arms up and down. "Whether it was his or her collection doesn't matter. They were creepy no matter who they belonged to."

"It's whom, dear," Mom said.

I looked at our mother and mouthed the word "whom" with emphasis on the "m."

Mom tried to suppress her laugh and waived me off.

"Why did the police call you about it?" Allie asked.

"He wrote a check to us on her account and apparently forged her signature. When it bounced, we went to his place to talk to him about it and found a whole lot of other things…"

"Including my new cat," K.C. said.

"Him too," I said. "Or her. Everything at that house was odd or suspicious, so we called the police."

"Do you think there was ever any real love there, or was he just in it for the money?" Mom said.

"That shrine might have been weird as all get-out," K.C. said. "But it was definitely the work of someone who was in love."

"I guess it depends upon your definition of love," I said.

"Speaking of that," Allie said, in a sing-song voice, "what's up with you and Alex?"

I cleared my throat, "Um, what do you mean?"

Oh, where to begin?

"Where is he for starters? I thought he was going to be one of the groomsmen in your wedding, K.C.," Allie said.

"He had to go home to—" I started to say.

The front door bell chimed and I looked up to see my dad, arms laden with bags of food. They were plain, white plastic grocery bags, so right away I knew they were from Skinny's. *Oh sweet scones, I've missed you so.*

I rushed to the front of the store to help with the bags. "That was perfect timing."

"Well, thank you. Your old dad does something right every now and again." He winked and smiled.

We cleared off the design table and gathered stools from the backroom and the basement to sit on. There was a calm quiet for a few minutes as hungry people devoured lunch. K.C. interrupted the silence. "You know, we never did find out how Harold Busby was killed. Jenny says she or Bruce didn't do it. If you can believe her."

"What about Jacqueline?" Allie said.

"Jenny told us her mother isn't involved in any of it. Jenny used her mother's love of Egyptian culture and history as a cover. She ordered the Egyptian Phragmites herself. Who better than a biologist who specializes in marsh habitat to order a plant like that? She worked as a researcher, so no one would raise an eyebrow at her bringing in a normally illegal plant species."

"I'm afraid I know the answer to who killed old Busbeak," Dad said. Mom shot him a glance and he held up his hands. "I mean poor old Harold." Dad looked at Mom apologetically. "According to Clint Wheeler, he and Harold got into a fist fight over some accusations that Harold was throwing at Clint about polluting the marsh and bribing a federal employee.

"He said Harold just wouldn't quit, and one day he came to the farm and Clint told him to leave, but Harold came at him. Clint says he was defending himself when he punched Harold in the face. It was enough to knock him back, but Clint said Harold never passed out. He just stormed off on his own in the direction of the visitor center. Apparently Harold passed out later and fell into the water. That's why Quincy found him—"

"Angus," Mom mercifully interrupted before we relived my discovery. "When did you speak with Clint Wheeler?"

"I didn't. Last night when I drove to see you, I passed Clint's farm and saw all the sheriff's trucks with their lights on. While I waited for you all to come out, I talked to one of the deputies I know..."

"What deputy do you know?" Mom asked.

"Jed Frazier. You know, Annette. Bill's son Jed, he used to deliver our paper."

"Oh, yes," Mom said. "How is Jed? Is he married? He's your same age Allie..."

I coughed a couple times. "Ahem. You were saying something about Clint's farm..."

"Yes, yes, as I was saying, Jed told me what Clint had said. He told them all this after he regained consciousness."

A collective, "What?" sounded throughout the room.

"One of his boys went looking for him when he saw the cows hadn't had their afternoon milking. He was in his office on the ground, behind his desk. He'd been knocked on the head. Lucky he wasn't killed."

"Who hit him?" Allie asked.

"He doesn't know. He was ambushed, but I bet we're all thinking it was Jenny," Dad said. Heads nodded in agreement.

"Poor Clint," K.C. said. "Here we were, thinking he was involved in the whole thing."

"We don't know that he wasn't," I muttered.

"Quinella McKay!" Mom's mouth had zipped into a tight line and she looked at me with her patented angry expression.

"What?" I said.

"That man almost died. You shouldn't be accusing him of things at a time like this."

"All I'm saying is that K.C. and I found that pond on his property. It was definitely being used to camouflage the polluting."

The discussion continued for a few minutes until we finished lunch and then it was back-to-work time. We had regular business to take care of as well as the wedding, and most of us worked until about eight o'clock that night.

My parents offered to take me and Allie to dinner, but I told them I had some leftovers at home and that I was too tired to go out. The second part of that was true. We had an early start planned for the next day, only one day before the big event. The first part was not true, unless half a jar of pickles and a spoonful of ice cream count as leftovers.

The truth was, I couldn't handle being around them and their recently rekindled romance when mine had been put on pause. I just wished Alex was back. I wished he'd been there in that parking lot, waiting for me with open arms. We would have gone home and talked into the night about all that had happened in California and here in Hillside while he was away. But he wasn't here and he hadn't called me. I assured myself he would call as *soon* as he was able.

I locked up after everyone and waited until all of them had left our parking lot before I hooked a right on Gentile Street and said, "Here's looking at you, Jenny," as I drove Zombie Sue straight to Bulgy Burger.

"I'll just have the regular," I said to my nemesis on the other end of the speaker.

I pulled up to the window with exact change in hand, gave it to him before he could say anything, and drove forward. I checked my bag to make sure the order was correct before I drove off. To my surprise a face was staring up at me. Two onion ring eyes, a tater tot nose and a curved French fry smile placed neatly on a folded up napkin. Under that was both fry sauce and ketchup.

Maybe the Bulgy Burger guy wasn't so bad after all.

CHAPTER TWENTY

"Tomorrow is the big day," I said to K.C. as she stood in the back room tying her apron strings. "Don't you have things to do today—*for your wedding?*"

"Well, yes," she said reluctantly. "It's just that I want to help out. You've all done so much for me and my guy, and I..." she started to choke up and pulled a lace-edged handkerchief out of what she referred to as the real Bank of America. In other words, her bra.

Allie came over and put her arm around K.C.'s shoulders. "Are you okay?"

"Oh sweetie, I'm fantabulous. You really are the best group of folks. I just get all misty about weddings, and here it is, my own. I guess I'm just going to mist all day long and into tomorrow."

Daphne came over and handed a box of tissues to K.C. "You can't be misty tomorrow. Your makeup will run."

K.C. smiled. "You're right. I'm just going to have to toughen up, buttercup, so I don't ruin the makeup job my granddaughter is going to do for me tomorrow."

"How are you going to wear your hair?" Allie said.

K.C. reached up to the bandana she wore on her head with the knot tied on top, just like Rosie the Riveter. "I haven't quite decided yet. I've got an appointment at the salon next door at noon. I hope I can make up my mind by then."

"Oh, before you *leave,* K.C., hint, hint," I looked at her and blinked innocently, "I've got some news."

"Lay it on me," K.C. said.

"I got a call from Jacqueline this morning," I said.

"No!" K.C., Allie, and Daphne said in near unison.

"She wanted to talk about the money she's already paid me. I take it she found out about Bruce and Jenny being…together…a few times. I assume that's why she said they won't need to decorate Bruce's condo anymore."

"But isn't her money non-refundable by now? She signed a contract, right?" Allie said.

"Officially, yes," I said. "But, I realized a refund gets me away from a screwed up bunch of people that much faster. I told Jacqueline I would gladly refund the money, minus what I've already spent on supplies and items that are non-returnable to my suppliers. It actually feels like a burden's been lifted."

"But what about your time, Boss? She sucked away hours of your time and you have nothing to show for it."

I sighed. "That's all part of the floral business. Besides, I hope karma will smile favorably upon me. Jacqueline—despite her annoying manner—is in a big mess right now."

"Do you think she was involved in the polluting cover up, or Brock's kidnapping?" Allie asked.

"I don't know. At this point she's not in jail, so I don't think she's involved with the kidnapping. I think Jenny would have told the police anything she could to get back at her mother. But as far as investigations into Bruce's company, I'm sure that will take a while. And," I did a little dance, "I don't care. Because I'm not involved with them *anymore*."

Daphne laughed at me and we all returned to work. Except for K.C. We finally convinced her to go so she could finish her errands, get her hair done, and get ready for the rehearsal dinner.

***

With little stamina left at closing time, I looked over all the arrangements we'd produced. It was hard to believe everything was finished, but I checked things off the list for the final time and everything was there.

I picked up the bridal bouquet I'd completed only a half hour before, and took it out of the cooler into better lighting to make sure everything still looked perfect. We'd chosen dramatic colors for the bouquet, to match K.C.'s personality. Billows of red garden roses and ranunculus were contrasted by orange pin-cushion protea. For whimsy, we added fern curls and chocolate cosmos, and then finished it off with a pop of vibrant green cymbidium orchids.

I gazed at the bouquet for several moments then scanned over all the arrangements packed into our cooler and every other nook and cranny of available space in the store. To think this little shop had produced something so big was…inspiring. I finally felt just a tiny bit successful—at least for this one moment.

I should already have been home getting ready for the rehearsal dinner, but I couldn't help pausing and thinking about weddings as I held that bouquet. Would I ever get married again? I thought about it for a few moments, but I couldn't quite form a clear picture in mind—at least, not yet. For now, I would watch K.C. walk the aisle from my vantage point up front, standing next to the other bridesmaids. I practiced "aisle walking" on the way to the cooler; first step forward, feet together, next foot forward, feet together. I glanced down at the bouquet balanced between both hands. The expression "Always a bridesmaid, never a bride," popped into my mind. I couldn't decide whether I relished or feared the idea.

CHAPTER TWENTY-ONE

Sunlight poured over the marsh on the wedding day. It was eleven in the morning and everyone was on site setting up the flowers and decorations. Thanks to Danny's staff and Daphne and Allie's friends, I didn't have to worry about the floral installations at the visitor center or anywhere along the path at the marsh. Danny conducted the wedding rehearsal, and I took my place next to K.C.'s son, as directed, at the foot of the aisle leading to the archway where K.C. and Fred were to take their vows.

I carried a bouquet of discarded flower stems I'd gathered from the trash pile on my way out of the visitor center where we would hold the reception later on. The real bouquets wouldn't be used until the actual ceremony. The weather forecast called for all sunshine for the entire weekend, so the arch, chairs, and aisle runner had been set up outdoors for the ceremony.

Everyone, except for Danny of course, wore jeans and t-shirts for the rehearsal. He wore khaki's with a cornflower blue-checked button down shirt; his casual onsite work outfit. K.C. sported her electric blue cat-eye sunglasses, while her hair was wrapped in a scarf so no one, especially

Fred, could see her hair color choice before the wedding. She said it was bad luck.

After rehearsal, I helped put the finishing touches on all the décor and went to check on my mother, who was the designated supervisor of the small kitchen where the caterers would set up for the reception. I walked in and found her making out with my father, which was incredibly disturbing, yet surprisingly normal and right at the same time. I still broke a speed record exiting that little room.

I helped Allie place the women's flowers in the small classroom-turned-brides room, and took the men's flowers to Danny, who would help pin them on lapels. The men's dressing room was a utility shed that had been cleaned out of tools and other items for the wedding.

"Well Eliza, did you bring the proper attire to compliment that beautiful gown you get to wear?" Danny asked.

"Don't worry, I've got it covered."

"If you're wearing that abomination I saw you in at the police station, you'd better have it covered...for all our sakes."

"Very funny, friend. Is your kilt up to snuff? I can't wait to see your shins reflecting the sun."

"Not a chance, my fair lady. I'm not wearing a kilt, just the men in the bridal party. I'll be wearing Lauren. You better get going so you have time to get your hair done."

"Right." I turned to leave then turned back. "Danny?"

"Yes, dear?"

"Thank you. For everything."

"You are so welcome. It's always my pleasure."

We hugged and went our separate ways. My life was good. Good friends, a successful business, my parents back together, and Fred's case solved. There was only one piece missing, but today wasn't the day to focus on my absent boyfriend.

I joined K.C. and the other bridesmaids in the dressing room. I'd brought the Iron Maiden and managed to get her fastened with some help from K.C.'s daughter. K.C. wore a hair dresser's cape over her dress while she had her makeup done, and she'd revealed her hair, a lovely shade of auburn in a tame bouffant. She looked wonderful.

"This is it, kiddo," she said.

"You look beautiful," I said.

"So do you, Boss. You'll be a sight for sore eyes when that beau of yours lays his on you."

"Too bad he won't get to see me in this dress. I don't think I'll be wearing it again in the near future."

She formed her mouth to say something but stopped and turned her head. "Do you hear that?"

"Yes," I said, "what *is* it?"

"Grandma, it sounds like something is dying outside. Your wedding's gonna be ruined," her granddaughter said.

"Nonsense, you two. That's the sweetest sound I ever heard. The pipes are calling. It's time to line up."

I'd momentarily forgotten K.C. had hired a bagpiper to play as people arrived and for the procession. She'd been serious about a themed wedding.

I peeked out the window to watch the guests pass by on their way to the seating area around the corner. I caught a glimpse of my father, who wasn't an official groomsmen, but being a proud Scot, wore his McKay tartan and full regalia. The man from the Booby lecture was there with a beautiful woman on his arm. Several people went by, then out of the corner of my eye, I saw Brock.

I left my bouquet inside and snuck out to talk to him. "Brock," I called out.

He saw me and smiled. "Hey, Quincy! So good to see you."

"Where have you been? I'm so glad you're here—and alive!"

"Yeah, me too. It's a long story, but I woke up in a dark room somewhere in Mexico."

"No, I meant really, where have you been?"

"I'm not kidding. These guys conked me over the head when I went to talk to Gordon and Fred about how I'd been working with Clint Wheeler. Next thing I know, I'm waking up in some room in Tijuana. I snuck out and found the cops who took me to border patrol. It's been a while, but I finally made it home. Anyway, I talked to Gordon yesterday and he told me about everything that happened to him and Fred and how you and Jenny—"

I interrupted to save him the misery of explaining, "I'm so sorry about everything, Brock. I'm just happy you're okay."

"Quincy, it's time to start," Danny called out from the doorway. "Places, everyone."

"I've got to run—hey, did you say you were working *with* Clint Wheeler?"

"Yeah, Fred's wife," he nodded toward the flow of the crowd who were walking toward the seating, "I mean, almost wife, said you would be pretty excited to hear about Clint. He made a deal with some guys from the EPA that if he would give them proof like pictures and stuff, that Bruce's company was polluting the marsh, he wouldn't get fines and prison time for his retention pond. He also had to promise to clean it up. I was their messenger. Since I worked at the marsh every day, they thought it wouldn't be suspicious that I would be hanging around Clint's farm sometimes. He gave me copies of photos he took, since he didn't know how to email them."

The envelope Harold had seen Clint passing to Brock had been full of photos, not money. I said a silent prayer for Harold and for Clint, who had killed Harold by accident.

I promised to talk to Brock at the reception and hurried back into the building to take my place in line with the other women. My mind raced at all the information I'd just learned, but I had to clear it all out and focus. I was not going to be the person who tripped on the way up the aisle and ruined K.C.'s wedding extravaganza.

"Now, just like we practiced, ladies," Danny said. "I will give you the verbal cue, you will step out of these doors, and turn the corner to join your usher just behind the first set of chairs. Then you will take his arm and proceed down the aisle together. Please, don't look like a robot when you step and put your feet together, just walk gracefully. Smile pleasantly and keep your elbows at your waist, cradling the bouquet just below, otherwise your flowers will make their way up to your chin. It's all about composure."

I'd felt calm and collected until this point. What if I looked like a robot? What if I tripped? I waited my turn and began to sweat when the girl in front of me was sent through. What if I got sweat stains on my gown? I'd made fun of my mom when she told me to buy dress shields, as if they were some kind of antiquated feminine hygiene product, and now I was wishing I'd heeded her advice. *Focus, Quincy! Arms on hips, arms on hips.*

I stepped up to the designated spot, next to Danny.

"It's go time, Eliza D.," Danny said.

"Why am I so nervous?" I said.

"It's a wedding. You're supposed to be. Don't forget to smile."

Well that didn't make any sense. But it was time. I stepped outside and rounded the corner. I looked at my feet to make sure I didn't catch a heel and go tumbling over. I watched my feet all the way until I saw a polished pair of men's shoes. I held out my arm and when K.C.'s son took it I remembered I was supposed to look up and smile. I looked up and smiled…at Alex…who smiled back at me.

My heart pounded so fast and hard, I was sure the wedding guests could see it beating. We couldn't speak to each other, we were doing the wedding march! I looked out at the guests, so that I couldn't stare into Alex's beautiful brown eyes with the cute crinkles around the edges. I saw my mother, dabbing at tears, my father on her left, and my sisters and brother-in-law on her right.

Gordon Hawkes and his wife were there and the man who'd lectured about the birds, Jack Conway, sat next to him. Both men had given toasts to the memory of Harold Busby at the rehearsal dinner.

We were halfway down the aisle. It was excruciating being this close to Alex and not being able to even look at him. I glanced at him out of the corner of my eye. I couldn't see much, but I could tell he was grinning.

I surveyed the crowd on Alex's side and saw Elma with her dad, Skinny. I caught her puckering her hot pink lips and waggling her penciled-in eyebrows at Alex. She'd never quit trying.

We reached the top of the aisle and I had to go stand with the other women. I watched him walk away to take his place on the groom's side. His kilt swished back and forth as he walked.

The wedding procession continued and finally, K.C. entered the stage. She looked radiant as the bagpipes played the wedding march and she walked down the aisle. Fred looked close to passing out, but also incredibly happy.

Danny dabbed at his eyes throughout the entire ceremony, along with most of the other guests. Just as the officiant told Fred he could kiss the bride, a loud flapping noise started up from the marsh behind us. As if on cue, a giant white bird the size of a crane took off into the air and circled above the archway then flew away to the south.

"It's the Booby," Jack Conway cried out. "It really does exist!"

Everyone applauded and laughed, although I don't know if it was for the bird or because Fred and K.C. had finished their kiss and faced the guests as the new Mr. and Mrs. Carr.

They walked back toward the visitor center where an hors d'oeuvres and drink bar had been set up. The rest of the wedding party had been instructed to stay in place so a few more pictures could be taken while the guests mingled. I stole a quick glance over to the men's side of the archway and found Alex looking back at me. Butterflies took flight in my chest. I took a step forward to go and see him while we waited for the bride and groom to return, only to be chastised by the photographer who'd apparently graduated from the Drill Sergeant Photographers Academy. After pictures, the waiting crowd of guests returned to where we stood to offer their congratulations and I lost sight of Alex.

I mingled and chatted, all the while searching the crowd for a handsome head of golden brown hair. I spotted the back of his head. At least ten people stood between us. With as much politeness as possible, I shoved my way through the crowd until I reached a behatted bunch of older women. I eschewed their dirty looks, keeping my eyes on the prize as I plowed through the group.

I finally reached the brown hair, but found a nice looking man in gray slacks. The woman he was with asked me if I was the florist she'd heard so much about and started to tell me about her niece. She was supposedly really talented at making silk wreaths for the holidays and would I like her phone number?

Suddenly a hand grabbed my wrist and pulled me out of the trap. It kept pulling, guiding me to the back of the visitor center and I followed without a word. Once behind the building he turned to face me and I backed up against the building. His eyes flashed with an intensity that made me shiver.

He closed the space between us. The heat from his gaze seemed to fill my entire body. He cradled the back of my neck and tilted my head up, then kissed me. All the kisses we hadn't had while he was away were made up for in that one perfect moment.

My arms had found their way around his neck and his other hand reached around my waist and he pulled me to him. I paused for just a moment to look up at him and take in the image of the face I had been longing to see.

I took in a sharp breath, preparing to suggest we leave immediately and finish what we had started in a more private location. As I parted my lips to speak, I was interrupted by a sound so jarring, so disturbing, so…embarrassing…the memory of it haunts me to this day.

It was the sound of my father clearing his throat.

Alex closed his eyes and cringed, at the same time whipping his hands off of me and clasping them behind his back.

"Oh…did I…so sorry to interrupt," my father said through a grin, accompanied by wickedly twinkling eyes.

"Angus," Alex said, then did his own throat clearing. "We, um, haven't seen each other in a while." His hand darted out to shake with my father's.

"I can see that," Dad said as he gripped Alex's outstretched hand. "I really didn't mean to stop any…thing. I just came looking for you to see if you wouldn't mind lending a hand with all the folding chairs. But you two look mighty busy." He looked at me and winked.

I shook my head at him. So much heat radiated off my cheeks, I might give off sparks and set the building on fire.

"We were just…" There was no use in me trying to explain. It was quite obvious what we had been doing.

"I'll be right over to help," Alex said. He and my father exchanged nods. Apparently they'd had a visit to Mantown.

"I am so sorry," I said. My body was sorrier.

Alex sighed and then took my hand. He kissed the inside of my wrist and placed my palm on the side of his face with his hand resting on top. He leaned down and touched his forehead to mine. We stood there silent for a moment. He pulled away. "I'll see *you* a little later. I've got some manly duties to perform." He brushed a quick kiss across my lips.

Oh, if he only knew the thoughts that entered my mind when I heard him say "manly duties." I darn near self-combusted on the spot. He turned and I watched his kilt move back and forth as he walked a few steps. "Oh, Alex…"

"Yeah, babe?" he said, turning to look at me.

"I was right. You are just as hot in a dress as I thought you would be."

"That's probably the most disturbing thing you've ever said to me." A mischievous smile curled at the corners of his mouth. "But just wait 'til I'm outta this dress and see what you think then." He turned and jogged over to the seating area.

I picked my jaw up off the ground and went inside.

***

K.C. and Fred rocked and rolled at their reception, along with their guests. Round tables topped with garden-style floral centerpieces, complete with miniature pumpkins and gourds, filled the edges of the room. A center square had been reserved for dancing. And dance we did. A four piece band occupied a corner providing live music the entire night. My dad even stood in for a few numbers with his banjo. At one point, Fred and K.C. unveiled a secret dance routine that they had been practicing for weeks. They stepped, clapped, sashayed, and dipped to the song "Little Bitty Pretty One," then invited the rest of us to join in.

I had to wait at the end of a long line for my turn to dance with Alex. It seemed like every woman in the place wanted a turn. Allie and I sat at our table and watched as he fought off Elma's advances. After her hands wandered a little too close to the sporran on the front of his kilt I jumped up and cut in. There was an exchange of dirty looks between she and I and she muttered something that sounded like the word "banned" as she walked away. A line had been drawn in the sand and I'd crossed it. I'd chosen Alex over hot fluffy scones with honey-butter. I think I made the right decision.

We held each other as the music played. "You look a little flushed," I said.

"It was like dancing with an octopus. And why does she think I would enjoy having my ass pinched like that?"

"It is pretty irresistible." I gave him a little pat.

"Don't you get started too. I won't be able to sit down as it is."

Later, while Alex danced with my mom, I danced with my dad, and Allie danced with our brother-in-law Rick, K.C. took over the microphone. At the end of the song she asked for everyone's attention.

"Before anyone leaves, Fred and I want to thank all of you for coming. You've made this the most special day, and we're so happy we got to share it with all of our friends. Those of you holding drinks can help me toast to true love."

Everyone sitting at the tables held their glasses aloft and toasted.

"Now for some announcements. We've got this beautiful center reserved for another hour so party hardy everyone. Also, I wanted to share the good news that our wonderful friend, Gordon Hawkes, has recovered from his injuries, thank the Big Guy Upstairs. And that his daughter Stephanie just got engaged!" She pointed to Gordon and his wife, who sat next to Stephanie and her new fiancé, while the crowd applauded. "And one more piece of good news comes from my new second family—the McKays. Angus would you like to tell us what I just overheard from a little birdie?"

My father had draped his arm across my shoulders while we listened to K.C. I looked up at him in surprise at the news I'd heard nothing about. He spoke from where we stood, his voice booming loud enough for everyone in the room to hear without a mic. "K.C., I want to congratulate you and Fred before I give our big news. This has been one heck of a shindig." The crowd applauded in agreement. "I just learned some big news for our family." He looked at me and squeezed my shoulders. I glanced around in excited anticipation and noticed my mother's blank expression. Apparently it was news to her, too. "I'm going to be a proud grand pappy. My daughter is pregnant!"

My mother's eyes flashed open and she let out a wail I could hear above the noise of the applause.

"Quinella McKay!" she shrieked.

Even in the darkened room I could see her skin turn ghostly pale...right before she collapsed. Luckily, she'd just been dancing with Alex, and he caught her before she hit the floor. He eased her to the ground and looked up at me, his brown eyes registering a look of shock. His normally tanned skin matched the gray tone of my unconscious mother's complexion. His mouth hung agape.

"Dad!" I shouted. I felt like I would soon be following my mother's lead. I grew light-headed and grabbed onto my father's arm.

"Oh no, oh no, oh no," Dad said as he looked around franticly. He ran up to the mic stand. "Sorry folks, I should have clarified. My daughter Sandy is pregnant." He shot over to my mother and the group of people gathered around her. "Oh geez, Annette. I stuck my foot in that one," he said as he kneeled. He took over supporting my mom's head from Alex. She was already starting to come to. "I'm sorry, lad. I owe you one. Hell of a scare, wasn't it?" They exchanged a brief visual communication of some sort. Mantown again, I supposed.

***

Alex caught the garter and Elma caught the bouquet. No one was really surprised at that. In addition to blocking out like an NBA center, she'd threatened every eligible woman at the wedding long before the flowers were tossed. I'd tried to help clean up, but Danny insisted his crew was there to do the take-down so the rest of us could enjoy the remainder of the evening. My mother had recovered from her faint and been told which of us was really pregnant, but I still felt like she looked at me suspiciously the rest of the night.

Now that the wedding was over I could focus on the other thing that had been occupying my thoughts. I left Zombie Sue in the competent and watchful care of Danny and rode home with Alex. I was still in my dress and he was still in his kilt.

"That was a pretty mean trick your father played tonight," Alex said.

"That was no trick. I was just as surprised as you were."

"I don't think that's possible. I had to wonder what really happened while I was gone. I still don't really believe your manure story. You were driving around naked for some other reason. Who was it? I'll kill him."

"I told you what really happened. And K.C. was the one driving. And I wasn't naked. I was in my granny panties and a bra that Danny made me burn."

"It's probably better I don't know how Danny works into all of this. You didn't say you burned your granny's. Are you wearing them now?"

I laughed. "Wouldn't you like to know?"

He didn't say anything for a long time, then quietly said, "Oh, I intend to find out. Soon."

I took a big gulp of air. Heat rushed throughout my body and stayed in certain places. He turned off of the main road, away from my house, and in the direction of his. It was an unexpected change in plans.

"I thought we were going to my house," I said.

"I know. So does everyone else. That's why we're going to my place."

Chills of excitement took over my insides. "You know, you played your own dirty trick on me, telling me you weren't going to be there tonight. How long had K.C. known you were really coming?"

I saw him smile as we passed under a streetlamp. "A day or three."

"Three days! That traitor. She knew for that long? And you. It was torture waiting to hear from you. Why did you do it?"

He paused a beat. "The job in Boise was postponed and I came home as soon as I found out. I called ahead and told K.C. so she could plan on me, but I didn't actually get here until late yesterday."

"So…why didn't you call me?"

"I guess I wanted you to have to think about things. Decide if you really wanted to be with me, without me here clouding your judgment. You jumped to a huge conclusion about me and Samantha's son before I left. I didn't know exactly what you thought, but I knew it probably wasn't accurate."

"Well then why didn't you just tell me? No. Wait. I already know the answer to that. I didn't let you. I get that. See? I did think about things while you were gone. I thought about how I might have chased away the best thing that's ever happened to me."

"I…" He reached over to hold my hand. "I feel the same way about you, Quincy. In fact, I think I'm…in…l—"

He couldn't possibly be saying what I thought he was saying. But I wasn't so scared this time. Whatever kind of "L" word he was going to use, I was pretty sure I felt the same way.

"—like with you."

I was right. I did feel the same way about him and it was perfect. I didn't know how to reply, but I felt warm all over.

"Babe, I'm so sorry I wasn't here for you with that crazy bride. Why didn't John call me?"

"I made John swear not to tell you anything about Jacqueline or Jenny. I threatened to take another ride with K.C. if he leaked even one word."

"Well that did the trick. He didn't call."

"But seriously, I wanted to handle it myself. And Jenny took me completely by surprise. I did try to call you after they arrested her though."

"Sorry. I turned my phone off so I wouldn't be tempted to call you. I wanted to surprise you today."

"You certainly did."

Neither of us said anything until he pulled into his driveway.

"Did you think about anything...else while I was away?" he asked.

"Oh, you have no idea," I said in a low, breathy voice.

"Whoa." He parked the Scout and came around to my side and opened the door. He held his hand up for me to steady myself as I stepped out. I took his hand and he pulled me into him and kissed me. He backed me up against the car and pressed into me as we kissed some more. We gave Mrs. Bernhisel her money's worth and then grabbed our things out of the Scout and went in the house.

Once inside, he threw the locks on the doorknob and the deadbolt, and then checked the back door. He took his landline phone off the hook and held up his cell phone as he switched it off. I fished for my phone in my bag, saw that I had a text from my mother and gladly turned it off. I gave it to Alex, covered my eyes and told him to hide it wherever he wanted. He went through every room making sure the windows and blinds were closed. He clearly did not want to be disturbed this time and I was in full agreement.

We sat on his sleek, black sofa. He kicked off his shoes and socks, then scooped up my legs and dress and crossed them over his lap so we could sit closer. He let out a sigh, "Finally." He slid his left hand behind my neck and up to the French twist pinned into my hair. His right hand brushed the side of my breast and continued on to my back. He leaned in and barely brushed my lips with his. I leaned forward for more, but he backed away, teasing.

He pulled at the bobby pins that fastened my hair, and it fell down over my shoulders. His hand returned to the back of my neck then tangled through my hair as he pulled me to him again and kissed me, this time deeply.

I put my hands on his hard chest and grasped at the lapels of his Prince Charlie Jacket. Then I unbuttoned the jacket and slid the lapels up and over his shoulders.

"Quincy?" he said as he shrugged out of his jacket.

"Hmm?"

"Are you really wearing granny panties?"

I stood up. "You'll just have to find out for yourself."

He stood up too. "Challenge accepted. Take off your dress."

"You first," I said with a giggle.

He grinned and I took his hands and put them around my waist. Then I unbuttoned his tuxedo shirt and pulled the tails up and out from the kilt. I did a sharp intake of breath as I stood there looking at his muscled chest and abdomen. I ran my hands up along his chest and onto his back and he dipped down for another kiss. I pressed into him with my body and felt the electricity that seemed to pass between us. He trailed kisses down my neck, and onto my chest, then stopped where he was, his hot breath burning directly over my heart. I let out a little moan.

"I can't take it anymore. I've got to see what's under there." He took my hand and pulled me into the hallway toward his bedroom. We stopped halfway there and kissed again, his hands traveling and exploring my body.

Eventually, we made it to his bedroom. The Iron Maiden made her appearance, and while she was a tough opponent, she was no match for the man in the kilt. There was no hesitation from either of us. In fact, quite the opposite. And much to my pleasure and surprise that evening, I found out it's true what they say about what goes on beneath those kilts.

EPILOGUE

The next morning I woke up in Alex's bed to the smell of coffee brewing and bacon cooking. I slipped into his tuxedo shirt, which hung just barely to my mid-thigh, and tip-toed into the kitchen. He stood at the counter in a gray t-shirt and jeans, his back to me.

I snuck up, reached around his waist, and hugged him from behind. "What, no more kilt?" I felt his deep laugh echo through his chest.

"The kilt is retiring. He's worn out," he said and turned to look at me. "Oh man, what are you wearing?"

"You like it?"

"I love it." He wrapped his arms around me. "But a man's gotta eat sometime. Are you hungry?"

I was. He dished out the food and we sat together at the table and ate. We talked about everything that had happened while he was gone and he told me about his family back home.

"They all want to meet you," he said.

"Really? Why?"

He chuckled. "Apparently I mentioned you a few hundred times."

I couldn't help but grin. "Awww. You missed me."

He came over and tugged me out of my chair, pulling me into him. "Oh, I missed you, Miss McKay." He flashed a look at me with those deep pools of melting chocolate as his hands began to wander. "A lot."

I started to tell him how much I'd missed him, but he covered my mouth with his, so I decided to show him instead. I grabbed the bottom of his shirt and he lifted his arms, so I could rip it up and over his head. I slowly ran my hands down over his tight pectorals then onto his hard abs, which made me shudder inside.

He held my head, both hands tangled in my hair, and looked into my eyes for a couple of beats before he kissed me again.

I felt him smile against my mouth. He slid his hands under my bottom and lifted against the backs of my thighs. I took his cue and hopped up, wrapping my legs around his waist. We eventually made it to the hallway leading to the bedroom. He stopped halfway and leaned me back against the wall. I drew in a breath as he kissed my neck and then slowly dragged his lips to the top button of my shirt. He stopped then straightened up and looked down at me with a mischievous smile. After what seemed like an eternity, he unfastened the top button in tortuous slow motion. Then, he returned his mouth to where he left off and dragged his lips to the next button.

A knock sounded on the front door.

He stopped kissing my buttons and looked at me with raised eyebrows.

I shrugged. "I didn't tell anyone I was here, I swear," I whispered. A scowl took over his face.

"I'm gonna pretend I didn't hear it," he said. "Now, remind me what was I just doing?"

I leaned in to nuzzle next to his ear before I whispered the answer.

The knocking came again, this time closer to pounding.

Alex tipped his head back and sighed at the ceiling. "You've *got* to be kidding me." He held me as I slid my legs to the floor then he gave me a desperate kiss. "I'll be right back. *Please* don't move." He stomped toward the front door. I clasped my shirt closed then stood and listened.

As soon as I heard the visitor's voice, a cold panic flooded my insides and rose to the base of my throat. I froze in a moment of indecision, then rushed into the living room just in time to hear Alex say, "I'm her boyfriend. Who the hell are you?"

"I'm her husband."

ABOUT THE AUTHOR

Annie Adams is the bestselling author of THE FINAL ARRANGEMENT, 1st in The Flower Shop Mystery Series

And

A CHRISTMAS ARRANGEMENT, a romance novella, which is also part of The Flower Shop Mystery Series

She lives in Northern Utah at the foot of the Wasatch with her husband, two dogs and two cats. She loves to hear from readers. Connect online:

Twitter/annieadamsauthr

Facebook/annieadamstheauthor

Pinterest/annieadamstheauthor

www.annieadamstheauthor.com

If you enjoyed DEADLY ARRANGEMENTS, please spread the word. Tell your friends and book clubs. Write a review on Amazon or Goodreads. Please email me at annie@annieadamstheauthor.com when you write a review so I may thank you personally in an email.

Thank You!!
Annie

Made in the USA
San Bernardino, CA
25 September 2018